DEATH OVERDUE

Praise for David S. Pederson

Lambda Literary Award Finalist *Death Takes a Bow*

"[T]here's also a lovely scene near the end of the book that puts into words the feelings that Alan and Heath share for one another, but can't openly share because of the time they live in and their jobs in law enforcement. All in all, an interesting murder/mystery and an apt depiction of the times."
—*Gay Book Reviews*

"This is a mystery in its purest form…If you like murder mysteries and are particularly interested in the old-school type, you'll love this book!"—*Kinzie Things*

Lambda Literary Award Finalist *Death Checks In*

"David Pederson does a great job with this classic murder mystery set in 1947 and the attention to its details…"—*The Novel Approach*

"This noir whodunit is a worthwhile getaway with that old-black-and-white-movie feel that you know you love, and it's sweetly chaste, in a late-1940s way…"—*Outsmart Magazine*

"This is a classic murder mystery; an old-fashioned style mystery à la Agatha Christie…"—*Reviews by Amos Lassen*

Death Comes Darkly

"Agatha Christie…if Miss Marple were a gay police detective in post–WWII Milwaukee."—*PrideSource: Between the Lines*

"The mystery is one that isn't easily solved. It's a cozy mystery unraveled in the drawing room type of story, but well worked out."—*Bookwinked*

"If you LOVE Agatha Christie, you shouldn't miss this one. The writing is very pleasant, the mystery is old-fashioned, but in a good meaning, intriguing plot, well developed characters. I'd like to read more of Heath Barrington and Alan Keyes in the future. This couple has a big potential."—*Gay Book Reviews*

"[A] thoroughly entertaining read from beginning to end. A detective story in the best Agatha Christie tradition with all the trimmings."—*Sinfully Gay Romance Book Review*

Death Goes Overboard

"[A]uthor David S. Pederson has packed a lot in this novel. You don't normally find a soft-sided, poetry-writing mobster in a noir mystery, for instance, but he's here…this novel is both predictable and not, making it a nice diversion for a weekend or vacation."—*Washington Blade*

"Pederson takes a lot of the tropes of mysteries and utilizes them to the fullest, giving the story a knowable form. However, the unique characters and accurate portrayal of the struggles of gay relationships in 1940s America make this an enjoyable, thought-provoking read."—*Gay, Lesbian, Bisexual, and Transgender Round Table of the American Library Association*

"You've got mobsters, a fedora-wearing detective in a pinstriped suit, seemingly prim matrons, and man-hungry blondes eager for marriage. It's like an old black-and-white movie in book form….a nice diversion for a weekend or vacation."—*Windy City Times*

By the Author

Death Comes Darkly

Death Goes Overboard

Death Checks In

Death Takes A Bow

Death Overdue

Visit us at www.boldstrokesbooks.com

DEATH OVERDUE

by

David S. Pederson

2020

DEATH OVERDUE
© 2020 By David S. Pederson. All Rights Reserved.

ISBN 13: 978-1-63555-711-4

This Trade Paperback Original Is Published By
Bold Strokes Books, Inc.
P.O. Box 249
Valley Falls, NY 12185

First Edition: July 2020

CREDITS
Editors: Jerry L. Wheeler and Stacia Seaman
Production Design: Stacia Seaman
Cover Design by Sheri (HINDSIGHTGRAPHICS@GMAIL.COM)

Acknowledgments

Thank you to my husband, Alan Karbel, always, for his love and support.

Special thanks to all my friends, who are my chosen family, and all my readers. Thank you!!!

And of course my mom and my biological family. You're the best.

Finally, thanks also to Jerry Wheeler, my editor with the most-est, and everyone at Bold Strokes Books who have helped me so much, especially Radclyffe, Carsen, Sandy, Cindy, Stacia, and Ruth.

CHAPTER ONE

Thursday Afternoon, August 7, 1947

I know what you are.

Those five words sent absolute chills through my body and made me shiver despite the blistering August heat. I looked up from the note and glanced around the mailroom of the police station to make sure no one was nearby, then, with a shaky hand, I continued reading.

I know about you and Alan Keyes. Come to my apartment, alone, on Saturday, August 9, one p.m., to discuss, or else. 1812 W State Street, apartment 201.

It was signed Lawrence Crow, a name I knew well, unfortunately. He had been married to my cousin Liz many years ago, though I'll never know what she saw in him. I don't think she knows either, and it's a relationship she certainly regrets. In a roundabout way, I played a part in them ever getting together in the first place.

I was a young Milwaukee police officer, and Larry was a janitor at the precinct where I was stationed. He was just coming on duty as I was leaving, and Liz, looking radiant as always, was waiting for me so we could go for an ice cream soda. I couldn't blame Larry for stopping dead in his tracks when he saw her. He wiped his hands on his coveralls and came up to us on the pretense of saying hello to me, which he had never done before. They started going steady and married just five months later.

It didn't take long before trouble surfaced—an argument over money, a disagreement about her cooking skills. But soon he tried to isolate her from her friends, her family, and even me. He worked nights at the station and slept most of the day, so she spent a lot of time alone, and he didn't like her going out by herself or having people over, especially me. I was relieved when she finally filed for divorce, though he didn't take it very well.

They went their separate ways, but I still had to see him occasionally at the precinct, usually when I ended up staying late, which was more and more frequently after my promotion to detective. Larry quickly went back to his pre-Liz ways. He was sullen and angry, and he held a grudge against me and Liz. I was frankly afraid of him, and worried about what he might do to her. Then, a little over two years ago, he remarried. I was relieved, and I think Liz was, too. But now, this. This.

I read the note again, handwritten in a messy, masculine penmanship, the ink smeared but still legible, on torn, lined notebook paper. It had been slipped into a used, dirty envelope that was probably fished from the trash. My name was written on the outside of it, and it was left in my mailbox at the station.

"Whatcha reading, Barrington? Got a love letter?" Spelling said as he walked up behind me. I jumped at the sound of his voice. Spelling was a fellow detective and rather annoying.

I quickly folded the letter over and shoved it back in the envelope. "I wish it was. Just a note from Train in scheduling. He wants me to pull an extra shift next week." It was a lie, of course, but a fairly good one.

"That stinks, but better you than me," Spelling said. He got his mail and messages, shifted through them briefly, and sauntered away.

"Yeah," I said to myself, letting out a deep breath. I stuffed the envelope into my coat pocket and wondered what I should do next.

CHAPTER TWO

Thursday Evening, August 7, 1947

The weather was trying hard to match my mood. The sky alternately drizzled, spat, misted, and poured rain on and off throughout most of the morning and afternoon, and the precipitation had done nothing to cool the excessive summer heat. In fact, it had only increased the humidity. I was tired, damp, sweaty, and cranky by the time I finally reached my apartment building on Prospect Avenue, and the mysterious note in my pocket weighed heavily on my mind.

It was almost seven, and Oscar, Mrs. Ferguson's cat, was waiting for me at the top of the third floor stairs, just outside my door. I bent down and gave him a scratch behind the ears, and it cheered me up to see his furry face. He started purring as he followed me into my apartment. I dropped the mail on the hall table along with the envelope with the note in it from Larry Crow, and I hung up my hat. Oscar, not one to be ignored, let out a soft meow I knew meant he was looking for a saucer of milk. I got him one, and then I changed into some dry, comfortable clothes before fixing myself a tall sandwich with a beer and a pickle for dinner. The two of us ate quickly. Oscar finished before I did, so he crawled up into my lap to see if maybe he could have a bite of my sandwich, too.

"Sorry, pal, not tonight. I know Mrs. Ferguson feeds you well enough. I heard a rumor the other day that you totally ignored a mouse Mr. Gillette saw in the basement last week."

Oscar looked up at me, licked his pink nose, and then meowed.

"Don't deny it, old boy," I said, scratching him behind the ears again. He purred softly once more and kneaded my thighs with his claws. "Besides, I'm just about finished eating, and you have more roaming to do." I disengaged his claws from my wool trousers and carried him to the hall, where he took a few steps, looked back at me once, then sauntered away fat and contented, his tail held high and swishing from side to side. I closed the door and returned to the kitchen to wash the dishes and get another beer. I turned out the overhead light and walked back to the telephone in the front hall to call Alan Keyes, my partner in crime, my partner in life. I was glad he was home.

"Hey, Heath, you're home late tonight. I tried calling you earlier, but there was no answer."

"Yeah, I know. Working on a petty larceny case. Lots of details to get through and not many leads at this point."

"Ah, I see. That's the way of it when you're a police detective. Us flatfoots don't have that problem. We pull someone over, we write a ticket, that's it. We go home at the end of our shift and forget all about it."

"I envy and miss that sometimes."

"Yeah, but it's not without its own set of problems, as you most certainly remember."

"True, every job has its ups and downs, I suppose." I picked up a piece of unopened mail from the desk next to the phone and fanned myself with it, glancing at the return address, written in neat script. It was a letter from Brockenhurst, England, via airmail. My old friend Simon Quimby of Heatherwick. I smiled in spite of my mood and set it down again to read later, next to the monthly telephone bill.

"That's true," Alan said. "You sound kinda down in the dumps. Anything wrong?"

"Hmm, just distracted. The weather's not helping."

"Ugh, I know. I had traffic duty today. Miserable. Even with my rain gear on, the water seeped in everywhere, right down to my boxer shorts and socks. And that rubber raincoat and galoshes I had to wear was torture in this heat. I was glad to get home and have a shower. Wish you could have joined me."

"Uh-huh," I replied, studying myself in the mirror above the hall table and still fanning my face. I suddenly looked even older than I felt. And was that a gray hair?

"Uh-huh? Is that all you have to say? Gee, I must be losing my touch."

"What? Sorry."

"You are definitely distracted. I was saying it would have been nice if you could have joined me in the shower."

"Oh, right. Yes, that would have been nice." I looked closer. It was definitely a gray hair, maybe two.

"Okay, what gives, Detective? There's something you're not telling me."

I paused for just a moment before answering. "Oh, I got a message in my mailbox at work today. Not a good one." I leaned against the wall next to the mirror. I felt anxious and tired.

"A message? From who? What's this all about? I'm curious, and I'm all ears. So spill the beans."

"All right, I'll read it to you." The soiled envelope from Crow was still on the table next to the phone and the other mail. I picked it up, pulled out the note, cleared my throat, and read it aloud, glad that police officers have private lines. When I had finished, Alan whistled softly.

"Jeepers. Larry Crow, I know that name from somewhere. Who is he?"

"One of the janitors at the station. He used to be married to my cousin Liz."

"Oh yeah, you've mentioned him before. I've seen him around the precinct. He's rather a sullen fellow, not very friendly, but attractive in a dark way."

"That's the one."

"How does he know about us?"

"I don't know. It's concerning."

"You think he knows, knows?"

"I just told you, I don't know," I said, annoyed.

"Okay, okay, don't get mad at me. I'm concerned and involved, too, you know. He mentioned me by name."

I sighed. "I know. I'm sorry. That's part of what has me the most upset, knowing you're involved."

"It's all right. We'll figure it out together."

"Thanks, Alan," I said. Just hearing him say those words helped a lot.

"So, what are we going to do?"

"Good question. I think I have to see him this Saturday."

"I think *we* should see him. I have patrol that day, but I could call in sick."

"Absolutely not. I'll go alone," I said sternly, straightening myself up.

"Why? Two against one is better odds."

"If we show up together, it will only prove his point, give him more evidence."

"I bet he doesn't have any real evidence, Heath. He's all talk."

"But people listen to talk, to rumors. A lot of people believe them. They can be easily persuaded. We don't know what he has on us, on me. It could be bad."

"Like what?"

"Once again, I don't know, but I want to find out. Besides, the note said for me to come alone."

"Maybe I could wait in the hall or outside, or at least in the car, just in case you need me."

"In case he gets rough? Don't worry, I can handle him. I'll call you Saturday as soon as I can after I leave his place, okay?"

"I'll be waiting. I get off patrol at five, and I should be home no later than five thirty."

"All right."

"And try to get some sleep tonight, though I know you. You'll be tossing and turning and fretting until dawn."

I laughed half-heartedly. "You *do* know me. Very well."

"And that, I think, is a very good thing. Don't worry, it will be fine. He's probably all talk, just wants to scare you into giving him some money."

"Could be, maybe. I wish I had your optimism."

"Oh, I'll be doing enough tossing and turning myself until I hear from you on Saturday, worrying about you mostly."

"I appreciate your concern, but I'll be fine. We'll both be fine. Ironically, Liz is getting home tomorrow."

"You mentioned that the other day. She's been in Paris."

"Yeah, lucky lady. I replied to her cable and told her I'd pick her up from the train station in the morning."

"Does she know about her louse of an ex-husband and this letter?"

"No, I'm sure not. She's been out of the country for months. But I think I should tell her."

"Really?"

"She's like a sister to me, maybe closer. I know you've never met her, but you'll adore her. Everyone does. And her opinion of Larry Crow is only slightly worse than mine."

"Okay, you know best. But does she know? About you, I mean? And about us?"

"No, we've never talked about it. I tried once or twice, but I just couldn't."

"So what are you going to tell her about why he wants to see you?"

"I don't know. I'll think of something. But I think she needs to know about the letter, at least in part."

"If she's the kind of person you say she is, it will be fine. Now, go curl up with a good book and take your mind off things."

"Yes, sir, and you do the same. I just started reading *Gentlemen's Agreement*, by Laura Z. Hobson. I'm up to chapter three. If I can't sleep, I may have it finished by morning."

Alan laughed softly. "Just get some sleep and call me tomorrow."

"Right. Sweet dreams, tomorrow."

"Sweet dreams, tomorrow?"

"You said to call you tomorrow."

"Wise guy. Good night."

"Night, Alan. And Alan? Thanks." I hung up the phone and got ready for bed, undressing and brushing my teeth. That done, I opened the bedroom window, checking to make sure the rain had stopped. I pulled down the shade and turned on the electric fan in the corner. I don't like sleeping with the window open as a rule, but my bedroom was hot and sticky and it seemed a slight breeze was blowing in as it rustled the shade against the window frame. Next, I headed for the icebox to retrieve my pillowcase, an old trick my aunt Verbina had taught me. Then, with at least my head nice and cool, and the electric fan in the corner moving the still air about some, I settled in for the night with my book.

CHAPTER THREE

Friday Morning, August 8, 1947

True to my nature, I did not sleep well, and I did not have sweet dreams. Quite the opposite, in fact. I dreamt I was being chased through the dark, gray, deserted corridors of the police station by an oversized, sinister tomcat that bore a strange resemblance to Larry Crow. The more I ran, the faster he ran, all four of his massive paws galloping silently after me, long whiskers twitching with anticipation. Every door in the corridor was locked, every corner I went around was a dead end, and I didn't know where else to turn. I tried to cry out for help, but no sound came from my lips—my throat was constricted.

When I looked up, that big black cat was staring down at me, grinning like the famous Cheshire, his narrow, green-yellow eyes glowing in the dark. He had stopped, knowing I was trapped. He licked his triangular nose, once, twice, three times, but he never took his gaze off me. Slowly now, one paw in front of the other, claws out, tail swishing from side to side, he started coming toward me, growling low, crouching closer and closer. I spun about, but there was nowhere to go. I stared into the cat's mouth and saw his long, sharp fangs. I felt his breath puffing over me, in and out. And then I woke up in a cold sweat, my bed soaked, my hair plastered to my head. The fan in the corner was blowing air over my body and making me shiver.

I sat up, took a deep breath, and glanced at the clock. Six fifteen in the hot, still morning. I threw back the covers and folded them down to allow the bed to air out and dry, and I raised the shade above the open window, taking just a moment to glance out at the dawn over the lake to my right. The skies had cleared, but it was going to be another hot, sticky day. With a shake of my head, as if to exorcise the dream from my consciousness, I turned and padded softly to the bathroom.

I felt a little better after I had showered and shaved, but my energy level and spirits were as low as a snake's belly, as my father would say. I draped a towel around my midsection and retrieved the morning newspaper from the hall, glad none of my neighbors were about just yet. Out in the kitchen, still wearing only a towel, I fished out the quart of milk the milkman had left in the box and then put it and my pillowcase back in the icebox for the day.

Despite the fact that my apartment was about ninety degrees, I downed a cup of hot black coffee, some freshly squeezed orange juice, a bowl of oatmeal, and a banana, though my stomach was in knots. I ate standing at the kitchen counter, perusing an interesting article about the *Kon-Tiki* raft expedition in the *Milwaukee Sentinel*. After a hundred and one days and over four thousand miles, it apparently had smashed into a reef sometime yesterday at Raroia in the Tuamotus. I marveled to myself at how quickly news traveled around the globe nowadays and made a mental note to myself to consult my atlas as to exactly where Raroia and Tuamotus were located. I listened to Mrs. Murphy in the apartment below me through the kitchen vent next to the stove. She was up early, too, and in a foul temper as she banged pots and pans around and shrieked at her husband, who was most likely on their living room sofa.

The stifling heat was putting everyone in a bad mood, but little could be done about it. I scraped the last of the oatmeal out of the bowl, did the dishes, and wrapped the coffee grounds in the newspaper, which I then deposited in the trash. That done, I left a note for the milkman and decided I should get dressed. I put on my blue single-breasted suit with a yellow tie and matching pocket square and double-checked my reflection. I looked weary and worried, so I pinched my cheeks a bit for color and forced a smile. Better, but not great. It was seven forty five as I switched off the electric fan in the corner of the bedroom and headed out the front door. As I retrieved my hat from its hook, the phone on the table next to the door started ringing. I hung my hat back up and picked up on the second ring, wondering who would be calling me so early in the day.

"Hello?"

"Oh, you're still home," I heard my mother say.

"Yes, obviously. You just caught me, why?"

"You're supposed to be picking up Elizabeth from the station today, aren't you?"

"I'm picking up Liz, yes. The cable she sent said she'd be on the eight thirty from Chicago. I was just about to leave."

"I didn't want you to forget. It's almost eight now."

"I know. I didn't forget," I replied, trying to keep the irritation out of my voice. "Like I said, I was just leaving when you called. It's a fifteen-minute drive from here. I'll actually be early."

"Good thing I called to remind you, then."

"Sure, Mom, thanks." I rolled my eyes.

"Tell her we want to see her as soon as she's settled. We'll have her over for dinner next week. I want to hear all about Paris. You can come, too."

"Gee, swell. I'll tell her, Mom. Anything else?"

"Just that we missed her, and we're glad she's home."

"I will, Mom."

"I still can't believe she went all the way to Paris by herself, without a chaperone."

"It's 1947, Mom, not 1912, and Liz can take care of herself."

"I know, but a single young woman all alone in a strange country and only a couple years after the war…I just didn't like the idea."

"You made that very clear before she left. But she was fine. You had nothing to worry about. Besides, she stayed part of the time with Dad's cousins."

"Your father's relatives are hardly good influences. And they're French."

"Lots of French people in Paris."

"Don't be smart, Heath."

"Sorry. You can box my ears next time you see me, but I should get going."

"All right, dear, drive safely. You never know about traffic this time of day, you know."

"Right. I've got plenty of time if you don't keep me on the phone much longer."

She made that clicking sound with her teeth. "I didn't know I was bothering you, dear."

"You're not bothering me, I just need to go."

"But you said you have plenty of time."

"I did and I do, if I leave now. I'll give you a call later. Say hi to Dad for me."

"I will, Heath. I can't get him to do anything lately. The torpor of summer, you know."

"The what?"

"The torpor. It means sluggish from the heat."

"I see. And you've been just waiting for a chance to use that word, haven't you?"

Her teeth went click, click, click. "I don't know what you mean. I read it in a book the other day is all, and I thought it was a very useful word, especially now. It certainly fits your father lately."

I thought of my long-suffering father, being barraged with teeth clicking and words like "torpor" on a daily basis. "Well, Dad works hard, Mom. He's allowed to be sluggish once in a while."

"I work hard, too, dear. People think keeping house and raising a child is easy, but it's not. I work from sunup to sundown."

"I know, Mom. Dad and I appreciate all you do. And all you have done."

"I'm glad someone does. By the way, don't forget to drink your water. It's important to stay hydrated in this heat, you know."

"I won't forget. I really need to get going now, though."

"Oh, all right. Call me later. Bye, dear."

"Bye, Mom." I hung up the receiver, picked up my fedora once more, and headed out the door, down the stairs to the lobby, and then out to the street where my car was parked beneath a great-grandmother of an elm tree on the boulevard. I glanced up at the cerulean sky and found it cloudless. There would be no respite from the heat today, either. Cerulean—my mother would be proud, I thought, and I chuckled to myself.

CHAPTER FOUR

Friday Morning, August 8, 1947, Continued

Even leaving early, I made it to the station just in time, and I hurried to the platform eagerly, the anticipation of seeing Liz again boosting my spirits. The train from Chicago pulled in slowly, its wheels grinding against the shiny blue steel tracks as the engineer braked. Steam hissed all around, and smoke billowed from the engine, like a giant dragon coming to rest after a long journey. The engine rolled on, followed by several cars, each one moving slower than the one before it, until finally the dragon halted, more steam was released from the head farther up the tracks, and a great sigh could be heard from the crowd of people gathered on the platform.

I pushed forward and waited. As people began to disembark from the car nearest me, I scanned each face in turn. Was that her? No, she couldn't have changed that much. The pretty one in lavender then, but quickly she turned and no, that wasn't her, either. I took a step back, wondering if Liz had missed the train or if I was on the wrong platform. But then, suddenly, there she was, striding toward me, holding her train case in her right hand and her black leather envelope clutch in her left. She must have gotten off from a different car farther back. She wore her scarlet hair pulled away from her face, and on top was a small green wool hat with a bowknot. As usual, she was smiling broadly. Liz was a happy person, and it was contagious. No matter my mood, I couldn't help but feel joyful when I was near her.

"Hey you! Welcome home!" I called out, my smile instantly matching hers. She rushed to meet me, sidestepping a large man with a bowler hat who had stopped to light a cigar, and we embraced, kissing each other on each cheek, as they do on the Continent. I read that in a book last year.

"Thanks, and thanks for picking me up," she said, her voice light and cheerful.

"The least I could do for my favorite cousin."

"Your only cousin."

"You're my only *first* cousin, so that makes you my favorite by default."

She laughed gaily. "It's so good to see you. It seems I was gone for ages."

"Nearly six months, long enough. Too long. I missed you tons. How was the crossing?"

"Oh, fine. Smooth seas, pretty much. I was on the *Ile de France*—second class, but still grand."

"A great ship."

"Agreed, I love the French line."

"One of the best. So what's buzzin', cousin?" I said. It was my standard question for her, and I waited for her standard reply.

"Me! Buzz, buzz!"

We both laughed.

"Except this bee is tired. The ship docked in New York just yesterday morning. I caught the overnight train to Chicago, and then this one."

"Let's get your bags and get you home, then."

"Sounds good to me. I like the sound of home and my own bed, even though I had a wonderful time. I have so much to tell you."

"And I can't wait to hear it. I have a lot to tell you, too!" We strode down the platform to the baggage car, where a porter was carelessly unloading the various satchels, valises, bags, trunks and suitcases as two others piled them into heaps and piles. We claimed hers as another porter, anxious to help, put a dolly under her steamer trunk, which was covered in stickers from faraway places.

"Gee, Liz, what have you got in here? Bricks?" I said, a tan leather suitcase in each hand.

"Wise guy. Just some of the latest Paris fashions to dazzle you and my admirers with."

"And you have so many admirers. But you don't need fancy dresses to dazzle them or me with. The light in your eyes is more than enough. You positively sparkle."

"Sweet talker. Get another porter if they're too much. I'll pay the tip."

"No, I can manage. But I don't recall them being this heavy when I dropped you at the station six months ago. And I can only imagine what you have in that trunk." I jerked my head toward it and the porter, who seemed to be struggling as much as I was.

"Presents for everyone, of course. Now let's go, cousin."

She looped her arm through mine and we moved down the platform and into the station, the porter with the trunk trailing slowly behind as we jostled through the crowd.

"So, how was Paris?"

She stared up at me with those velvet blue eyes and sighed, and her whole body sighed with her, but it was a contented, happy, relaxed sigh.

"Oh, Heath, it was lovely. Just lovely. It's as if the war never happened there. Oh, it's not the same. The people aren't the same, probably never will be after what they went through, what we *all* went through, but there's a beauty there, a magic that can't be taken away."

I gazed at her loveliness. "I'd say the beauty of Paris left on the *Ile de France* last week."

Liz laughed, so light, so gay. "Oh, Heath, you are such a dear."

"Everything go okay with my dad's cousins?"

"Yes. They're so kind and helpful and lovely."

"And French, as my mother pointed out this morning."

"Well, yes, delightfully so. *Tellement charmant.*"

"*Très bon.* Your French has improved."

The three of us passed through the station and out to the parking lot on the east side of the building, bathed in morning sunshine.

I unlocked the trunk of my Buick Century, and the porter and I hoisted in Liz's steamer. I gave him a silver dollar, and he thanked me profusely, hurrying away in search of other tips. I put Liz's other bags in the back seat and closed the door. "All set?"

She glanced around the parking lot, out toward the lake, and then to the city. "Yes, all set. It's good to be home, it really is. I missed Milwaukee, missed its smells, the good and the bad, but I shall miss Paris, too." She fanned herself then with her black leather envelope clutch. "Gosh, it's warm, isn't it? And it's not even nine in the morning yet."

"It's been in the high eighties and nineties for over a week. It rained yesterday, but I think it only made it worse. The humidity, you know."

"Doesn't matter. It was hot in Paris, too. It positively sizzled, but I loved it. By the way, I brought you something."

I looked at her, surprised. "You did? You didn't have to."

"I know. It's no fun when you have to. Like I said, I have presents for everyone. I hope you like them."

"Them?" I raised my eyebrows, curious and delighted, as she set her train case on the hood of my car and opened it. She rummaged around a bit before fishing out a small, oddly shaped package wrapped in brown paper and tied with white string. "Here it is!"

"You brought me rocks?"

She handed the package to me with both hands. "Very funny. You're lucky you're cute."

"Should I open it now? Here?"

"Of course. I can't wait to see what you think, my darling."

I undid the string carefully, knowing it was driving her crazy. Liz was the tear-it-off type of person.

"Oh, for Pete's sake, Heath, just rip it open."

Inside the packaging were two small wooden figurines, painted in black and white. They were identical to each other and odd looking, not male or female. I looked at Liz, puzzled, and she smiled, or rather continued to smile. Had she ever stopped?

"I found them in Montmartre, in a tiny little shop run by

a mysterious, wrinkled, old woman who must have been about a hundred. They're voodoo dolls, but not the kind you stick pins in. They bring you luck, darling."

"I love them," I said. Because they were fun and unique, because they were from Paris and from Liz, and because I love her.

"You must name them, of course."

"Of course! How about Billy and Cary?" I said, referencing two of my heartthrobs, William Haines and Cary Grant.

She wrinkled up her cute little nose. "Those are funny. How did you come up with that?"

I shrugged. "Just came to me. But maybe Health and Happiness would be better."

"Oh yes, I think so! Health and Happiness it is. I hope you like them."

"I adore them, and I adore you. And believe me, I can use all the luck I can get. I'm so glad you had a wonderful trip, but I'm even more glad you're home."

"Me too. By the way, I met a fellow on the *France* on the way home, and it turns out he's from Milwaukee, too."

"Really? That's a coincidence."

"Yes. Small world. He was on holiday, traveling all over France since June. He stayed in New York an extra day and will be back in Milwaukee tomorrow evening. He's rather dashing, I must say, quick witted, and smart."

"Oh, Liz, here you go again."

"Don't 'Oh, Liz' me, Heath, please. We had a nice time on the ship, and he's promised to call me. If he does, he does. If he doesn't, I have an extra voodoo doll that you *do* stick pins in."

"Liz!"

"I'm kidding, darling. His name is Mike Hart, know him?"

I shook my head. "Nope. But I can run his name at the station if you want, check the files."

Her eyes sparkled as she shook her head, her little green hat swaying along. "Thanks, but I'll take my chances. I think he's safe. He's just out of the Navy."

"I still think I'll check the files."

"Oh, Heath. You haven't changed. Always my protector."

"That's my lot in life. What's this guy do now that he's out of the service? How can he afford to be traveling all over France?"

"Jobs are hard to come by since the war ended, you know. All those servicemen coming home—"

"So he's unemployed, in other words."

"Temporarily unemployed. He said he used his savings to travel. He told me he wanted to see France as a civilian, to see Paris without swastikas flying from every building, and I can certainly understand that. How's your folks?" she said, clearly changing the subject.

I put the voodoo dolls carefully in my pocket along with the string and wrapping paper and opened the passenger door for her. Once she was settled in, I handed her the train case, which she balanced on her lap next to her clutch.

"They're fine." I slid in behind the wheel, put the car in gear, and headed out toward her apartment on Prospect Avenue, just a few blocks from my place. "Mom wants you to come to dinner sometime next week. She'll probably chastise you again for traveling to Europe alone. She still calls you Elizabeth and thinks of you as eternally twelve years old."

"I don't mind. And I do love Aunt Ramona's cooking."

"She said I could come, too."

"All the better. You look like you could use a few home-cooked meals."

"That's what Mom always says. And then she makes that clicking sound with her teeth." We laughed together, and I felt calmer. I hadn't realized how much I'd missed her.

"How's Aunt Verbina?"

"Oh she's grand, just grand. Hard to believe her and mother are sisters. Of course Verbina can be a bit eccentric, too. She's working on getting her third husband now, a banker."

"Goodness."

"Yeah, but he seems like a nice man. Lucky you come from Dad's side of the family. I think you missed the insanity!"

"Um, you may recall my father."

"Oh yes, I know. Uncle Leroy. He was a bit of a character. My dad was pretty ticked when his only sister married him."

"I remember Dad saying that. He and your dad never did get along."

"Two very different people. My dad is conservative, quiet, even shy. Uncle Leroy, well, just the opposite, to say the least."

"Remember when he got that job driving a city bus? One day he suddenly veered off the route and kept driving until he was in Kentucky. He said he just got the urge to visit his mother, my grandmother, who was in poor health."

"That's right. The bus company filed charges but eventually dropped them because of strong public support in his favor. At least he didn't have any passengers when he took off. How would they have reacted?"

"I can only imagine. He was a nut, but I miss my dad and mom a lot."

"I know. Eccentricities aside, your dad was a good man. And your mom was a sweetheart. The apple didn't fall far from the tree with you."

"Thanks, love," she said quietly. "Oh look, there's Juneau Park. Did you watch the fireworks this year?" Her mood brightened and her smile returned.

"Yes, Alan and I walked down here and sat by the statue of old Solomon. We had a great view."

She turned her head away from the window and looked at me, but I kept my eyes on the road.

"Who's Alan?"

"Someone I want you to meet."

"Oh?"

"Yeah. He's a police officer and has become a good friend. He's helped me on my last several cases."

"Your mother's written to me about your last few cases. I'm impressed, but she never mentioned anyone named Alan."

"I'm not surprised. They've never met, but I have told her

about him. That he's a friend. She thinks I spend too much time with him."

"I see. This Alan is handsome, I bet."

I felt myself blush a bit. "Some people might think so."

"I'm sure. I can't wait to meet him. And for you to meet Mike Hart." She put her hand on my shoulder, and suddenly I knew she knew, and I knew it was okay.

I allowed myself a quick glance in her direction. "Thanks, Liz. Truly."

"Of course, my darling. You're my protector, and I'm yours. Did you remember to water my plants? Manage not to kill any?"

I laughed again as we sat at a traffic light. "Managed to keep any alive is more like it. You know I don't have a green thumb, but I watered them dutifully."

"I knew I could count on you." A large fly buzzed in through the open car window and came to rest on the dash briefly before buzzing off and out the other side.

I grinned. "So, besides this Mike Hart, anything else memorable about your months abroad?"

"Oh, loads and loads. I have some pictures to show you, a divine little painting I bought from a funny old man along the Seine, and I discovered a new cocktail made with St. Germaine, Champagne, and sparkling water."

"Intriguing. Are you giving up on the Bee's Knees?" The Bee's Knees is a cocktail made with gin, fresh lemon juice and honey simple syrup, shaken and chilled with a twist. I introduced it to Liz on her twenty-first birthday, and it's been her drink ever since.

She glanced sideways at me. "Never, but a little diversity never hurt anyone. I suppose you're still drinking the Barrington."

"The what?"

"A vodka martini with a pickle, of course. I dubbed it the Barrington. I asked for one in Paris, and they thought I was mad."

"You are mad, Liz."

"Well, you said the apple didn't fall far from the tree with me." We both laughed, and it felt like she'd never left.

"So, what's been going on here?"

"Oh, you know, same old, same old. Murder, mayhem, and mystery. By the way, your ex-husband left a note yesterday in my mailbox at the station," I said, as casually as I could muster.

"Larry? A note? That doesn't sound like him. I didn't think he even knew how to write. Why would he be leaving you a note? You didn't tell him I was coming home today, did you?" She sounded alarmed all of a sudden.

I shook my head as the light changed to green. "No, of course not. I never speak to him except the occasional exchange of grunts if we happen to pass each other in the hall."

"So what did the louse want? Don't lend him money, Heath, if that's it. You'll never see it again. He's behind on his alimony payments. I intend to pay him a visit soon to discuss it."

I shook my head once more, and that uneasy feeling returned. "I'm not sure what he wants, but he wants to see me tomorrow afternoon at his apartment."

"That's really odd. It has to be he wants to borrow money or he heard I'm back in the country and he wants to find out about me. Oh, God, I want to be through with him."

"I don't think it's about you, Liz. He said something about knowing what I am. About knowing about me and Alan. I don't have a good feeling about it."

"Oh," she said, and suddenly she was quiet. "Are you going to see him?"

"He told me I'd regret it if I didn't." I gripped the steering wheel tightly, my knuckles turning white.

"Oh, Heath, I'm so sorry. But Larry's a bully. He's all talk and bluster, no substance. I don't think you need to worry."

"That's what Alan said, too."

"Alan sounds like a wise fellow."

"He is. Larry doesn't scare me, much. I feel sorry for his new wife, though."

I could see Liz biting her lip as I glanced in her direction once more.

"I do, too. I'd feel sorry for anyone married to him. I was young and foolish when Larry proposed, but it didn't take me long to come to my senses. He's a ruffian, a bully, and a drunk."

"I know. I thought when you two divorced, I'd also be through with him, but no such luck. Then when he finally did remarry, I thought once more we were through with him."

"There's only one way to be finished with people like him, and that's if they're finished for good, if you know what I mean, and I'm sure you do." She drummed her fingers fiercely atop her train case.

"Yeah, I suppose I do. Boy, our conversation sure turned dark quickly, Liz."

"Yeah, sorry. It's just that he keeps coming back like a bad penny. Guess I need a nap. Drop me out front. I can have the doorman help me with my bags and the trunk."

"Are you sure?"

"We have lots to catch up on and lots of time to do it, but for now I want a bath with lots of bubbles, a glass of wine, and my very own bed."

I pulled up in the loading zone in front of her building and set the parking brake, releasing my death grip on the steering wheel at last. I helped the doorman get the steamer trunk out, and as he wrestled it inside, I unloaded her other bags from the back seat. That done, I stood back to take another look at her. She might have been tired and weary, but she didn't show it. "I'll call you tomorrow afternoon and let you know how it went with Larry."

"You'd better. I expect a full report. In fact, why don't you drop over after and take me for an ice cream soda like we used to, and we can discuss it?"

"It's a deal, cousin. Get some rest. And welcome home again."

"Thanks, handsome, and thanks again for the lift."

"Anytime, and thank you for the lift in my spirits."

"Anytime. You're a killer-diller."

"And you're the bee's knees."

"Buzz, buzz."

The doorman returned and picked up her other bags and she

followed him up to the doorway. She turned then and waved, still smiling. I waved back, then released the parking brake, put my car in gear, and headed to the police station. As I drove I patted Health and Happiness in my suit pocket. 'Health and Happiness I can always use, but I hope you bring me good luck, too."

CHAPTER FIVE

Saturday Morning, August 9, 1947

I slept fitfully again, but thankfully no nightmares this time. I awoke groggy, and I unwillingly hoisted myself out of bed to the bathroom, where I showered and shaved. Breakfast consisted of a poached egg, orange juice, buttered toast, and strong, black coffee, which went down a little better than last night's dinner had. The drapes in the living room billowed in softly, indicating a fairly decent breeze had come up, so perhaps the insufferable heat had finally broken.

When I had finished the breakfast dishes and the morning *Sentinel*, I decided to do some laundry to take my mind off the clock, which was ticking and tocking ever so slowly toward one p.m. and my appointment with Mr. Larry Crow. I hauled my wicker basket down the three flights of stairs to the basement and put a load in, then climbed back up to my apartment, noting the time was just nine-thirty. Alan was on patrol, and Liz was probably still asleep, but I felt I needed to talk to someone, so I dialed my aunt Verbina's number. She picked up on the first ring.

"Verbina Partridge speaking."

"It's me, Auntie."

"Heath, how nice to hear from you."

"Thanks. I hope I'm not disturbing you."

"No, not at all. I have a lunch date with Mr. Finch."

"Quartus Finch, the eligible banker, of course."

"That's right. And I'm all dressed and ready."

"But it's not even ten yet."

"Oh, I'll probably change my clothes at least three times between now and noon."

"Whatever you wear, you'll knock his socks off."

"Thank you, dear. I understand Liz got home yesterday."

"Yes, it was wonderful to see her. I imagine she'll ring you up soon. She said something about having presents for everyone."

"How sweet. She didn't need to. She's such a charming girl. Did she have a nice time? Her letters and postcards certainly made it sound like she did."

"She had a wonderful time. Paris will never be the same."

"You two are so alike."

"So we've been told."

"It's true. Anything wrong, dear? You don't sound like yourself."

"I'm just distracted. I have a few things on my mind."

"Such as?"

"Such as Larry Crow."

"Larry Crow? You mean Liz's ex-husband?"

"The one and only."

"Such a nasty man. Why on earth are you thinking about him?"

"Because I'm meeting him this afternoon at one o'clock."

"Whatever for?"

"Nothing good, I'm afraid. I'll tell you all about it later."

"Why not tell me now? I have a good two hours before my date."

"I'm sorry, Auntie. I thought I was in the mood to talk about it, but I guess I'm not."

"Then call me later. You know I hate it when you toy with me like that."

"I'm sorry. And I will call you later. Maybe I'll even stop by and tell you in person. You have a party line, remember."

"Yes, but I can always tell when someone picks up and starts listening. Usually it's that nosy Mrs. Kramer."

"Nonetheless, I'd rather talk about it face-to-face."

"Suit yourself. You certainly have my curiosity aroused. Does Liz know about this?"

"Yes, I told her yesterday."

"Hmm. Well, ring me back tonight. I should be home after four, and we can make plans to have a drink or something."

"Home alone after four?"

"Cheeky! Yes, Mr. Finch has a bank function to go to."

"All right, I'll call you later. Bye for now."

"Take good care, Heath."

"I'll try to."

I hung up the phone and picked up Health and Happiness from the phone table where I'd left them yesterday, deciding they needed a proper home. The three of us walked around my entire apartment several times before I finally put them on my dresser in the bedroom, where they'd be the last thing I saw at night and the first thing I saw in the morning, depending on whether Alan was staying over or not. I read a chapter in my book, and then I checked on my laundry in the basement. I hung everything up to dry on the lines strung from the rafters and then climbed back upstairs, glad not to run into any of the neighbors.

By 11:45 I'd read another couple of chapters, then reread them because I couldn't recall what I had read, and then finally gave up, putting my bookmarker back where it had been the night before. At 12:35, I put on my tie and my service revolver and holster. Then I took the revolver and holster off again and locked them back in the nightstand. This was not official business, and I was not afraid of Larry Crow, I told myself, though I didn't really believe it. Finally, I put on my suit coat, grabbed my hat, and headed down the stairs and out the door to my car. The temperature was still quite warm, but the breeze from earlier had picked up and the clouds had increased.

It was about a twenty-minute drive, and I parked my car on State Street near the address he had given me. I crossed to the north side of the road, where a small row of relatively new four-unit apartment buildings stood that had been put up hurriedly after the war. Number 1812 was the third one from the corner, nondescript, basic, ordinary, and cheap. The front door of the building, centered between two sets of narrow windows, was unlocked, and the lock appeared to be broken. I went in and climbed the stairs to the dark second floor.

Apartment 201 was on the left, 202 on the right. I knocked on the door on the left. The building was obviously poorly made, and I could hear two men's voices from inside, but I couldn't make out what they were saying. I knocked again and waited. Finally, Larry Crow opened the door, wearing a dirty, sweat-stained undershirt and dark gray work trousers, no socks, no shoes. He actually wasn't a bad-looking sort, even attractive in a thuggish sort of tomcat way. Dark, curly hair, green/yellow eyes, a cleft chin under a day's beard. Too bad he was such a jerk.

"So, you came," he grunted, scratching his chest through the flimsy undershirt, his nipples protruding through the thin fabric.

"You asked me to," I said.

"Right. Wasn't sure you'd come, though."

"You said I'd regret it if I didn't."

"You would have," he replied, glancing over his shoulder into his apartment. He seemed agitated as he looked back at me. "You alone?"

"Yes, I am. Do I come in or what?"

The door to apartment 202 across the landing opened, and a pretty woman came out, peering at us. She was wearing a blue print dress with a sweetheart neckline, a full gathered skirt with pockets, and poufy short sleeves that showed off her slender, pale arms. Her cinnamon colored hair was gathered in back. Her lips were full, her cheeks rosy, and her blue eyes shining. She had an hourglass figure, and most men would call her a looker.

"Afternoon, dollface." Larry grinned lecherously at her over my shoulder. "You need something?"

"Nothing you have, Mr. Crow, and it's Mrs. Picking, if you don't mind."

"I don't mind at all, and I bet you wouldn't, either."

She scowled. "I have to go check on my laundry." She closed the door behind her and pounded down the steps.

When she had vanished from sight, I turned my head back to Larry, who looked back at me.

"Pretty Pickings, I call her, but she's not very friendly, if you get my drift."

"Nice-looking lady," I said.

"Yeah, a war widow. All alone, but she won't give me the time of day, yet."

"You're a married man."

"But I ain't dead, as the saying goes."

"If looks could kill, you would be. She was shooting daggers at you."

"Eh, one of these days. She's just playin' hard to get. Redheads." He looked over his shoulder into his apartment once again, and then back at me. "Come on in."

He stepped aside, so I walked in and he closed the door behind me. The apartment was small but tidy. The furnishings looked old and well used, possibly secondhand. The air was stale and smelled of cigarettes and cigars, and Larry had an odor of sweat and alcohol that oozed from his pores. "Is Mrs. Crow home?"

"Alice left about a half hour ago. Went to the damned library again, every single week."

"You have something against libraries?"

"She reads stuff she shouldn't, and that spinster librarian is always putting ideas into her head. I told her she could only keep going there if she reads something normal, like *Titus Groan*. That's a *real* book."

"Ah, yes. I heard he's writing a sequel and intends it to be a Gormenghast trilogy. I can see why you'd like that."

"I'm impressed you know it."

"I try to stay well-rounded."

"Yeah, I'm sure you do. Anyway, it's better than the stuff that librarian was giving her. I forbid Alice bringing that crap home anymore. But at least the library gets her out of my hair every Saturday."

I looked at him as I set my hat on a small wooden table by the door. "You alone, then?"

"Yeah, sure, why?"

"I heard voices when I was out in the hall, sounded like you and another man talking."

"I was on the phone, that's all."

"Funny, I distinctly heard two voices, both male."

"Might have been the radio, then. I just turned it off when you knocked. We should get down to business." He stole a look down the hall toward what I assumed was the bedroom and bathroom. He definitely seemed a tad nervous.

"What business would that be, Crow? I don't like the thought of doing business with you."

"That's not very friendly, Heath. You never did like me, did you? Of course, the feeling is mutual, as they say."

"There's not much to like about you, Larry. Mrs. Picking and I would seem to be in agreement on that. I guess you do a decent enough job of being janitor at the police station, but that's about all you have going for you."

He scowled. "So high and mighty, so smug. Liz got like that, too, after a while. I can't stand it."

"Then maybe I should be going."

"Not so fast, cousin-in-law."

"Ex-cousin-in-law. Liz came to her senses and divorced you, remember? What she ever saw in a lowlife like you is beyond me."

"She's a woman. Every woman needs a man, and dames like men like me."

"Clearly you don't know Liz, even though you were married to her for almost two years. I suppose you think every man needs a woman, too."

He grinned, showing straight, gray teeth, and his breath was foul. "Sure, but not in the same way women need a man. Men aren't meant to be tied down to one silly female. Most men, anyway, which brings me to why we are here. Have a seat." Once more he glanced down the hall.

I shook my head. "No thanks, I'd prefer to stand. I don't plan on staying long."

"Suit yourself." He flopped down into an oversized easy chair next to the radio and let out a belch. "God, I'm tired. Working nights is a bitch."

I paced about the room, peeked into the kitchen and then down the short hall. The door to what I assumed was the bedroom was closed. I walked back closer to him and put my hand on top of the radio console, noting it was cold. Interesting.

Crow's eyes followed me everywhere. "What the hell are you doing? Stop moving around," he growled.

I walked over to the sofa, which faced the doorway to the kitchen, and ran my hand along the back of it. The fabric was worn and the seams were separating. I picked up two long, red hairs and held them out for examination. I shuddered when I realized they were the same shade as Liz's. "Is your wife a redhead?"

"Not hardly. She's a brunette. Those probably belong to Peggy. Or maybe Bonnie."

"Friends of yours?"

"Just friendly. I like redheads."

"Yet you married a brunette."

"The second time, yeah. Alice was gonna have a baby, so I married her, but she lost it shortly after. Quit being nosy and let's get this over with so I can take a nap. I took a sleeping drought just before you got here, and it's starting to hit me."

I put the hairs in my suit coat pocket as nonchalantly as I could. "What are you talking about, Larry? Get what over with?"

He pointed one of his long fingers at me. "I'm talking about you. You don't need a woman in your life, do you? You've never had a woman in your life, and I don't think you want one. You're not the friendly type when it comes to females."

"What's that supposed to mean?" I felt a lump in my throat the size of a chicken egg.

"You tell me, Heath. Liz and me used to talk about it sometimes. She wondered, you know."

"Liz and I."

"Huh?" He scrunched up his face.

"Nothing. Wondered what?"

"You know. She may not know, but you do. So, tell me who

wears the dress? You or Alan Keyes? I bet you look real purty in pearls and a skirt."

I stared at him, hard. The lump in my throat plunged to my stomach and grew to the size of an ostrich egg. "That's not funny. Not in the least."

"I ain't laughing, am I? Maybe you take turns." He eased himself out of the chair and walked over to a sideboard to pour himself a drink, scratching his ass as he went. If I had to guess, I'd say he wasn't wearing underwear. "Bourbon, straight. Want one?"

"No."

"Figured as much. As I recall, you're a martini drinker. Bourbon is a man's drink."

"I drink bourbon sometimes, but I haven't even had lunch yet."

"Never stops me."

"I'm sure not. I wouldn't mix bourbon with a sleeping drought if I were you, and it appears you've already had at least one beer," I said, pointing to an empty Pabst bottle on the coffee table. "Or at least someone has."

"Your concern for me is touching, Barrington."

"Frankly, I couldn't care less. It's just in my nature to point out dangerous behaviors."

"Such a Boy Scout." He poured his drink and turned back to me.

"And you're reprehensible."

"Thanks."

"So, what's this all about, then, Larry? I don't have all day."

"I told you. It's you. It's all about you. You're a rising star on the force. Solved a few cases, bright, young. You have a future ahead of you. But if word got out, if rumors were confirmed—"

"Rumors are just rumors, Larry. I need to get going. I'd say it was nice seeing you, but..." I walked over to the door and picked up my hat.

"I've collected quite a file on you, you know, Heath. Ever since I found a note in the trash at the station from you to Mr. Keyes. Kind of a love note. You signed it with a little heart and both your initials. Real sweet."

I stopped in my tracks, clutching my hat in my hand and crushing the brim. I remembered that note instantly, as if I'd written it yesterday. I had absentmindedly drawn the heart and our initials at the bottom, then, realizing what I'd done, crumpled it up and stupidly thrown it in the trash. I should have burned it.

"After finding that note, I began to take notice of the two of you. I asked around a bit, too. A trip to Lake Geneva with Alan Keyes. A trip to Chicago with Alan Keyes. Lunches together, the theater, dinners out, just the two of you, neither of you ever seen with a lady friend. He's even spent the night at your apartment a few times, according to one of your neighbors."

I set my hat back on the table and turned to him, a scowl across my face, my eyes narrow. "We're just friends," I said tersely, interrupting him. "When he stays over, he sleeps on the couch. And I have been seen with a lady friend. Phyllis Waters from payroll."

He laughed the way a hyena would. "Yeah, I know."

"How do you know all this? Have you been spying on me? On us?"

He took a long drink before flopping down into the chair once more, legs spread apart as he leered up at me, his oversized feet bare and dirty. He set his glass on the table, next to the empty beer bottle and a ceramic ashtray that held a half-smoked cigar and four Camel cigarette butts. Next to the ashtray was a brand-new Willard Ponies cigar still in its wrapper, resting on top of a well-worn copy of *Girls Aplenty* magazine. "It's not difficult, Heath. You're not the only one with detective skills. I may be a lowly janitor, but I ain't stupid. I had a conversation with Miss Waters, too, you know. She found me rather attractive, most dames do, as I said before."

"Don't flatter yourself, Crow."

"I don't have to. The ladies do it all by themselves. So, Phyllis told me you're quite the gentleman."

"What's wrong with being a gentleman? Not that you'd know."

"Nothing in general. But you're a gentleman who never gets fresh, never asks for a kiss, never invites her to his apartment, never gropes—"

"I respect her, that's all. She's a lady."

Larry laughed once more and picked up his glass again. He took another drink, dribbling some of it on his chin, which he wiped away by pulling up on his undershirt. In spite of myself, I couldn't help but notice the dark trail of hair running up his stomach from the waist band of his pants when he did that. "Yeah, that's all, all right, respect. You know, Barrington, if I was to share my observations, that note, and Miss Waters's thoughts, people would believe things about you. I think you'd find yourself out of a job or worse. And Alan Keyes would be bounced, too. Maybe institutionalized. Lobotomized."

I shuddered involuntarily.

"People don't take kindly to people like you, Barrington."

"I'm just a man, Larry, like you."

He scowled. "Not like me. You're a man who likes other men. A pansy. A fairy, a poof, as they call 'em, and not a good one. Not that there is such a thing as a good one."

"What do you want from me?"

"Five hundred dollars would be nice." He took another drink as he stared at me, still grinning, waiting for a reaction.

I stared back, refusing to give him what he wanted. "It would be. I wish I had five hundred dollars."

"You can get it if you want. I know you can. Maybe you can split the cost with your boyfriend, two-fifty each. Seems fair. Do you want to pay up, Heath? Or should I make my notes and observations public?"

I grabbed my hat and put it back on my head, pulling it down tight as I clenched my fists. "That's blackmail, you know. It's against the law."

Larry finished his drink and set the glass on the coffee table next to the telephone. "So, arrest me or fork over five hundred bucks."

I shoved my fists in my pockets and scowled again, my eyes squinting even more, my forehead ridged. "I'll have to get back to you on that."

"I'll be here, but don't take too long. The clock is ticking, as they say. You've got until noon tomorrow."

A noise came from behind the closed door in the hall, like

something being knocked over, and both of us glanced in that direction.

"I thought you said you were alone."

"I am, must have been the stupid cat."

"I didn't know you had one. You keep him locked in the bedroom? That is the bedroom, I assume."

"Yeah. He doesn't like me."

"Smart cat."

Larry shrugged. "It's a male cat. Maybe he'd like you."

"Funny." I pointed toward the ashtray. "And the cat smokes Willard Ponies cigars?"

"That's mine."

"You didn't finish it. In fact, it looks like it's still burning."

We both gazed at it, a whiff of smoke rising up toward the ceiling.

"I got tired of it. I'm more of a cigarette man myself, but I like a cigar now and then."

"I'm sure you do. You still have a brand-new one lying there, too. Next to that beer bottle. It's almost like you *do* have company."

"I do, wise guy. You."

"Yes, and you're such a good host. So, where is this note you supposedly found? I'd like to see it."

Larry laughed. "I'm sure you would." He glanced about the apartment with a smirk on his face. "Don't worry, it's hidden safely away. Some place Alice won't even find it. Noon tomorrow, don't forget. Tick tock."

CHAPTER SIX

Saturday Afternoon, August 9, 1947

My throat was dry and parched. I could have used a drink, but not from him. I took my fists out of my pockets and left the apartment, not bothering to close the door. I took the stairs down two at a time, shoved my way out the front door, and almost ran across the street and down the sidewalk to my car. My heart was racing and my hands trembling as I got behind the wheel and started driving, not sure what to do or where to go.

I thought at first of calling Alan, but he was on patrol this afternoon. Verbina? No, she was on her lunch date with the banker. Liz, of course, I should call Liz. I promised her I would. But what to tell her? What to say? A few blocks away, I spotted the State of Mind on State Street, and I pulled over. It was a typical neighborhood corner bar, and I figured no one would know me there.

My eyes took a moment to adjust to the dim interior. The smell of cigarettes, booze, and stale beer filled my nostrils immediately. I took my fedora off and went to the bar, where a large middle-aged chap in a dirty white apron and shirtsleeves was drying glasses with a less than clean looking towel. The place was almost empty, just an old man nursing a beer at the other end and two fellows playing darts over by the jukebox, which was playing an Andrews Sisters tune I recognized but couldn't name.

"What will it be?" the man with the apron said as I positioned myself on one of the dark red leather stools and put my fedora on the one to my left. The man in the apron had tattoos of buxom mermaids on both of his hairy forearms.

"A Barrington."

"A what now?" he said, raising a bushy brown eyebrow that looked like a fat caterpillar.

"Sorry, just an inside joke between me and my friend."

The man with the apron glanced about and then nodded as he looked at me with a queer expression. "Oh, I see. And is this friend here with you now? Is that him sitting there?" He pointed to the stool with my hat on it.

I scowled. "No, of course not. I'm not crazy. Well, maybe I am. Just bring me a vodka martini with a pickle."

"A pickle."

"That's right, and make it a double."

"Sure thing, mister, whatever you say. Shaken or stirred?"

"Shaken, please."

"Okay." He moved slowly down the bar and scooped ice into a shaker, followed by vodka and a thimble full of vermouth. When he shook it, his whole body moved, and I smiled in spite of my dour mood. I was still smiling when he returned and set it before me.

"Well, you look like you're in better spirits already, buddy."

"I will be, when better spirits are in me. Bottoms up." I picked up the glass and downed a good third of it. "Got a phone in this place?"

"Through that door, next to the men's room." He jerked a thumb over his right shoulder.

"Thanks." I took another large drink and set the empty glass on the bar. "One more."

The man in the apron took the glass and sauntered away, returning shortly with another double martini and a sad-looking pickle on the side. "Here's to you."

"Likewise." I finished half of it and then went to the phone as I fished a nickel out of my pocket. It had been a while since I had telephoned Liz, so I couldn't remember the exchange at first, but then it came to me. I dialed her number and waited. She picked up on the third ring.

"Hello?"

"What's buzzin', cousin?"

"Heath! I've been waiting for your call. Did you see him?"

"You're supposed to say, 'Me, buzz, buzz.'"

"Honestly, darling, I love you but sometimes you can be infuriating. Did you see Larry or not?"

"I did."

"And?"

"He wants five hundred dollars."

I heard her gasp. "I knew it. Don't give it to him, please. He'll never repay you."

"It wouldn't exactly be a loan. He makes a rather compelling argument in favor of just giving it to him."

"Like what?"

"I can't discuss it right now, I'm on a pay phone, and you have a party line."

"Where are you?"

"Some bar on State Street, I forget the name."

"It's one thirty in the afternoon, Heath."

I pulled out my pocket watch and stared at it in the dim light. "That it is. One forty, to be exact."

"Don't you think it's a little early to be in a bar?"

"Tut, tut, cuz. I'm supporting my local economy."

"You're worried and upset, and so am I."

"Join me."

"That won't solve anything. I'm going to go see Larry, right now."

"Don't. It will just make things worse."

"He's behind on his alimony."

"Liz—"

"I can get Mr. Green to drive me."

"Who's Mr. Green?"

"The man downstairs from me, the one with the blotchy skin and the bad toupee."

"Oh, yeah, I remember. So, you haven't seen Larry since you've been back?" I said, fingering the two strands of red hair in my pocket.

"I just got home yesterday morning, as you should recall. When would I have had time?"

"I don't know, last night, this morning."

"Well, I didn't see him, but I'm going to now. I'll call you afterward. That's if you're home by then. Don't drink too much."

"There's no such thing."

"Yes, there is, Heath, believe me. And it sounds like you've already had enough."

"Only one and a half so far, though they were doubles, so technically I guess that's three. And too much is never enough. If you go to see him, be careful. I don't trust him, and I got the feeling he wasn't alone."

"In spite of what you think, I truly can take care of myself, cousin."

"I know that all too well. You're stubborn, independent, and fierce."

"And those are just some of my good qualities."

I laughed. "Indeed."

"Go home, Heath. I'll call you later."

"Right, bye."

"Bye, darling." I heard her hang up, then I did the same as my nickel dropped down with a clink into the depository. I felt a weight crushing down on me, and it was hard to breathe. I was scared and worried, not just for me but for Alan and for Liz, mostly for Alan and Liz. This was all my fault. If I paid Larry the five hundred dollars, I knew it would just be the beginning, and the end would only come when Alan and I were exposed and ruined or when Larry was finished for good. Liz's earlier words from yesterday came rushing back to me. I shivered and trembled, and noticed I was sweating.

I used the men's room, since I needed to and it was right there, and then I wandered back to my stool and finished my second cocktail. The checkered floor was sticky in spots.

"One more," I said to the big, aproned man with the hairy buxom mermaid forearms.

"Another double?"

"Absolutely."

"They're twenty-five cents apiece for a single, you know. Forty cents for a double."

I took out my wallet and placed a five dollar bill on the bar. "Keep 'em coming until that's gone, including your tip, my good fellow."

He shrugged. "Your funeral, chap." He picked up the money along with my empty glass again and sauntered away, only to return momentarily with a fresh drink. "Sorry, all out of pickles."

I shrugged. "That's all right. They just get in the way, anyway."

"Right. So, what is it?" he said, wiping his hands on his dirty apron.

"What is what?"

"What's got your goat? Girl trouble? Has to be something, a guy like you in a place like this, early in the afternoon on a Saturday."

"What's a guy like me?"

He shrugged. "You know. Nice looking, nice suit, nice way of talking. You was raised right, I can tell. Educated."

"My mother thanks you." I raised my glass to him and took a drink.

"So, what brings you in here? I'm just curious." He pulled on his mustache and dug his little finger into his left nostril before wiping his hand on the apron again.

I cringed just a little, but I don't think he noticed. "You're a curious fellow, all right. That's usually what they say about me." I finished the third drink. "Another, please."

He didn't say anything, just picked up my glass and moved off again. This time when he returned, he placed two full glasses in front of me. "Saves me a trip," he said with a deep laugh.

"Good thinking," I said, swallowing most of martini number four.

"Dames, right?"

"Right." Who was I to argue?

"Don't let 'em get to you, mac. They ain't worth it."

"Some are, I think."

He shook his head and folded his big arms across his chest, letting them rest on his ample stomach. "Eh, I've been married twice. I was widowed once, divorced once. Better off without 'em, I think. What do you do for a living? I'm pretty good at guessing, you know. I'm thinking you're a banker."

"Nope." I took another drink.

"Lawyer?"

"Nope." Another drink.

"Hmm. Undertaker."

I laughed, and it felt good. "I'm a police detective."

"Really? You don't say. I wouldn't have figured. Working on a case?"

"I am indeed. A case of vodka and vermouth, and I'm hot on the trail." I finished the fourth and picked up the fifth.

"Hope you can swim, mac, cause you're drowning in your troubles."

"Say, that's pretty good. What's your name, apron man?"

"Wally, yours?"

"Heath. Heath Barrington."

"A pleasure, Mr. Barrington."

"Likewise, Wally." I was halfway through the fifth at this point and feeling much better. "Set me up with two more, my good friend."

"You sure you can handle it?"

"Besides being a detective, I happen to be a first-class drinker."

"You're first-class, all right. I gotta open another bottle, back in a moment, Mr. B."

Funny thing about booze. It gives some men courage and strength, others fear and weakness. It makes some happy, some sad. And it makes most everyone do foolish things. In this case, for me anyway, it was a little of all of them. As I finished that last drink, I suddenly decided to go back to the Crow apartment and confront Larry, hopefully before Liz got there. The bartender sidled up to me, a wary look in his eye. He set down martinis six and seven. "You're up to two dollars and eighty cents, just so you know."

"Keep a dollar for yourself, Wally. You've earned it."

"Thanks, but after these I think you've had enough, friend."

I polished off number six and slid the glass toward him, but for some reason it went off to the left, and he only just caught it before it tumbled to the floor. I stared across the bar at him once more, but he was a tad blurry and out of focus. Why did he keep moving? And were the mermaids on his forearms dancing? "I'll be the judge of that, but yes, I think you're right, as soon as I finish number eight."

"Seven."

"If you say so. Who's counting?" I downed a good portion of it. "Besides, I have somewhere to be."

"Should I call you a cab?"

"I've been called worse."

"Right. Wait right there." He moved off, and I held on to the edge of the bar to steady myself. The floor had begun undulating in waves. When he returned, I was proud I had managed to stay upright on the stool.

"Gotcha a Boynton Yellow Cab. It's two ten now, should be here in about five or ten minutes."

"You, sir, are a gentleman and a scholar." I spun about on the stool, only to realize I had made a three-sixty and was facing the bar again and feeling even more dizzy.

"You okay?" Wally said, handing me a silver dollar and twenty cents. "I kept a dollar, like you said."

"Good. And I'm fine. Never better." This time I slid off the stool carefully and managed to put one foot in front of the other until I reached the door and stepped outside, the summer heat slapping me in the face the way a certain young man had done many years ago. What had happened to that nice breeze from before? I curled up into the corner of the doorway, in the little shade provided by the canvas awning, and waited. True to their word, a Yellow Cab pulled up shortly, and I climbed into the back seat and gave the driver the address of the Crow apartment. Things got a bit hazy after that.

CHAPTER SEVEN

Sunday Morning, August 10, 1947

A bell was ringing incessantly. And everything was dark, at least until I opened my eyes. I was in my bed, in my bedroom, though I didn't really recall how I got there. That bell! I sat upright, then staggered to the bathroom, where I threw up, fortunately in the toilet. The bell stopped, but my head continued to pound and throb. I took some aspirin with a large glass of water, stripped off my underwear, and got in the shower, as cold as I could stand it. Better.

I turned off the water, stepped gingerly out of the tub, shivering, and wrapped a large towel around my waist. My tongue felt like sandpaper, and I stuck it out at the haggard face staring back at me in the medicine cabinet mirror. It looked yellow, and so did my face. I covered my cheeks and chin with shaving lather and slowly scraped it off, using my straight razor. That was not a good idea, as my hand was shaking and I nicked myself in several places. I dotted the cuts with pieces of toilet tissue and washed the lather down the sink before returning to the bedroom.

The shade covering the window was up, and the bright sunlight streaming in hurt my eyes. I pulled the shade down. I seemed to remember it was dark when I finally got home last night. Where had I been? Then I remembered. I was at Larry Crow's place, and a bar, somewhere. Something about mermaids. And a cab, a Yellow Cab. And another bar and another cab. Everything was fuzzy. The damned bell started again, and this time I realized it was the telephone, so

I padded slowly out into the hall by the front door to answer it, leaving wet footprints behind me on the wood floor.

"Hello?"

"Heath?"

"Yes, hello, Alan."

"Thank God. I've been trying to reach you all morning. I tried several times last night, too. I was worried sick. You were supposed to call me after you saw Larry Crow yesterday."

"Yeah, I know. I'm sorry, I forgot. Yesterday was a little rough."

"You forgot? I didn't know what had happened to you or where you were. I even tried calling Larry Crow's place. Did you know there are four Lawrence Crows in Milwaukee? I called them all. Three were wrong numbers, the fourth there was no answer all night. I couldn't find your aunt Verbina in the phone book, and I don't know your cousin Liz's last name. I thought about your parents, but I figured they'd be the last to know. Finally, a little after nine, I called Mrs. Murphy, your downstairs neighbor. She said she hadn't seen or heard from you all night. You told me she knows everything that goes on in that building, so I asked her to call me the moment she heard from you, regardless of the time. I got a call from her just after eleven that you had stumbled in. Apparently, you were in quite a state, and caterwauling on the stairs as you went up to your apartment. What on earth got into you? What happened at the Crow place? And where did you go until eleven p.m.? Your appointment with Larry was for one, so you were missing for ten hours."

I shook my head, and it hurt. So many questions. "Ten hours? Yeah, I guess that's right, more or less. I left his place around twenty after one. I may have stopped at a few more bars. Somewhere along the way, I seem to recall getting something to eat at a fairly awful diner, and then I went for a walk in Washington Park. I may have fallen asleep there for a couple hours on a surprisingly comfortable park bench. I'm afraid it's all a bit hazy." I picked up my wallet from the table by the phone and noted it was empty of cash. I had over fifteen dollars in there yesterday.

"Geez, that doesn't sound like you at all. What happened with you and Mr. Crow?"

"What time is it?" I said, ignoring his question for the time being.

"Don't you know? It's after ten in the morning."

"Ugh, really? And lower your voice, if you don't mind."

"Are you okay?" he said, only slightly softer.

"I'm fine, more or less, though I don't look so hot. I guess I had a few too many martinis. Then after that, well, I'm not exactly sure, like I said."

"You really had me worried. You still have me worried, behaving like that. I barely slept last night."

"I'm sorry. Crow shook me up more than I thought he would, I guess."

"So, I take it you haven't heard the news, then."

"Heard what? What news?"

"Larry Crow. He was found dead in his apartment late yesterday afternoon. They announced it on the radio this morning. Must have happened shortly after you left him. Explains why there was no answer at the fourth Lawrence Crow number I tried."

I nearly dropped the phone. I felt the blood draining from my cheeks. "I'm sorry, Alan, I thought you said Crow was found dead."

"I *did* say that. He was found dead in his apartment. What's the matter with you?"

I shook my head, and it hurt again. "It's just hard to believe, that's all. I thought I was hearing things. I mean, I just saw him yesterday."

"I know. Good thing I didn't know it last night, or I would have been a real mess."

"Do they know who killed him?"

"I never said he was murdered, Heath. I just said he's dead."

My brain pounded and throbbed. Why was Alan still talking so loud?

"Well, yeah, but he was a young man, and he was, well, Larry Crow, not well liked. I just assumed."

"Right, I know. I phoned the station after I heard about it on WBSM. Bergstrom told me Green's got the case."

"Alvin Green's a good detective. He'll get to the bottom of it."

"No doubt. Are you sure you're okay? Maybe I should come over."

I looked at myself in the mirror above the hall table. My face was barely recognizable. My eyes were bloodshot, my complexion was white as snow, and my skin was craggy and dotted with little red and white toilet tissue pieces. "No, no need. I'm okay, I guess. I'm just in a bit of a shock." As I gazed at my reflection, the vision of Larry Crow lying dead on his sofa came to me. I was standing over him, and there was blood everywhere. Someone was coming. I heard a voice, calling me.

"Understandable. Are you going into the station today, Heath? Heath? Are you there?"

I snapped out of it, though I still felt as if I was in a deep fog, and I thought perhaps I was going to be sick again.

"I'm here, sorry, just lost in thought."

"I was asking if you plan on going in today."

"Hmm? Oh, yes, I'd better. I'm off today, but I have a few things to check on. I'll have to get a ride in, though. If I remember correctly I took a cab home last night."

"Where's your car?"

"I'm not sure exactly. Somewhere in the vicinity of that bar, I think. The first one."

"Gee, Heath. You should have called me. I could borrow my landlord's jalopy and pick you up if you need a ride to the station."

"Thanks, but I can walk over to Farwell and hop the streetcar, then walk to the precinct from the stop. The fresh air and exercise will probably do me good."

"Okay, if you're sure."

"Yeah, I'm sure, but thanks. I suppose I'll have to let Liz know what's happened."

"She probably already knows. Bergstrom told me it's in the morning paper, too."

"The boys at the *Sentinel* don't waste time."

"No, they don't. So, what happened at Crow's apartment yesterday, anyway? You still haven't told me."

"I need to talk to you about that, but not over the phone."

"Okay, maybe we can meet for lunch. I'm off today, too."

"Sounds good, if you don't mind eating late. I have a few things to get done first. How about we meet at Schwimmer's at one thirty? I should hopefully have my car back by then. If you get there before me, grab a booth by the window."

"It's a date, see you then. Feel better."

"Right." I hung up the phone and looked at myself one final time, but the reflection staring back at me was Larry Crow's. I shuddered as I stared at his lifeless face, covered in blood, eyes half open. What did it mean? He was alive the last time I saw him. Wasn't he? Shaking it off, I walked back to the bathroom, combed my hair using my Kreml hair tonic, and slowly removed the tissues from my face, glad that the bleeding had stopped. I made myself a bromide and forced it down, then I raised the shade in the bedroom and put on my dark green suit with a striped tie. I had tossed the blue suit and tie I had worn yesterday on the chair in the corner. I walked back to the entry hall and retrieved the newspaper, which I dropped on the dining table.

I boiled a couple eggs and had a piece of toast and some of my mother's grape jam, a glass of orange juice, and a large cup of coffee. I put a note for the milkman in the milk box and read the paper at the table while I ate. Standard stuff on Crow, stating the facts, not much else, but then, I supposed they didn't know much else yet. After I finished and had cleaned up the kitchen, I decided to give Liz a call.

"Morning, cousin, what's buzzin'?" I said, though my inflection lacked its usual enthusiasm.

"Me. Buzz, buzz. Though not really," she replied flatly. "I'm glad to hear from you at last. Did you see the morning *Sentinel*?"

"I did. It's hard to believe."

"I know. Couldn't have happened to a nicer person, though."

"Liz…"

"Sorry. It's just you didn't know him like I did. You weren't married to the creep."

"I know, I'm sorry. I seem to recall phoning you from the tavern. You said you were going to go see him. Did you?"

"I did, or at least I tried to. No one answered the door, so Mr. Green drove me back home."

"Mr. Green didn't try to get fresh?"

"He suggested we stop for a drink, of course. I told him no in no uncertain terms."

"I bet you did."

"Of course I did. And I telephoned you afterward, as promised, but you didn't answer. I was worried about you."

"I had a rough night."

"A rough afternoon, I'd say. You started early."

"True, and I must admit parts of it are a bit hazy. What time did you get to the Crow apartment?"

"About a quarter after two, why?"

"Just wondering. I got there about one p.m. and stayed twenty minutes or so."

"And then you went to the bar."

"I did. But I think I went back to Crow's place later, I'm not sure when. It must have been about two thirty."

"Why would you go back there?"

"I was angry and a bit drunk. And I was concerned when you said you were going to go see him. I wanted to be there."

"Oh, Heath. To protect me? I told you I can take care of myself. Just ask Mr. Green."

"Yeah, I know, but still—"

"I'm not twelve anymore, cousin. So what happened?"

"I'm honestly not sure. I remember getting in a cab and giving Crow's address, but after that it's all a blank, more or less."

"Like you said, you were a bit drunk."

"Very drunk by that point. Double martinis on an empty stomach."

"You were pretty shook up, and I don't blame you, but it's not like you to drink like that."

"It wasn't just me I was worried about, Liz. It was you, like I said, and Alan, the fellow I was telling you about in the car. He was implicated in all this, too."

"Implicated in what? You mentioned yesterday Larry had made a compelling argument in favor of you just giving him five hundred dollars."

"I can't discuss it on the phone."

"It's all right, I think I can guess. You said it involves you and Alan, and knowing Larry like I do, well, a type of mail that starts with the letter B comes to mind."

"That's a pretty good guess."

"And you wanted to protect Alan."

"Yeah." The sight of blood everywhere came back to me once more. "I feel like I may have done something. I keep getting these flashbacks, these visions…"

"Of what?"

"Of him. Of Larry, lying there on the sofa, dead, blood all over the place."

"You didn't kill him, if that's what you're thinking. It's just your imagination."

"I wish I could be so sure."

"Don't be ridiculous. You probably went back to his apartment, knocked on the door, and no one answered, just like no one answered for me fifteen minutes prior, so you got back in your cab and left."

"Yeah, maybe. Maybe it is just my active imagination, like you said."

"Of course it is, darling. Don't give it another thought, okay?"

"Okay. Anyway, I just wanted to make sure you'd heard. I need to get going."

"All right, my cousin, just take care of yourself first and foremost, understand? At least you don't have Larry Crow to worry about anymore, and neither do I."

"Right."

"I saw Verbina yesterday evening, by the way. She said you were supposed to call her after four."

"Damn. I guess I forgot to call her, too."

"At least I'm in good company. I didn't mention the drunken phone call from the bar. I just told her you had called from someplace and had probably got delayed."

"Thanks for that. I'll give her a call later. Bye for now." I hung up the phone and went back to the bedroom. I picked up my blue suit and brushed it off, as it was dirty and wrinkled, and it had a small rip in the shoulder seam. It would have to go to the cleaners, along with the tie, which looked like I had used it as a handkerchief, so I set them both aside and picked up the white dress shirt I had been wearing. There was a large stain on the front of it, brownish red in color. The stain didn't seem to have an odor, but I knew from experience what a dried bloodstain looked like. Where had it come from? I examined my face in the mirror over the dresser but could find no scratches or nicks except for those I self-inflicted that morning while shaving, and I hadn't noticed any injuries elsewhere on my body while I was showering. I wondered what blood type Larry Crow had, and I shuddered. I crumpled the shirt into a ball and stuffed it in the far corner of my closet.

CHAPTER EIGHT

Sunday Afternoon, August 10, 1947

I took the streetcar to the precinct, signed in downstairs, then headed up to the detective's room, where I spoke briefly with Alvin Green, who was assigned to the Larry Crow case. He verified Crow was murdered in his apartment sometime yesterday afternoon. Larry's wife found the body, and there was a lot of blood. Grisly. Since he didn't seem to have any other information he was willing to share, I inquired about my missing car at the sergeant's desk. The boys had located it parked outside a bar called State of Mind on State Street, which sounded vaguely familiar. I thanked them for the information, then headed to my desk to do a little work on my current case.

After about an hour or so, I signed out again and got Grant Riker, an up-and-coming police officer I had worked with on a case a few months ago, to give me a lift over to the bar so I could pick up my car. Of course, a parking ticket had been tucked under the windshield wiper. I'd have to get Lois at the precinct to fix that. I shoved the ticket in my pocket, thanked Riker for the ride, and steered my car toward the east side and Schwimmer's restaurant.

Alan was waiting for me outside the door, his hat pulled low to shade his eyes from the afternoon sun. I was five minutes late.

"Sorry, I had trouble parking. Quite a crowd at Saint Mary's late Sunday service this afternoon, apparently."

"Yeah, and I think half the congregation is inside Schwimmer's. The after-church brunch crowd, you know. But I slipped the maître d' a silver dollar, and he said he'd save us a booth by the window."

"Excellent work, Officer. Shall we?" I held the door open for him and we went inside, removing our hats. The place was indeed bustling, but true to his word, the host ushered us over to a small booth in the back by a window after a brief wait.

"You're looking spiffy, Alan. New suit? I don't remember you wearing a navy double-breasted before," I said after we had hung up our hats and settled in across from each other.

Alan beamed. "Glad you noticed. Thought I'd better try keeping up with you, though I think that's a losing battle."

"Nonsense. You, sir, are a sharp dressed man."

"Well, thanks. How are you feeling? Any better?"

I sat upright and cracked my back and my neck. "Ugh, better than I did this morning, but not great. Remind me not to drink anymore."

Alan laughed. "Duly noted, for what it's worth. Drink some water, it helps."

"Right." I took a large gulp from one of the water glasses the waiter had deposited with the menus before he had hurried away. "What looks good?"

"Normally I'd say you, but not today. You don't look so hot, kind of pale. And what happened to your face? Get attacked by a rogue squirrel?"

"Funny. Remind me to buy a safety razor. I'm officially retiring my straight razor after today."

"Sounds like a good idea. I always hated using a straight razor. Those things are wicked."

"Especially after a night of heavy drinking. So, what are you going to have to eat?"

Alan glanced back at his menu, which had a pink piece of paper clipped to it listing the daily special. "Grilled cheese on rye and a bowl of tomato soup, I think, and a Coke."

"The lunch special for a dollar thirty-five. Sounds good, make it two."

"Right." Alan signaled for the waiter, a young, lanky chap with a quick smile and dark brown wavy hair who was fast on his feet.

He couldn't have been more than eighteen or nineteen. His name tag read David.

"What will it be, fellas?"

"You're awfully young to be working in a place like this," I said.

"My dad owns the joint. He's got me working six days a week, mostly for tips. I never get to hang out with my friends at the coffee shop anymore. We're hopping today, so what can I get you?" He tapped his pencil on his order pad impatiently.

"Two lunch specials, two Cokes," Alan said.

"Got it." He shoved his pencil behind his ear, grabbed our menus, and zoomed away.

He was certainly much quicker and younger than the waiter we had the last time we ate here.

"Did you get to the precinct?" Alan said.

I nodded as I took two more aspirin out of a tin and popped them in my mouth along with a swig of water. "I did. They found my car outside a bar on State Street. Riker gave me a ride over there."

"Well, that's something anyway. How is Officer Riker?"

"Fine. He said to say hello. He's bucking for detective, and I think he'll make it."

"Good for him."

I felt the aspirin slide down my throat. "Yeah. I talked to Green briefly, too. He didn't have much to say."

"I suppose not. Still all too new."

"But he verified Crow was murdered."

"Did he say how?"

I shook my head. "No, but he indicated there was a lot of blood everywhere." I closed my eyes, and the vision of Larry lying on the sofa covered in blood darted through my head again. I opened my eyes quickly and blinked several times.

"What is it?"

"Nothing. Something, maybe. I don't know. I'm not sure I want to know, to be honest."

The waiter dropped off the sandwiches and soups along with the

Cokes and stood impatiently with his hands on his hips. "Anything else?"

"No, thank you, this will do for now," Alan said.

"I'll be back in a bit to check on you." He was gone before he had finished the sentence, his words trailing behind him like steam from a locomotive as he sped off to the next table.

"Did you talk to your cousin?" Alan said, blowing on a spoonful of tomato soup.

"Liz? Yes, I called her right after you. She was in shock, too. It's all so unbelievable." I tried the soup. It needed salt.

"Who would kill him? I mean, I think a lot of people wanted him dead, but to murder him in cold blood—"

"A lot of people *did* want him dead," I said, shaking salt into my bowl. "Including me and Liz."

Alan didn't say anything for a moment. He took the shaker from me once I had finished and salted his own bowl, then took another spoonful. "Better, and you're right about people wanting him dead. I must admit even I was kind of glad to hear the news, but still…"

I tried the grilled cheese, finding it perfect. "I know, Alan, I know."

"So, what happened when you went to his apartment yesterday? What did he want? What did he say? What did you say?"

I took another bite of the sandwich, a drink of water, a sip of my Coke, and then a spoonful of soup. "It's complicated, I think. I don't even remember exactly. He wanted me to give him five hundred dollars."

Alan dropped his soup spoon into his bowl, causing some of it to splash up on his new suit coat. "Cheese and crackers!" He dipped his napkin into his water glass and dabbed at the spot. "This will have to go to the cleaners."

"I'm afraid so."

"First time I've worn it, too."

"They'll get it out."

"I suppose, but still. My napkin's in my lap, but the soup just *had* to splash above it."

"Always the way."

"Yeah. So, he wanted five hundred dollars. Golly, that's a lot of money," Alan said softly, still dabbing at the spot.

"That was his demand."

"What did you say?"

"I told him I didn't have five hundred dollars, which is the truth. He gave me until noon today to come up with the money."

"Why did he think you'd give him that kind of dough?"

"Because of you. And me. You and me. He found a note I'd written to you a while ago and had stupidly thrown in the trash. It was a love note of sorts."

"Oh." Alan stopped dabbing at his suit and stared across the table at me. "So, that's what he meant by knowing about us."

"Yes. It's all my fault. After he found that note, he started keeping tabs on us. Places we went together, things we did. He interviewed one of my neighbors, and he even talked to Phyllis Waters from payroll."

"Why her?"

"She and I went out a few times a while ago. To the movies and stuff. Mainly just to keep up my reputation, you know? Keep people from talking. I guess it didn't work so hot. I was too much of a gentleman."

"Probably would have worked with anyone but Phyllis Waters. So, he investigated until he felt he had enough evidence to blackmail you."

I finished my sandwich and pushed the plate away. "Exactly. You have no idea how scared I was, Alan, for both of us. And how scared I still am."

Alan slowly pushed his plate and bowl away, too, dropping the soggy napkin next to them. He loosened his tie and reached his hand partway across the table, as if to touch me or hold my hand, but then realized where we were and retracted it quickly. "Heath, I know you didn't kill Larry Crow, if you're thinking that's what I'm thinking." His voice was just loud enough for me to hear, but no one else in the noisy restaurant.

I looked at his fresh-scrubbed face with just a hint of stubble, his brilliant blue eyes, his jet-black hair, his tender lips, and I couldn't help but smile.

"That makes one of us, then. Actually, two. Liz also thinks I'm innocent."

"She's right. Why would you doubt yourself?"

"Because I went back to his apartment after I left that bar, at least I think I did. And I keep seeing images of him lying dead on his sofa, covered in blood."

Alan didn't say anything for a moment. "Why did you go back?"

"Because Liz said she was going there, and I was worried about what he might do to her, and about what she might do to him. And because I was angry, and just a tad tipsy."

He gazed at me tenderly. "I know you. You rescue earthworms off the sidewalk after it rains. You could never kill someone."

"Larry Crow was lower than an earthworm."

"Maybe so, but he was still a living being, and it's not in your nature to be cruel."

"I'm not so sure anymore. It wasn't just me who was in danger. Even your friendly neighborhood dog will bite if her pup is threatened."

"And I'm your pup?" He cocked his head in that adorable way of his.

"Well, you're a cute pup, as someone once said. And I would bite to kill if you were threatened."

"I doubt Larry Crow was bitten to death."

"You know what I mean."

Alan took a last drink of water before pushing the glass away next to his plate and bowl. "I do know what you mean, and likewise. But I still don't think you murdered him." He picked up his Coke and played with the straw, alternately sucking on it and biting it. I found it quite distracting.

"Then who did?"

"That, my friend, remains to be seen, as you always say," Alan said.

"There's something else about that day. Yesterday. When I was in the Crow apartment for our meeting, I got the impression someone else was there besides me and Larry."

Alan raised an eyebrow. "Oh? Who? His wife?"

I shook my head. "No, she'd gone out, at his request. It was a man, I think. I saw a cigar in the ashtray and another unsmoked one next to it."

"Maybe Larry smoked cigars."

"Maybe. That's what he claimed, but I got the impression he was lying. Larry appeared rather flustered when I first arrived, and it took him a while to get to the door. I had to knock twice. I could hear two men conversing behind the door, but I couldn't quite make out what they were saying. He said he was on the phone, but when I mentioned I distinctly heard two voices, he claimed it must have been the radio, which he said he'd just turned off, but the top of the console was cold."

"So he *was* lying."

"Like a rug. Also, the bedroom door was closed, and I heard a noise from within. Larry said it was a cat. And there was an empty beer bottle on the coffee table, but Larry was drinking bourbon."

"Well, your instincts are usually pretty good. I wonder who it was. The murderer?"

"A good possibility."

"All finished?" The waiter had reappeared and was scooping up our bowls, plates, and glasses before we could answer. He left our Cokes, since we were holding them.

"Dessert?" the waiter said, almost as an afterthought.

Alan looked at me, but I shook my head. "No, just the check, please."

"Sure thing." He whisked the other dishes away with a flourish, and I had to admit I envied his youthful energy. He returned quickly enough with the bill, which Alan insisted on paying. This time I didn't put up too much of an argument.

"Want to catch a movie or something?" Alan said as we finished our Cokes and gathered up our hats from the hooks on the wall.

I shook my head once more. It still hurt, but not quite as badly. "Thanks, but I'm not in the mood right now. I think I'm going to go home and lie down for a bit."

"All right, get some rest and try not to worry."

"That's like telling a fish not to swim, but I'll try. You do the same. Need a ride home?"

"Nah, I can hop the streetcar, but thanks. Call me later, okay?"

"All right, I will, I promise."

"Don't forget this time."

"I won't," I said.

We walked out into the sunshine and pulled our hats low to shade our eyes. I wished, as I had on so many occasions, that I could embrace him, kiss him, and hold him tight, right there on the sidewalk in public, in broad daylight. But instead, we shook hands and went our separate ways, glancing over our shoulders at each other once or twice. The breeze had returned.

CHAPTER NINE

Sunday Late Afternoon, August 10, 1947

I drove home slowly, my head and stomach both aching. Luckily my favorite parking spot under the great-grandmother elm tree just up the street was available. I pulled into it easily enough, the whitewall tires just kissing the high curb. I left the vent windows open a crack and then headed up the steps and across the walk to the front door.

Mrs. Murphy was in the lobby, seated in a well-worn, overstuffed floral club chair next to the mailboxes. Her eyes were closed and her head was back as I entered. She was snoring softly, her mouth agape. She had on a yellow light cotton dress and pink house slippers, her legs crossed at the ankles, her face flushed. She looked warm and tired, as I imagined I did, too. She awoke with a start as the door closed behind me and sat bolt upright, snorting and sniffling as she did so, like an asthmatic bulldog.

"Good afternoon, Mrs. Murphy," I said, taking off my hat and wiping my brow.

"Oh, hello, Mr. Barrington, I was just having a little rest." She glanced up at me and wiped away a bit of drool from the corner of her mouth with a handkerchief she'd extracted from her ample bosom. "Enjoying your Sunday?"

"It's been rather warm again."

"It has indeed. Though the breeze helps some."

"Yes, but it comes and goes. It's just started up again a little while ago."

"Ugh." She fanned her face with her right hand. "Mr. Murphy hasn't moved from the sofa all day, and he refuses to get dressed. He just lies there in his undershirt and boxer shorts."

That was a mental picture I really didn't need. "Yes, well, supposedly it's going to cool off tomorrow. I'm afraid I have a bit of a headache, so I'm going to go lie down myself."

"That's a good idea. You don't look too good, and frankly I'm not surprised after last night."

Now it was my turn to be embarrassed. "Right, well, if you'll excuse me—"

"You know I like to mind my own business, but Mr. Murphy was exasperated over your friend telephoning us at such a late hour last night. I think it was that fellow you work with, the one I see you with sometimes. He gave his name but I've forgotten. Keene, maybe."

"Keyes, Alan Keyes. And I'm so sorry."

"Yes, that's it, Keyes. It was after nine o'clock, you know. No one telephones after nine, unless it's bad news. It was most distressing. And of course, I couldn't tell him anything. I had no idea where you were, and I hadn't heard a peep from your apartment through the kitchen vent all evening."

"I was out having a few drinks."

"A few? You woke us up when you finally did come home. I think you woke up the whole building, singing some woeful song as you made your way, stumbling and falling up the stairs. I got right up out of bed. Such a ruckus! And I'd promised that Mr. Keyes I'd call him back when and if I heard you were home, no matter what time it was. So I put on my robe and my glasses and did just that. He was relieved you were all right, though that was a matter of opinion. He said he'd call you this morning."

"He did. And once again, I'm very sorry to have disturbed you and Mr. Murphy and anyone else."

"That's not all, you know. You left all your laundry on the lines in the basement, Mr. B. That's not like you, not like you at all. None of this is. You're usually so quiet, considerate, and polite. I knew it was your laundry because I recognized some of your clothes, and of course your wicker basket was on the chair."

"Oh, my goodness, that's right. I hung it up down there yesterday and forgot all about it. I've got a lot on my mind lately."

"You're the only person I know with a monogrammed laundry basket. H.B. So fancy."

"It's just an old luggage marker I attached after my first one mysteriously disappeared from the laundry room last year. I'll go down and get it right away."

She held up one of her little hands, the one she had been using to fan her face. "No need, I took care of it for you. I took it all down, folded it, took the basket upstairs to your apartment, and left it outside your door."

"Gee, that was awfully nice of you, Mrs. Murphy. You didn't have to."

"I *did* have to because there wasn't any room on the lines for my things, and Sunday is my wash day, you know. You're not the only one in this building. Very inconsiderate, and as I said, not like you at all," she chastised me, wagging one of her fingers in my direction, and I felt terrible.

"I do apologize," I said earnestly once more. "It was just an oversight. Thank you again for taking care of it for me."

"You're welcome. It's a lot of stairs, though, from the basement all the way up to your apartment on three, and then I had to go all the way back down and hang up my things. I have sciatica, you know, quite painful. And on top of that, you waking us up in the middle of the night. Mr. Murphy was able to fall back asleep but not me. Once I'm up, I'm up. I'm just resting here until my laundry is dry."

"I do so appreciate it, and I'm sorry again you had to go out of your way like that."

She shrugged ever so slightly and shifted her weight. "Eh, it's what neighbors do. You'd do the same for me, I'm sure." Her tone had softened some.

"Of course." Though the thought of handling and folding Mrs.

Murphy's delicates did not much appeal to me. "I promise there won't be a repeat of last night, either."

"I should hope not. I need my beauty sleep, you know."

"That, Mrs. Murphy, is one thing you don't need. You are ever lovely," I said, and I meant it. She was a kind, beautiful person.

She blushed and tittered, and I could tell I was forgiven.

"I'd better get upstairs and put everything away," I said. "Have a good afternoon."

"You do the same." She shifted her weight a little in the chair once more, laid her head back, and closed her eyes again.

When I reached the third floor, I saw my laundry basket was indeed outside my door, and Oscar, Mrs. Ferguson's cat, was enjoying a catnap on top of my clean clothes. "All right, you. Wake up and on your way. No saucer of milk right now."

Oscar gazed languidly up at me, licked his nose, and meowed softly, but he didn't budge. I sighed. This weather was making everyone cranky and tired, and Oscar was probably no exception.

"You're getting too fat and lazy, mister, and you're getting hair all over my things. Up with you." I tilted the basket a little and he obliged by climbing down onto the floor, where he promptly stretched out once more and flicked his tail back and forth to let me know he was most annoyed at having been disturbed. I unlocked my door, picked up the basket, and went inside. As I turned to close the door, Oscar looked up at me and meowed.

"Same to you."

I hung up my hat and took the basket to my bedroom. As I put my shirts, towels, socks and underwear away, I recalled the dress shirt with the bloodstain that I had shoved in my closet. When the clean clothes were stashed, I pulled it out again and looked at it. Once more, visions of Larry Crow dead and covered in blood flashed through my mind, and I shivered in spite of the fact my apartment was warm and stuffy. I put it back in the corner of the closet, shut the door, undressed, and flopped down on my bed, making a mental note to call Alan later, but I still couldn't decide if I wanted to tell him about the bloodstained shirt or not.

I napped until almost five and awoke with a start, covered in sweat. I took a shower, got dressed once more, and listened to the radio for a bit, but there wasn't much good on, and I couldn't concentrate anyway. Finally I gave up, turned it off, and made myself a light dinner. After finishing up the dishes, I gave my aunt Verbina a call.

"Verbina Partridge speaking."

"Hello, Auntie. It's me, Heath."

"Well, about time you decided to phone, over twenty-four hours later than promised."

I sighed. "I'm sorry, it was a crazy day, a crazy night."

"I see. I was worried sick, of course. Even more so when I read this morning's paper."

"I know, entirely my fault for not calling. I simply forgot."

"That's not like you, dear. Are you all right?"

"I'm fine," I lied. "Just tired."

"So, what happened? Why did you go to see that nasty man in the first place?"

I didn't answer immediately, as I pondered just how much I really wanted to tell her. I decided less would be better, especially over the phone. The details would have to wait until I saw her in person. "He wanted money. He was behind on his rent, his alimony, and a couple of other debts, I guess."

"How much money? And why on earth would he think he could get money from you?"

"A fair amount. We were family once, of sorts, you know. He probably ran out of people to ask."

"I certainly hope you told him no."

"I told him I'd think about it."

"Good heavens. Well, now you don't have to think about it. What happened to him, anyway? How did he die? He was a fairly young man."

"I only know what you know, Auntie. Just what I read in the papers. Alvin Green has the case, not me."

"He was alive when you left him, of course."

"Yes, very much alive." At least the first time I left him, I thought.

"Do keep me posted, please. I worry about you."

"Thanks, Aunt Bina."

"Liz came to see me last night," she said. "We had a light supper in the China Cupboard restaurant downstairs. She brought me the most delightful Parisian scarf, stunning colors. It was lovely to see her again. She positively glowed."

"Yes, being abroad seems to have agreed with her."

"She also mentioned you had telephoned her and you weren't at home, but she neglected to give me any details."

Good ol' Liz. I could always count on her to have my back. "I stopped for a drink after I left Larry's, and I gave her a call, that's all."

"But you didn't call me."

"I should have, but it was around one thirty or so, and I figured you were still on your lunch date with the eligible banker."

"That's true, I was. But I expected you to call around four, so I made sure I was home. You and I were supposed to make plans to get together. I was concerned about you. I tried phoning, but there was no answer."

"I'm sorry. I got home later than expected. How was the lunch?"

"Very nice. We ate at the Pfister Hotel. Charming. We must do tea there again soon. We've gotten out of the habit, Heath."

"Yes, that would be nice. Things have been so busy lately. But I always enjoy our tea dates."

"So do I, dear. I always have time for you."

"Thanks," I replied, feeling guilty all of a sudden. "Anyway, I must go for now, but we'll set up a tea date soon, I promise."

"All right, I look forward to it. Ciao for now."

I hung up the phone and breathed in and out a few times as deeply as I could. After a few moments, I gave Alan a call, as I promised, but I still didn't mention the bloodstained shirt. I told myself I would, but the timing just wasn't right, not yet. We chatted about Mrs. Murphy, Aunt Verbina, and even Oscar, but he could tell I was distracted and worried. He did his best to reassure me and even offered to come over and spend the night, but I wanted to be alone to think and brood, and I most likely wouldn't sleep much again.

CHAPTER TEN

Monday Morning, August 11, 1947

I slept fitfully, as I had predicted. Sometime in the wee small hours of the night, I got up, used the bathroom, and fixed myself a cheese sandwich, but I could only eat half of it. I wrapped the other half in wax paper and put it in the icebox and then went back to bed. When the alarm went off at seven thirty, I must have been somewhat fast asleep, as I awoke with a jolt, knocking the alarm clock off the nightstand, where it crashed into pieces on the hardwood floor. I sighed. A brilliant way to start my Monday.

Once showered, shaved, and dressed, I felt a little better. My headache was gone, but I still didn't look so hot. I didn't cut myself with my straight razor this morning, but I held to my vow to get rid of it, as yesterday's nicks were still visible. I put on my brown suit and green tie.

Coffee and breakfast helped my mood, and I perused the morning *Sentinel* as I ate. Nothing new on the *Kon-Tiki* or Larry Crow's death. I cleaned up the dishes, retrieved my quart of milk from the milk box, grabbed my hat and my soiled blue suit and tie, and headed downstairs and out the front door of the building. It had cooled off to a much more comfortable seventy-five degrees or so. With a nod to a haggard-looking Fuller Brush salesman who was lugging his battered black leather sample case laboriously up the sidewalk, I climbed in behind the wheel of my car and turned it toward the police station, with a brief detour at the dry cleaners.

Mr. Howard at Sparkle Laundry seemed a bit surprised by the condition of my suit and tie, as I am usually fastidious with my apparel, but nonetheless he asked no questions and promised to have it ready by Thursday. That done, I arrived at the station only slightly behind schedule and entered via the Eighth Street door, signing in on the blackboard. Sparrow was behind the desk.

"Morning, Sam, how was your weekend?"

He glanced up at me and grunted. "Nonexistent, Barrington. I was here. I've been putting in some overtime."

"Sorry to hear it."

"Eh, it's okay. I can use the money. Lucy's expecting again." He looked tired. He was only in his thirties but already had bags and sags under his red, puffy eyes and a bit of a paunch around his middle.

"Congratulations. Your fourth?"

Sparrow groaned. "Fifth. Maybe this time we'll have a boy."

"I'll buy you a cigar. Say, do me a favor, will you, Sparrow? Run a check on a Michael Hart and see if anything turns up. He lives somewhere in town, recently out of the Navy, currently unemployed."

"Sure, why?"

"Just curious. He's interested romantically in my cousin. They met on the *Ile de France* last week, Cherbourg to New York."

"Will do." He scribbled a reminder to himself on a pad and then looked up at me again. "By the way, the chief wants to see you, right away."

I cocked my head. "Oh? What for?"

"Don't know, not my business. He got in early. Told me to tell you to go right up."

"Thanks. See you later."

"Right."

I checked my mail slot, stuffed a few notes in my pocket, and then climbed the stairs to the detectives' room and put my hat on the rack behind my desk. That done, I proceeded to the chief's office, a knot in my stomach once more. I felt like a naughty boy being summoned to the principal.

"Come in," he called out in answer to my rap on the glass.

He was seated behind his massive oak desk, his collar open, suit coat and tattered old hat on the rack behind him. His shirt sleeves were rolled up, revealing hairy forearms, and his necktie was undone. Even though it was just after nine a.m., his ashtray already had about four cigarette butts in it. Apparently his attempts to quit had not been successful.

His office was a decent size, full of the usual accoutrements one would expect. Besides the large desk, there was his chair, a couple of side chairs, and some filing cabinets, all well used and broken in. A dingy, yellowed strip of flypaper hung in the corner of the room, with little black corpses clinging to it as it spun lazily about. A rusty fan sat atop one of the filing cabinets and moved the smoky air around the room. The window behind his desk was open about four inches, and the metal blinds clattered occasionally with the breeze.

"Good morning," I said, hopefully.

He looked up at me, his bushy caterpillar eyebrows forming a V. "That remains to be seen. Have a seat."

I dragged a wooden chair across the scuffed linoleum floor, pulled it up to his desk, and sat down rather uncomfortably.

"You heard about Larry Crow?" he said.

"Yes. Sure is a shock."

"Is it?" He looked at me hard across the surface of his desk, cluttered with inkwells, fountain pens, pencils, telephones, file folders, and papers.

I felt my stomach do a back flip. "Well, sure. I mean sudden death is always a shock, isn't it?"

"I suppose. His murder is Green's case, of course. Since Crow worked here at the station, it wasn't hard for him to find out a few things. Green's preliminary report got me curious." He tapped a manila file on his desktop with his left index finger.

"Alvin Green's a good detective."

"He is. And so are you. Crow was married to your cousin, wasn't he?"

"Yes, a few years ago. He remarried."

"I read that. I didn't really know this Crow fellow, but from what Green's told me he was rather a shady character. Someone we probably shouldn't have had working here, even as a janitor."

"Larry was a tough cookie, Chief. Not well liked."

"I can understand why. Green found out he was involved with Vinnie the Horse, too."

I raised my eyebrows in surprise. "The gangster? I hadn't heard that."

"If I'd heard that before yesterday, Crow would have been unemployed in a heartbeat. No one tells me anything, at least not until it's too late."

"I suppose those in charge are often the last to know."

"Anything *you* want to tell me, Barrington?" he said, leaning forward and staring me in the eye.

I swallowed. "Can't think of anything."

He didn't speak for a moment, but continued to stare at me. Finally he leaned back in his chair. "Okay. So, Melvin Horshauer, aka Vinnie the Horse. Vinnie used to be in cahoots with Benny Ballentine and Gregor Slavinsky, but he went his own way, for better or worse. Preliminary reports also show Larry Crow mixed up in some shady dealings of his own, and it's possible he and Vinnie were partners in a bad business or businesses."

"Like what?"

"Fight fixing, racketeering, gambling, loan sharking, just to name a few. Larry was into Vinnie for some big bucks, according to what Green found out from one of Vinnie's associates."

I whistled softly. "Sounds like Larry was in all kinds of trouble."

"And trouble begets trouble."

"Meaning?"

"Meaning Vinnie puts the screws to Larry for money, so Larry puts the screws to others for money, or something like that."

My stomach was now doing triple somersaults. "You think Vinnie killed Crow?"

"It's one of Green's theories. A man matching Vinnie's description was seen entering the Crow apartment the day of the murder."

I took a deep breath. "That would make sense. Vinnie the Horse has murdered before."

"Manslaughter. And he was put away for it, but he got out not long ago, on parole."

"So, he could have done it."

"He could have. We're trying to locate him for questioning. He's no longer at the address he gave when he got out, and he didn't leave a new one, which is against his parole instructions. We could lock him up again just for that, and we just may, once we find him again."

"If he did bump off Crow, he's probably left town," I said.

"Probably, if he did kill him." The chief leaned forward and rested his hairy left arm on the desk top as he stroked his chin, fingering the stubble of his beard. "But I can't figure out why he'd kill him. Break his leg, or an arm, maybe. Cut off one of his fingers, possibly. Smash his nose, perhaps. All options that would get his point across but still leave Crow alive to get Vinnie his money. With Crow dead, Vinnie's got nothing."

"I suppose. Do you have any other suspects besides Vinnie the Horse?"

He picked up a pencil and moved it about in his hand as he leaned back in his chair again, which creaked and groaned accordingly. "I can't discuss it, not your case."

"You're already discussing it with me."

He chewed on the pencil, which already looked like a beaver had had it for lunch. Finally he tossed it in the trash and lit up a cigarette. "The wife's still trying to get me to quit, but it's not going well. Days like this don't help."

"I'm sorry."

He blew the smoke toward an errant fly, who did a lazy spin and landed on one of the file cabinets. "I don't know of any other suspects yet."

I looked at him again across the wide expanse of his desk. "Why do I feel like you do, but you're not saying."

The chief took another long drag on his cigarette and returned my stare. "All right. You're one of my best detectives. Green asked around some. You and Crow didn't exactly care for each other, and he was married to your cousin at one time. And a notebook was found in the apartment."

"What kind of a notebook?"

"A list of names. People he was apparently blackmailing or who owed him money. Your name was in it, along with an appointment time of Saturday, August ninth, one p.m. The day he was murdered. There weren't any other appointments listed for that day."

I swallowed again, hard this time. "I see. What else?"

"You tell me. In fact, I really wish you would. I've given you a couple of chances already but you wouldn't bite. If it were anybody else but you, you'd have been arrested by now on suspicion of murder, and you still may be. So, tell me why Larry Crow would be blackmailing you? What did he have on you?"

My stomach was done doing backflips and somersaults and had collapsed in exhaustion. "Nothing. He was all bluster. He sent me a note telling me he had something on me and that he wanted to see me at his apartment, so I went."

"If it was all bluster, why did you go?"

"Curiosity, I guess. I wanted to see what he had dreamed up."

"Is that on the level, Barrington? You know Green's going to dig more things up, and if there's something you don't want dug up, you better tell me now. You're a Milwaukee Police detective, and what happens to you happens to the entire department, me included, understand?"

"Yes, sir, I understand."

"Good. So spill it. What did Crow have on you? Or at least think he had on you?"

My stomach lay flat, dead, and bloated. And I felt a bead of sweat pop out on my forehead again. "He, uh, imagined I'd had some unsavory relations with someone in the department." I dabbed at my forehead once more with my handkerchief before stuffing it back into my suit pocket.

The chief raised his bushy eyebrows into an M shape this time and picked up an unchewed pencil, turning it over and over between his fingers, the cigarette dangling from his lips. "What kind of unsavory relations and with who?"

"He, uh, didn't say who. I'm thinking maybe he meant Phyllis Waters in payroll. She and I have gone out a few times."

"Why would Crow care about you and Miss Waters? And why would he think anyone else would care?"

"She's a divorcée and has a sullied reputation." I felt terrible bringing Phyllis into this, but I had to protect Alan if I could. And I had to protect myself. Besides, Phyllis apparently hadn't hesitated to spill the beans about me to Larry Crow.

"I'm aware of Miss Waters and her reputation, but that hardly seems like something anyone would think they could blackmail someone over." He dropped the pencil and finished off the cigarette, grinding it out in the ashtray.

"Larry was grasping at straws. He needed money and was desperate. He was behind on his rent, he owed alimony to my cousin, and he apparently owed quite a bit to Vinnie the Horse, as you just told me."

"Yeah, apparently. So, you went to see him the day he was murdered."

"In hindsight it was a pretty stupid thing to do."

"Lots of things are stupid in hindsight, Barrington. What happened?"

"He'd been drinking and was unreasonable, to say the least. I tried to convince him he had nothing on me, but he kept insisting, though he wouldn't tell me exactly what it was he supposedly had. He asked for money, and I denied him. Finally, I left."

The chief groaned audibly. "Jeez, Barrington. Why didn't you come to me right away with this?"

"I don't know. I should have."

"Yes, you should have. You realize you're a suspect now. Even if you're not arrested, I could place you on leave until the case is resolved."

"But you said a man matching Vinnie's description was seen entering Crow's apartment on Saturday."

The chief consulted the folder on his desk containing a typewritten report. "I did say that. Green talked to one of the neighbors, a Mrs. Picking."

I felt my face go white. The pretty lady that lived across the hall from Crow. Fortunately, the chief had his nose in the folder and didn't notice the sweat break out on my brow again, which I quickly wiped off with my handkerchief.

The chief continued reading. "It says here the man was tall, dark, well dressed, slim waisted, and broad shouldered, wearing a dark suit, gray fedora, and smoking a cigar. Rather a general description. She didn't get a good look at his face as he had his back to her."

I felt a little sick, knowing that description fit me to a T, except for the cigar. I recalled instantly the cigar in the ashtray and on the table in the Crow apartment.

"Vinnie the Horse has always been known for being a sharp dresser, and he is tall, dark, and slim."

The chief nodded. "He is. And cigars are his trademark. Willard Ponies, to be exact. Vinnie the Horse, Willard Ponies cigars, get it?"

"Yeah, clever. Did Crow smoke them, too?"

"Hell if I know, why?"

I shook my head. "Just wondering. I got the impression someone else was in the apartment while I was there, hiding in the bedroom."

"What makes you think that?"

"I heard two men talking right before I knocked, and there were two cigars on the table, one in the ashtray, and a new one next to it, the band still on it. The brand was Willard Ponies. When you mentioned the neighbor lady saying the man she saw was smoking a cigar, well…"

The chief's bushy eyebrows shot up. "Vinnie the Horse."

"It might have been."

"But you never saw him?"

I shook my head. "No, but the bedroom door was closed, and I heard a noise from within, like he accidentally knocked something over."

"Interesting. If he was there, then Vinnie figures to be a prime suspect."

I sighed, somewhat relieved.

"But the neighbor's description was rather general," the chief continued. "I can't help but notice that it even matches you."

I laughed, though it came out as more of a titter, and the chief shot me an odd look. "But I don't smoke cigars."

"Not that I know of. You're a smart man. You may have made up the whole thing about someone hiding in the apartment." He sorted through the file once more and perused some of the photographs. "Green's report doesn't mention finding any cigars, and the pictures of the crime scene don't show any in the ashtray."

"I didn't make any of that up, Chief, on the level, I swear. The mystery man must have taken them with him. He probably finished the one in the ashtray and put the unsmoked one back in his pocket. The ashtray could be checked for cigar ash."

He grunted again. "Type up a statement and get it to Green, pronto. Don't leave anything out. He'll contact the lab and have that ashtray and its contents examined."

"Yes, sir, I'll get right on it. I'll ask around and see if Crow was known to smoke cigars, too, but I don't think he did."

"Let Green do the asking around, Barrington. This is not your case, do I make myself clear?"

"Yes, sir. Not my case."

"Just type up your report and get it to Green."

"I will. Anything else?" I said, hoping he was finished.

"So, this fellow, possibly Vinnie the Horse, you think was presumably still in the Crow apartment with Larry when you left, is that correct?"

"I believe so, yes."

"And Larry was alive and in good health the last time you saw him?"

"Yes, of course."

"Right. And what time was that?"

"I got to his place about one, and I left him around one twenty."

"To go where?"

"A bar, a neighborhood bar."

"That doesn't sound like you, Barrington." He picked up the pencil again and absentmindedly started chewing on it.

"Again, stupid in hindsight."

"So, someone in the bar can provide you with an alibi?"

"Yeah, sure. The barkeep. He and I were friendly. There weren't too many others in there that time of day."

"Okay, good. What time did you leave the bar?"

"I don't recall exactly, but I think it was almost two thirty. Maybe twenty or twenty-five after."

The chief frowned. "That doesn't exactly help your case, Barrington. Mrs. Crow didn't get home and find the body until two forty."

I felt like I was going to throw up. "It might have been later, I'm not sure. The bartender called me a cab. I left my car there."

"I see. Green will want to talk to him, so get him the name of the place and any other details you can remember. What cab company did you use?"

"I honestly don't recall."

"The bartender will know, Green will find out. Where did you go after you left the bar?"

"I don't really remember that, either. Another bar, I think," I said, which wasn't a total lie. "I also ended up in Washington Park for a few hours, and I grabbed something to eat along the way."

"The cab company should have a record of where they took you."

"Sure, Chief, but you can't seriously think I killed Larry Crow, do you?"

He snapped the pencil in half and threw it in the garbage can under his desk next to the corpse of the other one. "I like you, Barrington. You're a good man. And if I didn't trust you, you wouldn't be sitting here right now. So you're not an official suspect, and I want to keep it that way, but you are a suspect. Do I believe you bumped him off? No. But it doesn't matter what I think. What matters is what Alvin Green finds out, and I expect you to cooperate with him to the fullest, understand?"

"Yes, sir, and thanks."

"For what?"

"For saying you don't believe I did it."

"Forget about it. I don't believe television will ever replace radio, either. But that doesn't mean it won't."

CHAPTER ELEVEN

Monday Afternoon, August 11, 1947

After leaving the chief's office, I stopped in the men's lavatory, where I had the dry heaves. I splashed some cold water on my face, but it didn't help me feel much better. I then headed back to the detectives' room, where I noticed most of the other guys hadn't made it in yet.

I returned to my desk, where I quickly typed up my statement as best as I could remember it, leaving out the details of the note Crow had found. That done, I pulled it out of my typewriter, put the carbon copy in my filing cabinet, and hand-delivered the original to Alvin Green at his desk. He was also typing something up, using the hunt-and-peck method and swearing under his breath.

"You know, if you asked nicely, I bet Betty would type that for you," I said, walking up to him.

He glared at me. "I can do it."

"Suit yourself. I just came from the chief's office. He asked me to give you my statement on what happened at the Crow apartment when I was there on Saturday." I held out my one double-spaced page, and he took it from me without looking at it, setting it down on his desktop as he continued his assault on the typewriter.

"Thanks. I was going to ask you for it."

"Glad to be of help. He also told me about your preliminary report and what you found on me."

"Nothing personal," he replied as he continued to hunt and peck. "Where's the damned 'W'?"

"Next to the 'Q,' upper left."

"Thanks." He glanced up at me then. "You don't look so hot."

I sighed. "I've been told that a lot lately. I don't feel the greatest, either. Anyway, the chief told me you'd want the name of the bar I went to after I left Crow's place."

He abandoned his typing temporarily. "I already know that. It was the State of Mind on State Street. Your car was found outside of it yesterday morning with a ticket on it."

"Like I told the chief, you're a good detective."

"Some people think so. Lois will fix the ticket for you."

"Yeah, thanks. I picked my car up yesterday afternoon after I talked to you. The desk sergeant told me where to find it."

"I could have told you if you'd asked. Did the chief give you any details of my report?"

I sat down in one of the wooden chairs next to his desk and leaned in, my arm resting on the scuffed top. "He told me my name was in the notebook you found with an appointment time of one for the day of the murder."

"I'm surprised he'd share that with you. But then, he always did have a soft spot for you, you know. I bet you remind him of his son or something."

"Maybe. Anyway, no hard feelings, okay? I mean about what you put in the report."

"I appreciate that. I found out a lot in a short period of time. A few things I really didn't want to, but you know, I'm just doing my job."

"I would have done the same if the situation was reversed," I said.

Alvin looked at me hard. "The situation would never be reversed."

I moved my arm off his desk. "Never say never, Alvin. Of course, you searched the apartment thoroughly."

"Of course, once we found the notebook. Me and the boys spent most of a nice Saturday afternoon and evening in that smelly, dumpy little place, photographing the crime scene, dusting for fingerprints, and checking and rechecking every nook and cranny.

We went through every drawer and every cupboard, looked behind the cheap paintings on the walls, went through her hatboxes and shoes, his collection of magazines, and even checked the icebox. We took a thorough inventory, right down to her unmentionables and his dirty socks."

"Anything else turn up?"

"Like what?"

"Oh, I don't know. You found that notebook. Was there anything with it?"

"Nothing of note, not that it's any of your business. I'm going through the list of names that were in it, contacting them, finding out where they were on Saturday. Standard procedure, in case you weren't aware."

"Funny guy. How's your wife? How's Janey?"

"Mother and daughter are both fine. It's Janey's birthday today."

"Happy birthday to her. I'll buy her a balloon."

"Sure. The wife said we should have you over for dinner one of these days."

"I'm always up for a good meal."

"You could use it, you're too thin. So, what the hell did Crow have on you? Why did he want to see you?"

I shook my head. "Nothing, really. He was all talk. I already told the chief, and it's in my report there."

"I'm not buying it."

"I'm not selling it."

"Aren't you? I think you're trying hard to sell it. Maybe even to yourself." He picked up my report and started reading, his lips moving along with each line. When he'd finished, he dropped it back down and looked over at me. "So, you think someone else was hiding in the apartment the same time you were there?"

"I do. And it makes sense that it may have been Vinnie the Horse."

"Because of the cigars you mentioned."

"That and the fact that the two of them were running some shady operations, and Larry owed Vinnie a good chunk of change."

"The chief tell you that, too?"

"It just came up. Plus, the neighbor said the man she saw was smoking a cigar."

"I see. Well, we didn't find any cigars in the apartment. The only butts in that ashtray were cigarettes, all Camels."

"All the more proof someone was hiding in the bedroom. He took his cigars with him when he left, maybe after killing Larry. The chief thought you could have the ashes in the ashtray analyzed and see if any of them came from a Willard Ponies."

"You remember seeing the brand of cigar, huh? That's impressive."

"The cigar band was still on the fresh one next to the ashtray. Willard Ponies are distinctive."

"And Vinnie the Horse is known for smoking them. Convenient you remember such detail."

"I admit parts of that afternoon and evening are a bit hazy, but if I could get back in there and have a look around, it might clear things up."

"Back in where?"

"Larry Crow's place."

Alvin laughed. "Not a chance."

"Come on, Alvin. I need access to the Crow apartment." I wanted to locate the note Crow had hidden and destroy it before it saw the light of day.

"You're a suspect in this murder. I can't give you access to the crime scene."

"I'm not an official suspect."

"Not yet, and only because the chief likes you. If you were a suspect, you'd be on leave. That still may happen whether he likes it or not."

I leaned in again and looked him in the eye. "Don't we always take care of our own? We've worked together for a while now. You're a great detective, so you should know I didn't murder Larry Crow. Help me clear my name, please? You can come with me. I just want to look around. Maybe I can help you find the real murderer. Like you said, you and the boys have been over everything thoroughly, so what's it going to hurt? Besides, didn't you say you owed me one for taking the case at the Davidson Theater for you when your daughter was sick?"

"Geez, Heath. You have to have a reason for wanting to get in there so bad. What is it? Something you left behind that we overlooked? Something incriminating?"

"It doesn't sound like you overlooked anything. I just want to see if the place triggers any memories. Besides, it will give you a chance to pick up that ashtray and bring it back to the lab."

"Willard Ponies, huh? You realize if I don't find any cigar ashes or remnants, you move up on the suspect list. The chief will have no choice but to suspend you, and I will make sure he does."

"Ten minutes is all I ask. I'll bring you a bottle of wine when I come for dinner."

"Mrs. Crow is staying with a friend for the time being, a Miss Evelyn Caldwell. The locks to the Crow apartment have been changed."

"And you have the keys."

He rolled his eyes. "As I told you, it's Janey's birthday today. So we have to make it quick, understand? The chief gave me the afternoon off."

I smiled at him, relieved. "Quick as a wink. Like I said, ten minutes."

"It's against my better judgment, but I am definitely coming with you."

"Two's company."

"And you'd better make it two bottles of wine."

CHAPTER TWELVE

Later Afternoon, Monday, August 11, 1947

We stopped by the police lab for an evidence bag and then signed ourselves out. We took Alvin's car, parking just up the street from the Crows' apartment building. Once more the front door was unlocked, so we entered unannounced and climbed the dimly lit stairs to the second floor. I glanced across the hall toward Mrs. Picking's apartment, hoping she wouldn't open the door. Thankfully she didn't. Maybe she was out.

"I'm asking you again, Barrington, what are you hoping to find here?" Alvin said as he unlocked Crow's apartment and stepped inside, pocketing the key.

I followed him in and looked around, closing the door behind me. There were no apparent signs of a struggle and nothing out of place that I could ascertain. The living room was much the same as it was when I'd last seen it, except for the bloodstains on the carpet and sofa, which were now just a muddy brown, like someone spilled a chocolate soda. It reminded me eerily of the stain on my white dress shirt, still stuffed in the corner of my closet. The air was heavy with several foul odors, more so than last time. "I don't know, Alvin, really. But maybe something will come back to me." I certainly wasn't going to tell him what I was actually looking for.

"I see. I get the impression you're looking for something specific, like I said before, maybe something you inadvertently dropped when you were here Saturday, but I can't imagine what. We scoured every square inch of this place already. The boys found the notebook, and the murder weapon, and they picked up lots of fingerprints, including yours, but not much else."

"It's no secret I was here that day, so naturally my fingerprints would be on things."

"Naturally."

I ignored his comment and walked over to the sofa. "So, he was found here?"

"That's right. How did you know that?" Green shot me a funny look, but I wasn't laughing.

I shrugged, wondering myself, though it was all so clear in my mind. "I don't know exactly. All the bloodstains appear to be here on the sofa, I guess." I noticed another long strand of red hair on the back of the sofa. I could swear it wasn't there when I left him on Saturday, but maybe I'd just overlooked it.

"Well, that's where we found him all right. His head near the lamp, throat cut clean. He'd been drinking. There was an empty beer bottle on the table along with an empty glass of bourbon, and the coroner found a sleeping draught in his system, phenobarbital. The wife said he took that regularly."

"Yes, that's right. I remember the beer bottle being next to the ashtray, but Larry was drinking bourbon."

Alvin pushed his hat back on his head. "And you think that means someone else was here, hiding."

I bristled. "It's just a clue, Alvin. Or possibly a clue, that's all. What was the murder weapon?"

"A kitchen knife."

"Any prints on it?"

"Not yours, I already checked."

"Funny. Anybody else's?"

"Just Mrs. Crow's. Whoever did the deed probably used gloves."

"Makes sense. And I doubt Mr. Crow was the type to help out in the kitchen, so his wouldn't be on it. How did the killer get in?"

"Mrs. Crow was at the library. When she got home, she said the back door was unlocked and ajar."

"Curious."

Alvin shrugged. "Not really. She said they usually left it open during the day. Unlocked, anyway. The front door, too. People never lock their doors in this town. It drives me crazy. She probably didn't close it all the way when she left."

"Yeah, I know. I'm always after my mom and pop to lock up the house, even when they're home, but they always say the same thing, 'This is a safe neighborhood.'"

"Yup, sounds familiar. Of course, according to your theory, the killer was already in the apartment when you arrived and still there when you left."

"Vinnie the Horse. Again, it's a theory, Alvin. Not my only one."

"And not a good one, I'd say. Mrs. Crow got a phone call from her husband at approximately two twenty at the library. He was alive at that point."

"So?"

"So you left at one twenty, according to your report you so neatly typed up. That would mean the killer stayed in the apartment another hour, only to kill him shortly after he phoned his wife telling her to come home. Seems far-fetched. If the killer was still there, why would Crow make the telephone call?"

"But if Vinnie wasn't there, if Crow was alone after I left, why would he wait until two twenty to phone his wife?"

"Maybe he wanted to get in a nap first because he'd taken that sleeping stuff."

"Or maybe he wasn't alone after I left."

"Possibly, though Mrs. Crow told us she phoned in a grocery delivery order before she left on Saturday. The grocer, a Mr. Jarvis, dropped off the items at two p.m., according to his statement. He said Mr. Crow was sleeping soundly on the sofa at that time, and snoring loudly. No one else appeared to be home."

"Hmm. Well, Vinnie could have heard the grocer coming and hid until he left. Maybe he was still hiding when Larry woke up and placed the call, so he didn't know Vinnie was still there."

Green raised his eyebrows. "And then Larry fell back asleep and Vinnie popped out and slit his throat, just like that."

"Well, it's plausible."

"Not very. You leave, Crow falls asleep knowing there's a gangster in his apartment, and the gangster waits almost an hour before killing him?"

"It's still possible. What else did she say? Mrs. Crow, I mean."

"She left the apartment about twelve thirty, as Larry had told her he had a meeting with someone at one, and she was to stay away until he called her."

"And that someone he had the appointment with was me, of course."

"Yeah, according to the notebook he had you down for one p.m. Saturday."

"I was on time."

"Bully for you. There was no one else listed for that day."

"Maybe, if it was Vinnie, he just showed up. Vinnie the Horse isn't the type to make appointments or leave calling cards."

"You've got an answer for everything."

"Just stating possibilities, Alvin."

"Yeah. So, anyway, Mrs. Crow left through the back door and stopped to chat with the neighbor lady, Mrs. Picking, who was hanging up her wash on the back porch."

"She went directly to the library after that?"

"That's right. I checked with the librarian there, a Miss Caldwell, who's apparently a friend of hers. Mrs. Crow is staying at her place until this is all cleared up. Quite the character, that Miss Caldwell. If you look up spinster in the dictionary, I bet you'll find her picture."

"Oh?" I moved my hat back on my head and wiped my brow with my handkerchief.

"Yeah. She's in her early thirties, I'd guess, rather severe looking, plain, manly even. It's like she doesn't even try to be feminine. She even smelled of tobacco, I think."

"None of which makes any difference," I said.

"It does to me. I don't like women like that. But she did verify Mrs. Crow arrived at the library at approximately twelve forty and stayed until about two thirty p.m. She also witnessed the call Mrs. Crow received from her husband at around two twenty, telling her she could come home."

"What happened when she got back here?"

"What do you mean? She came in the back way and saw him. It's a straight line of vision from the back door to the living room sofa."

"She saw him right away, then?"

"Hard not to. You'll see for yourself if you go in the kitchen and look back. Mrs. Crow saw him and all the blood immediately and screamed. Typical dame. The Picking lady was out on the back porch taking down her laundry, heard her, and came running."

"Must have been quite a shock for both of them."

"Naturally. You don't expect to come home and find your husband murdered with his throat slit."

"Naturally. So he was alive at two twenty when he phoned, but dead when she came back, about two forty," I said.

"That's right, a pretty narrow window of time. And you supposedly left him at one twenty."

"I did. I went from here to that bar on State Street."

"I plan on talking to that bartender this afternoon on my way home."

"Please do," I said. "He can vouch for me."

"What time did you leave the bar?"

I looked away from him. "About two-thirty, I think, or close to it."

"That would be enough time to hightail it back over here, kill Crow, and get back out before the wife got home. That bar's not far from here."

"Maybe so, but that's not what happened."

"I'd like to think not, but we'll see. Your report mentioned the bartender called you a cab—"

"Yeah, I'd had a couple of cocktails."

"Rather early in the day for that. But I can check with the cab company easily enough, see what time he picked you up, and where he took you."

I felt suddenly sick. "Vinnie could have easily done it, Alvin, you know that."

Alvin pointed a finger at me, like a gun. "So could you, if you'd come back."

I opened my mouth to reply, but no words came out. I *had* come back, and Alvin would find that out soon enough. The cab company kept records, and the driver could probably identify me. And then there was the blood that wasn't mine on my dress shirt. If they arrested me, they'd get a warrant and search my place. I vowed to get rid of that shirt one way or another. I closed my mouth and turned away from Alvin. "Mind if I use the bathroom?"

"If you have to. It's off the bedroom."

"Right, thanks." I walked down the short hall, glancing back at Alvin, expecting him to follow me at least as far as the bedroom, but he had picked up the girlie magazine and was temporarily distracted. I stepped into the bedroom and glanced about. The full bed was unmade, and a pair of scuffed-up men's black shoes were tucked under a chair in the corner, but otherwise nothing appeared out of place.

As discreetly and quickly as I could, I opened a couple of the drawers of the dresser and rifled through Alvin's underthings and socks, but the note wasn't there. I looked under the bed and mattress. All I found in the closet were clothes and hatboxes of assorted shapes and sizes stacked on the shelf. On the floor of the closet were three pairs of well-worn women's shoes, nothing else. The bathroom was spotless and shiny, with pink and black tiles, but otherwise it yielded nothing. The toilet seat was up, shower and soap dry, totally normal, and the medicine cabinet held only medicine, some feminine things, tooth powder, and two toothbrushes. The towel bar, I noted, was empty, the toilet tissue roll was full. I flushed the toilet, ran the water in the sink, and went back out into the hall.

"Are you ready to go?" Alvin had dropped the magazine back on the table and was putting something in his wallet as I walked back into the living room. "Janey's birthday, you know, and I still have to stop by that bar."

"Right. Where was the notebook found, by the way?"

"The bottom of a cigar box in the hall closet."

I glanced back down the hall I'd just come from and saw the closet across from the bedroom, but there was no way I could go back without arousing Alvin's suspicions. "You said the knife was a kitchen knife?"

"Correct. Mrs. Crow identified it. She's got a knife block on the kitchen counter."

"Handy but deadly."

"They can be, in the wrong hands."

"Yes. What happened to the beer bottle and the glass that were on the coffee table?" I glanced at the old wooden table and noticed several off-white glass and bottle rings covering it like pock marks. The girlie magazine probably hid a lot of them. The telephone and the ceramic ashtray with the cigarette butts were still there, but both the half-smoked cigar and the fresh one were missing, just as Alvin had said.

"We took the bottle and glass down to the lab for prints and contents analysis. The only prints on the glass were his."

"What about the beer bottle?"

"A few prints on there, actually. Some matching Mrs. Crow, some Larry Crow's, and a set as yet unidentified."

I raised my eyebrows. "Perhaps the mystery man in hiding."

Alvin looked annoyed. "Perhaps. We'll run them against Vinnie the Horse's this afternoon. Could just be the prints of the fellow at the liquor store."

"Let me know, will you?"

"It will be in my report to the chief, classified."

"Have you gotten the autopsy results back yet?"

"I'm surprised you don't already know, seeing as how the chief coroner, Fletcher, is such a good friend of yours."

"Fletch would never disclose information to me I wasn't privileged to, Alvin. He's top notch."

Alvin took his hat off, ran his fingers through his hair, and then put it back on. "He does a decent job. I guess there's no harm in telling you the basic facts as there was nothing unusual in the autopsy report. Death by loss of blood caused by large laceration to the throat. A barbiturate was found in his bloodstream, the sleeping draught."

"Anything else in his stomach?"

"I don't remember all the details, Barrington. Bourbon, some pieces of undigested sandwich he probably had for lunch. That's about all, I think."

"So, no beer," I said.

"I don't believe so, no."

"Then who drank the beer?"

"It might have passed from his system before he was killed. No telling how long that bottle was sitting on the table."

"I suppose." I walked into the small kitchen off the living room and stopped just inside the doorway.

"Careful," Alvin said from behind me. "Nothing's been touched or moved except to be fingerprinted, and then it was put back right where it was, except for the murder weapon and the glass and bottle from the living room. We've been over everything, but it's still a crime scene."

On the counter closest to the door were a bunch of carrots, a can of peas, and a bag of sugar whose seam had split. I noticed a small line of tiny brown ants in a procession from a crack in the backsplash out to the sugar, and another procession heading from the bag back home.

"Did Mrs. Crow say why she left these groceries on the counter?"

"She didn't leave them there. Those are the items the grocer dropped off at two, according to his records. He unpacked the box as a courtesy and then left. He heard Larry snoring on the sofa."

"Interesting." The kitchen was clean and neat, with a small metal and Formica table beneath the window and two matching chairs whose seats were ripped and taped. A gas stove, sink, and icebox stood in a row on the opposite wall. Alvin was watching me, so I had to be discreet in my search. If I were to hide a small note, where would I put it? I opened a few of the drawers below the counter, but found nothing unusual, just the typical kitchen cutlery and gadgets. There was a pan soaking in the sink, half filled with now cold, murky water. Nothing under the sink except a metal bucket, some rags, and cleaning supplies.

Next to the icebox was the cabinet that held the ironing board, and on the counter to the left of the icebox sat an old electric iron and a sewing basket, along with some well-worn clothes in a neat pile. I opened the icebox door next. A carton of vanilla ice cream was in the freezer compartment, along with a tray of ice. I'd read of a case once where a man hid a small ring in a cube of ice, but it wouldn't make sense to hide a handwritten note there. Below the freezer, a half-filled bottle of milk stood next to a pitcher of orange juice, a stick of butter, some bottles of Pabst and Miller beer, and half a roast chicken. I closed the door and glanced about the kitchen once more.

"What, are you hungry, Barrington? Looking for a snack? Or something else? I'd really like to know."

I glanced at him, still standing in the kitchen doorway, watching me. "I'm just curious, Alvin, that's all." On the other side of the sink was a green metal bread box. Inside was a half a loaf of bread, wrapped neatly in wax paper. Next to the bread box was a library book, *The Company She Keeps*, and just beyond that stood the knife block, the largest slot empty. "So, this is where the murder weapon came from."

"Brilliant deduction, Detective."

On the other side of the icebox from where the iron and mended clothes sat, were three metal canisters, all with matching yellow lids, with red roses on their fronts against a white background. I peeked in each one, in turn, filled to the top with sugar, flour, and coffee, but nothing else. I replaced the lids and walked over to the back door, next to the table.

I unlocked it and peered out onto the back porch, which ran the width of the building, and a wooden staircase that led down to the alley below. There was a door to the other apartment off the porch, too, just down the way on the other side of the staircase. A laundry line was strung above the railing on each side. It was all very familiar to me.

"Easy for anyone from one of the other apartments to slip in here this way. Either from the one next door or up the back stairs," I said.

"I suppose. Only two apartments on this floor. Two more on the first floor."

"Interesting."

"If you say so."

"I do say so. If not one of the other apartments, then basically anyone, really. All they'd have to do is come down the alley and up the stairs."

"Big risk of being seen."

"Did anyone report seeing anyone?"

"The neighbor lady, that Mrs. Picking, reported an unsavory chap hanging about the alley the last couple days. She didn't get a good look at him, though, but she did say he was smoking cigars. And as you know, she mentioned the guy with the cigar in the hall past twelve thirty, shortly after Mrs. Crow had left."

"Twelve thirty? Are you sure?"

"That's what the neighbor lady said. He was out in the hall, knocking on the door of the Crow apartment. His cigar smoke hung heavy in the air. As she came out of her apartment and went down the stairs to the first floor and the basement, he whistled at her."

"Huh. But that fits with the mystery man I think was hiding in the bedroom, cigar smoke and all."

"Vinnie the Horse."

"Yes, it definitely could have been him in the alley and the hall. If he arrived just past twelve thirty, after Mrs. Crow left, he most likely would have still been there when I arrived at one."

"So, why would he hide in the bedroom?"

"Larry probably told him to. Larry wasn't expecting him. Vinnie probably came to put the screws to him, as the chief said. When I knocked, Larry told him to hide, as I'm a police detective."

"I have to admit that does make sense. But about a half hour later the mystery man was back in the hall, according to Mrs. P, talking to Crow when she came out of her apartment once more to go back down to the basement."

"About one o'clock," I said. "It wasn't the same man. It was me the second time. She was just confused as she didn't really see either of our faces."

"Or maybe they were both really you, and you made up the story about a man hiding in the bedroom."

"But Mrs. Picking said the man was smoking cigars. I don't smoke them, but Vinnie does. Vinnie the Horse and I are of similar build, and we were both wearing dark suits that day."

"Convenient," Alvin said. He walked over to the coffee table and carefully collected the ashtray, putting it in the evidence bag and sealing it shut. That done, he looked over at me. "So I got your precious ashtray, ashes and all. You about finished here? Find what you were looking for?"

"No. I mean, I don't really know what I was looking for."

"Right. Let's get out of here then, 'cause like I said—"

"I know, I know, Janey's birthday, and you have to corroborate my story with the bartender on your way home." I fished in my pocket and brought out a dime, which I held out to him. "Here, buy her that balloon from me. I'm all finished, let's go."

"I'll get her a blue one. Blue is her favorite color."

"I prefer green, but it's her birthday." The note, wherever it was, would hopefully remain hidden, as I couldn't search for it any more today and most likely wouldn't be able to get back in again, at least not any time soon.

We left the apartment together, and I watched while Alvin secured the door. Just as he was finishing, the door to apartment 202 opened and I flinched.

Alvin turned around and forced a smile, tipping his hat. "Good day, Mrs. Picking."

"Oh, it's you, the detective," she replied. "I heard someone out here, just wanted to check. There's been so many men coming and going lately."

I turned then and tipped my hat, also.

"This is Detective Barrington, Mrs. Picking."

"How do you do?"

"How do you do?" I replied.

She was staring at me, but finally she shook her head and turned to Alvin.

"By the way, Detective, I forgot to mention someone else was here on Saturday, besides that one fellow."

"Oh?"

"Yes, a young lady. Very smartly dressed, red hair, slim, nice figure. I heard her knocking on the door of the Crow apartment so I glanced out the peephole, you know."

My mind went immediately to Liz. She said she had stopped over. And then there was the red hair I'd found on the sofa.

"What time was that?" Green said.

"Oh, about two fifteen or two twenty or so."

"And?"

"No one answered, so she turned and left. I didn't think much of it at the time. Larry was known for entertaining women when Alice was out, though this one looked classier than his usual troupe. He was such a disgusting man."

"Could you identify her if you saw her again?"

"No, I'm sorry. I couldn't see her well through the peephole."

I breathed a sigh of relief. "It sounds like you didn't care for Mr. Crow, Mrs. Picking."

She looked at me again. "No, I didn't. Always leering at me, making rude comments, brushing up against me on the stairs or by the mailboxes, calling me dollface or other vile names. Alice is a friend of mine, which just made it worse. I've only lived here a little less than a year. I'm a widow, my husband was killed in the war."

"Our condolences," Green said.

"Thank you, it's been over four years now. Mr. Crow wasn't nice to Alice, either, you know. He kept her isolated, alone. I was one of her only friends, me and that librarian woman, Miss Caldwell. Alice talks about her all the time. Alice phoned me this morning and told me she's staying with her temporarily."

"I see. You were discussing Mr. Crow…"

"Oh, he was vile and nasty. I think he even hit Alice on occasion, though she was always saying she'd bumped into something. And of course, he cheated on her regularly."

"Do you think Mrs. Crow knew about his infidelities?" Alvin said.

"I imagine, though she never talked about it. The day of the murder, she came out on the back porch on her way to the library, like she does every Saturday, though a bit earlier than normal. Alice told me Larry had ordered her out and to not come back until he phoned her because he had an appointment with someone. I figured it was a girl, but I didn't say anything."

"But it wasn't a girl," I said.

"No, it was a man, smoking a cigar." She looked at me again, up and down. "He looked a lot like you, actually."

I felt my face flush. "I understand it was a rather general description."

She shrugged. "Yeah, I suppose so. The hall's kind of dark, as you can see. I didn't like Larry Crow one bit, obviously, and I think he got just what he deserved. But to be murdered in his own apartment? In broad daylight? It just gives me the creeps. I'm keeping my doors locked from now on."

"Always a wise precaution, Mrs. Picking," Alvin said. "You were on the back porch when Mr. Jarvis delivered the groceries?"

"Yes. It was just a few minutes after two, I think. It was such a nice day, though a bit warm. Of course, I like it hot."

"Some people do," I said.

"Yeah. I had my stockings off and my feet up. That Mr. Jarvis is kind of creepy, too. Always with the looks, staring, commenting. I pick up my own groceries because I don't want him in my house. Men, you know? No offense."

"None taken," Alvin said.

"He's always working an angle, Just like Larry used to. In that regard, he and Crow were birds of a feather, if you'll pardon the expression."

"How do you mean?" I said.

"He bets on the horses, just like Mr. Crow. Waste of money in my opinion. And he's always looking to make extra dough, but not by working hard, that's for sure. He's lazy, if you ask me. He'd offer to take your trash down to the alley, but with a hand out for a tip, you see? That kind of a fella. If he were my husband I'd kick him out, but he's nobody's husband, thankfully."

"Did you speak with him that day?" Alvin said.

"Sure. I don't care for him, but I'm not rude. I remember I told him Alice must be planning on doing a lot of cooking, as the box was near overflowing, more than she usually gets at one time. I could see the top of the carrots from where I sat. When he came out again with the box, he made some off-color remark about it being hot and what nice legs I have. He also said Larry was on the sofa, snoring like a buzz saw. He didn't like Larry much, and vice versa."

"Why is that?"

"Bad blood between them, I guess. Larry accused him of overcharging Alice once, and I think Larry thought Jarvis was too familiar with his wife. There was also something about a bad tip on a horse one of them gave the other, but I don't know the details. They got into an argument about it all once or twice, each of them threatening the other. I couldn't help but overhear, of course."

"Naturally."

"So, Mr. Jarvis snuck out kinda quiet like that day. I imagine he didn't want Larry waking up. Oh, and I remember him asking me the time, it was about ten after two. He was concerned about being gone too long as he'd locked up his shop to make the delivery."

"Do you recall what time it was when Mrs. Crow returned?"

"Sure, it was around two forty. She looked done in. She had her handbag on one arm and a new book she must have just checked out under the other. I'd just put a cake in the oven and set the timer on the stove for forty-five minutes. I recall thinking it would be done about three twenty-five. The oven runs hot, so I have to be careful. I spoke to the landlord about it, but he doesn't care."

"That's too bad," Alvin said.

"He knows he could re-rent this place for more money in a heartbeat, what with the housing shortage and all. He's a jerk. But anyway, I told Alice I had a cake in the oven and it would be done soon if she wanted to come over for a slice and some coffee."

"What did she say?" I said.

"She thanked me but said Larry was waiting for her."

"But we all know by now he was dead at that point," Alvin said.

"As a doornail. Still kind of a shock," Mrs. Picking replied. "She went inside and screamed almost immediately. I came running as fast as I could. I hurried her right out the front door and over to my apartment. Then I locked both my doors and called the police. You never know, the murderer might have still have been in there! I heard a program on *Murder at Midnight* where something like that happened."

"Yes, smart thinking on your part," Alvin said, glancing at his watch. I knew he was anxious to get going.

"And that strange man hanging around the alley the last few days, and once or twice last week. Just plain creepy. He might have been the murderer, you know. Just waiting for a chance."

"What did he look like?" I said. "Can you describe him?"

"A little shorter than average, solid build. Dark suit, hat pulled down low, hands in his pockets, leaning on the light pole, smoking cigars. He was clean shaven, I think. Mid-thirties if I had to hazard a guess."

"Could it have been the same man you saw in the hall?"

"I don't think so. He was shorter and stockier than the hall fella. Lots of men smoke cigars, Detective."

"I suppose. The alley is an odd place to hang around in the middle of the afternoon," I said.

"I thought so, too, and he stayed quite a while. But none of my business, I thought at the time. I thought maybe he was a private dick on a case, you know, like in the movies? But now I think, what if he was the murderer? It gives me chills."

"I suggest putting a sweater on. I'm afraid we must be going, but if you think of anything else, Mrs. Picking, you have my card," Alvin said.

"I will. Nice meeting you, Mr. Barrington."

"Likewise." We both tipped our hats once more, then descended the stairs and back out to his car.

As we drove back to the station, I fiddled aimlessly with my pocket watch, turning it over and over in my hands. "That Mrs. Picking sure is something," I said at last.

Alvin glanced over at me. "She is indeed. A pretty lady, but a bit of a busybody and a gossip."

"Well sure, she is that. But I mean, it sounds like she loathed Larry Crow. Enough, I think, to kill him."

"You think so? A dame doesn't go around killing guys just because they whistle at her or make a pass."

"No, not normally. But it sounds like Larry often did more than that. It sounds like he was harassing her. On top of that, Mrs. P. was friends with Mrs. Crow, and she felt sorry for her. She said Larry hit Alice more than once."

"I see where you're going with this. Another theory. It's possible, too, I'll admit."

I turned my watch over again and stared at it for a while. "I mean, she knew Alice was out. She probably saw or heard me leave at one twenty. Vinnie most likely stuck around until one thirty or so, then Larry fell asleep on the sofa and was still sleeping when the grocer arrived." I put my watch back in my pocket. "Mrs. Picking said she was on the back porch and saw Jarvis leave about two ten. He told her Larry was sound asleep on the sofa, so she figured it was a perfect opportunity. She slipped in right after the phone call at two twenty, grabbed a kitchen knife, and slit his throat."

"Maybe."

"Sure. Once his throat was cut, there was bound to be more blood than she anticipated. So, she dropped the knife and fled out the back door, leaving it ajar. She went into her own apartment to change her clothes and wait for the body to be discovered."

Alvin drummed his fingers on the steering wheel as we waited at a red light. "Once again it makes sense."

"You might want to talk to that Jarvis, see if he recalls what exactly Mrs. P. was wearing that afternoon, and check those clothes for bloodstains. Maybe even check with Mrs. Crow and see if she recalls what Picking was wearing when she got home, and if it matches with what she had on when she had left."

Green growled. "Stop telling me how to do my job."

"Sorry, just trying to help. Of course, there's also the strange man Mrs. Picking saw lurking about the alley, too. She said she was in and out from the porch all afternoon. He could have come up and slipped into the Crow apartment unseen."

"*If* there was a man in the alley," Alvin said as we proceeded through the now green light and down the block toward the police station. "I think that lady has an active imagination."

"Good point. But maybe if it wasn't Vinnie, it was one of Larry's so-called associates casing the joint, figuring out when Larry would be home alone, or she may have made it up to throw suspicion off her. I think we should talk with this Jarvis chap and see if he noticed anyone, and then ask him about Picking's clothes, too."

Alvin brought the car to a stop abruptly in front of the station and I jerked forward, putting my hand on the dash to keep my head from slamming into the windshield.

"I already talked to him once, and if anyone's going to talk to him again it will be me, alone. You're going to go upstairs and work on your petty larceny case. I've already shared way too much with you, Barrington. You're still a suspect."

"Officially?"

Alvin looked away from me. "No, but maybe soon. I don't know yet. I'll admit that yes, it's possible Vinnie the Horse was in the Crow apartment while you were there, and murdered him after you left. It's also possible the neighbor lady did it, and perhaps even the grocer, or this mystery man, but it's also possible you did it and you're just throwing all these other ideas and theories around to confuse me. I have a lot of thinking to do. But right now I have a few things to finish at my desk, then I need to get over to that bar, and finally home to Janey."

"Don't forget to buy her that blue balloon," I said, getting out of the car.

"Right," Alvin replied, slamming his car door hard and striding up the steps of the station.

I followed behind. I had a lot of thinking to do, too, and I had to think fast, before Alvin got around to checking with the cab company and finding out I actually had gone back to Larry Crow's place. If that happened, I'd definitely be placed on leave pending the outcome of the case.

CHAPTER THIRTEEN

Monday Evening, August 11, 1947

I sat at my desk in the detectives' room and reviewed the larceny case file ten or twelve times. After reading it over and over and making some notes, I realized I hadn't focused on any of it, couldn't make heads or tails of what I'd written, and had to start again. Finally, I gave up. I couldn't concentrate on larceny when Crow's murderer was out there somewhere, or worse, right here inside my suit, so I checked myself out on the board downstairs and left the building.

I stopped briefly at the hardware store up the street to buy a new alarm clock and a safety razor and blades, and then I headed home. It was just coming six when I unlocked my door and picked up the evening paper, Oscar nowhere in sight tonight. I hung up my hat next to the mirror in the hall and locked my service revolver away in the nightstand, placing my new clock on top of it. The safety razor and spare blades went in the medicine cabinet and the old straight razor in the trash. I changed into more casual slacks and a short-sleeve print shirt, mint green with fishing lures on it, that my mom had bought me for Christmas last year. I couldn't figure out why she had chosen that shirt for me, as she knew I had only been fishing once in my life and hated it. Still, being the dutiful son, I wore it on occasion, mostly around the house or on visits to their house.

A slight breeze was coming in from the north-facing windows, so I left the electric fan in the corner off for the time being and decided to make myself a cocktail before dinner. I was just shaking the vodka and vermouth when there was a knock on my door. I froze in mid-shake. I didn't get many unexpected visitors, and my mind went immediately to the police. Did Green talk to the cab company already? Was I being taken into custody for the murder of Larry Crow? And that bloodstained dress shirt was still on the floor of my closet. The knock came again, more aggressive this time, so I set the shaker down on the kitchen counter, wiped my hands on the towel next to the sink, and walked to the front hall, feeling suddenly sick.

"Who is it?" I called out tentatively. If it was the police I wasn't sure what I'd do or how I'd react. I certainly couldn't flee, so best to cooperate, not say anything, admit to nothing, and hire the best lawyer I could afford.

"It's Mrs. Murphy from downstairs, dear."

I breathed a huge sigh of relief, wiped the sweat from my palms on my slacks, and opened the door. She effectively took up the entire door frame, swathed in a black dress with pink peonies all over it, and red shoes. She was breathing rather heavily and carrying a wicker basket, covered in a checked cloth.

"Good evening, Mrs. Murphy. This is a surprise."

She put her left hand to her breast and breathed deeply, her ample bosom rising up and down. "Goodness, those stairs are going to be the death of me. It's just one flight up here from our place, but still, carrying this basket and all, and my sciatica, you know. I told Mr. Murphy we ought to think about moving to some place with an elevator, but he's so stubborn."

"Yes, I'm sure. Won't you come in?"

"Oh thank you, I can't stay, mind you, but I'd just love to see what you've done with the place."

I stepped aside as she walked in, still catching her breath, and continued into the living room. Closest to the door from the hall, between the doorway and the living room closet, was my console radio, which I had tuned in to the *Bing Crosby Hour*. On the wall directly in front of the hall doorway was a low-backed dark green sofa just the right length for afternoon naps when I got the chance. Opposite that, on either side of the doorway to the dining room/kitchen, were two wingback chairs, upholstered in a tan chintz with red roses. On the hardwood floor was a basic, oversized rug, and there were end tables next to one of the wingchairs and on each end of the sofa. Solid color cream drapes with a green border hung on each of the three windows in the bay. A small tufted bench, covered in a soft orange velvet, sat under one of the windows, a favorite place of mine to read.

"Oh my, Mr. Barrington. It's so modern, so colorful. You do have an eye, don't you?"

"Thank you, Mrs. Murphy. I like it."

"Oh yes, so do I. It's just so right, just so you. My, my, my," she said, moving her head slowly from side to side. She had caught her breath at last.

"So, what may I do for you?"

"Hmm? Oh, yes. I felt bad about being cross with you over your, shall we say, boisterous late-night arrival and the laundry incident."

I held up my hand in protest. "Oh no, please don't give that another thought. I was discourteous in my midnight revelry and my forgetfulness in the laundry room, and you were kind enough to fold everything for me and bring it up here. You have nothing to feel badly over."

"Nonetheless, I baked you some bread and fried some doughnuts for you this morning. Well, I fried them for Mr. Murphy, but I put a few aside for you," She smiled broadly at me as she handed me the basket. It was surprisingly heavy.

"How very kind," I said, shifting the basket to my other hand.

"I put off baking while it was so hot, but now that it's cooled down again, I thought I should get to it. I hope you enjoy them."

"I'm sure I will." I lifted the basket up and took a sniff under the red and white checkered cloth. "Everything smells wonderful." And it truly did.

"Good, I'm glad. Just one loaf of bread and six doughnuts. Drop the basket and cloth off whenever you get the chance. I'd better get going for now. Mr. Murphy needs his dinner, roasted chicken tonight. At least he's finally put some clothes on."

"Thank you again, Mrs. Murphy, for all you do. You're a good neighbor."

She blushed. "I do what I can."

We walked back to the door, and I opened it for her. "Tell your husband hello for me," I said.

"I'll do that. Ta ta!" She walked to the top of the stairs, turned, and gave a little wave before starting her descent. When her head had disappeared from view, I closed the door and took the basket to the kitchen, where I put the bread and doughnuts into the breadbox and stashed the basket and cloth under the sink. My mother told me never to return a plate or anything else that someone has loaned you empty, so I made a mental note to pick up a few fresh oranges or something to fill it with before taking it back to her.

I finished shaking my cocktail and made myself some dinner. I settled in at the dining room table with my plate and my glass to read the evening *Milwaukee Journal* and eat. After I finished my spaghetti, complete with a thick slice of Mrs. Murphy's bread and a slab of butter, I indulged in one of her doughnuts and a cup of coffee. Simply delicious. I cleaned up the dishes, put the newspaper in the bin, turned off the radio, and decided to give Alan a call. But before I did that, I pulled out the phone book from the little shelf under the table and flipped it open to the C's. When I found what I was looking for, I made a little note on the pad I keep next to the phone and then dialed Kings Lake 5-2835 and let it ring once, twice, then three times before he picked up.

"Hello?"

"Hey, Officer."

"Heath. I was just thinking about you."

"Likewise, always. Am I interrupting anything?"

"No, I just finished dinner and was going to take a stroll. My landlady got a new puppy, and she asked if I'd go walking with her and the dog."

"Nice. What kind of pup?"

"No idea. She found him in the alley behind the building. Poor little guy was covered in fleas and thin as a rail. She's had him about a month now, I guess. He's probably seven or eight months old, and doing much better."

"I'm glad he's got a good home."

"Me too. She's named him Binkley. So, how did your day go?"

"Ugh, It was a Monday. I broke my alarm clock, for one thing. Knocked it off the nightstand this morning. Then I got called into the chief's office."

"Oh? What for?"

"Larry Crow. They found a notebook in his apartment. Apparently Crow kept a list of people he was blackmailing or extorting money from."

"I'm impressed. I didn't think he'd be that organized."

"Unfortunately, he was. Fortunately, your name didn't come up."

"But yours did."

I breathed deeply, then out. "Yeah. My name was in that notebook. He had even made a note of our appointment the day of his murder."

"Damn. And the note you had written to me that he was trying to blackmail you with?"

"I don't think it's been found, and hopefully it won't be."

"That's good. So, now what? What did the chief say?"

"He actually told me he doesn't believe I was involved in Crow's death, but he wanted to know what Crow had on me. I lied, made up some story off the cuff. Sounded believable, I think."

"Jeepers, Heath. You think that's wise, lying to the chief?"

"As opposed to what? Telling him the truth? That you and I are involved? I'd be fired on the spot, and so would you. They may even arrest us for it or have us institutionalized."

I could hear him sigh. "I guess you're right. But still, what's going to happen?"

"I honestly don't know. Both Green and the chief know all about Crow being married to Liz at one point, and they know Larry and I didn't get along very well and that he had something on me, like I said. Beyond that, the investigation is ongoing, but I'm not an official suspect yet."

"Who do they suspect?"

"Vinnie the Horse is high on the list."

"The gangster? I thought he was in prison."

"He was. They had him on manslaughter, but he got out a few months ago and went right back to his old tricks. He and Crow were involved in all kinds of illegal activities, and Crow owed him a good deal of money. Vinnie's been known to loan shark as well as act as a bookie."

"Gee, he sounds like a prime suspect, all right. I always wondered why they called him Vinnie the Horse. Do you know?"

I laughed. "No one knows for sure. Some say it's because he's got a long nose, others say it's because he's lean and fast. He claims it's because he's endowed like one. Personally, I think it's just a play on his last name, Horshauer. His first name is actually Melvin."

"I think your answer is the correct one, but the third one is intriguing."

"Funny. But he's not the only suspect. There's the neighbor lady, a Mrs. Picking, too. She disliked Crow intensely for a variety of reasons, and she had opportunity."

"I would think just about everyone disliked Larry Crow," Alan said, "for a variety of reasons."

"True indeed. There's also a grocer that works at the Grundy Market on Twenty-seventh and State. Name of Jarvis. He apparently also disliked Mr. Crow and was at the apartment right before the murder."

"Hmm. So, Vinnie the Horse, Mrs. Pickling—"

"Picking."

"Oh, right. Picking. Funny name. Anyway, Vinnie the Horse, Mrs. Picking, and the Grundy Market guy."

"There's also my cousin, Liz," I said, though I really didn't want to utter the words out loud.

There was a pause. "You really think so? You adore her."

"I know I do. But she was also at the Crow apartment the day of the murder."

"What was she doing there?"

"He owed her back alimony and she was angry about him trying to blackmail me. The neighbor lady said she saw a woman fitting Liz's description knocking on the door about two fifteen or two twenty. According to Picking, the woman knocked, there was no answer, and she left, which matches with what Liz herself told me."

"So she's off the hook."

"Maybe. But Liz is a smart cookie. She may have faked knocking on the door. She might have got there, done the deed, then stepped out into the hall. She heard Mrs. P. coming, so she turned around and knocked on the Crow apartment door, pretending to have just arrived. The grocer had made a delivery at approximately two, and Larry was still alive at that point. If Liz arrived shortly after that, she could have killed him."

"Jeepers, Heath. Do you really think Liz would have murdered him?"

"No, honestly I don't. Any more than I think you would have or could have, but I have to look at all the facts."

"I suppose. That makes four strong suspects."

"There's also a strange chap the neighbor lady saw hanging about the alley the last few days."

"That's a curious place to hang around."

"Yeah, I thought so, too. She thinks he may have been a private dick, but it's possible he may have been one of Crow's associates, just waiting for a chance."

"So, five good suspects."

"Six, actually."

"Six?"

I took a deep breath in and let it out slowly before answering. "Yeah, official or not, Green still thinks I had something to do with it."

"You didn't."

"How can you be so sure? I'm not even sure myself, Alan. I'm more sure you and Liz had nothing to do with it than I am of me."

"I know you didn't do it because I know you, that's how."

I paused, thinking, contemplating, just breathing.

"Are you there, Heath? Hello?"

Finally, I spoke. "Sorry, I was just mulling something over."

"Like what?"

"Like there's something I haven't told you yet. Something

I haven't told anyone. When I got up Sunday morning, with that terrible hangover, I found my suit and tie on the chair in my bedroom."

"So, you weren't your usual tidy self when you went to bed. You were drunk, so what?"

"So, under the suit was the white dress shirt I had been wearing on Saturday. It had a dark reddish brown stain on the front of it, a bloodstain, I'm sure."

There was a moment of silence on his side of the line this time, and then Alan finally spoke. "It may not be blood, or it could have been your own blood."

"I thought about that, but I can't see anywhere where I would have cut myself, and I know what a bloodstain looks like by now, I've seen my share."

"You got a bloody nose then. It happens. You may have bumped into a door or something when you were getting ready for bed, and you just forgot, or didn't even realize it, given the state you were in that night."

"Maybe, but I didn't see any remnants of dried blood on my nose or nostrils or anywhere else in my apartment. And it was a lot of blood on the shirt."

"Where's the shirt now?"

"On the floor of my closet, bunched up in the corner, but I'm thinking I should dispose of it."

"That may be a good idea, but I still say you're innocent."

"Thanks. But there's more."

Silence again. "What?"

"I talked Alvin into letting me go back to the Crow apartment to have a look this morning. I knew instinctively he'd been murdered on the sofa. And it matched with these visions I keep getting of Larry lying there covered in blood. I mean, I knew exactly where his body was, even which end of the sofa his head was at."

"Why did you want to go back there?"

"Because of the note."

"You mean *the* note?"

"Yes, the one Crow was using to blackmail me, or trying to. He never showed it to me, but I figured he may have had it hidden in the apartment. It must not have been with the notebook Crow kept."

"So, you went to look for it but couldn't find it."

"It may be hidden elsewhere, but with Alvin standing over me and following me around, I didn't have much of a chance to look. A small piece of paper like that could be hidden anywhere."

"True. You don't think his wife knew about him and his shady dealings?"

"I don't know. I've never met her. But I don't think you could be married to someone like Larry Crow and not figure it out before too long. How much she knew, or chose not to, is anybody's guess."

"Well, we'll just have to wait until Green finishes his investigation. I know you didn't kill Crow, Heath, and the real murderer will be found out. Green's a good detective."

"He is a good detective, but so am I. I'm going to do some investigating of my own."

Once more, silence on the other end of the line. And then, finally, "I don't think that's a good idea, Heath. You could get yourself into all kinds of trouble."

"I think I'm already in all kinds of trouble. I want to talk to Mrs. Crow and see what she has to say. Alvin mentioned she's staying with a friend, a Miss Evelyn Caldwell. I've got some free time tomorrow, so I think I'll pay her a visit."

"If Green or the chief find out you've been meddling—"

"Just a friendly visit. I'll let you know how it goes."

Another pause, shorter this time. "You won't have to, because I'll be there with you. I can take some time off, I've got it coming. A long lunch hour, anyway."

"I don't want you involved, Alan."

"I'm already involved, with you and with this case. What time tomorrow, and where should I meet you?"

I sighed, but I was actually relieved to have his support. "All right, if you insist. Are you on patrol tomorrow?"

"No, I've got traffic duty again. The corner of Wisconsin and Water, but I can get Chet to give me a break, he owes me one."

"All right. How about twelve thirty on the corner of Knapp and

Franklin Place? You can take the bus down Wisconsin to Prospect and get off on Prospect and Juneau, just east of the Knickerbocker Hotel. It's just a block walk from there."

"Sure, but why there?"

"According to the phone book, a Miss E. Caldwell lives at 829 East Knapp."

"Sounds like you've been researching this already."

"I like to be prepared."

"I know you do. I'll see you at twelve thirty tomorrow, Detective. Sleep well."

"You do the same. And Alan?"

"Yes?"

"Thanks. For believing in me."

"Always. We're a team. There's no me without you."

"And vice versa. Sweet dreams. Good night."

"Night, Heath."

I hung up the phone and studied myself in the mirror. Some color had returned to my face, and I looked calmer. Amazing what love can do.

I decided then to give Liz a call.

She answered on the second ring. "What's buzzin', cousin?" I said.

"Buzz, buzz. How are you, cuz?"

"The same. You?"

"Catching up. It seems like I was gone forever. I'm just sorting through all my mail I had held while I was in Paris."

"A big project, I'm sure. By the way, you said no one answered the door when you went to Larry's place Saturday afternoon, right?"

"That's right, why?"

"Just making sure. Did you try the door to see if it was locked?"

"Why would I do that? He didn't answer when I knocked, so I left."

"I found two red hairs on the sofa in his apartment is all, when I was there meeting with him the first time, and Mrs. Crow is a brunette. And I noticed a second long red hair when I was back in there with Detective Green."

"I see. And so you think they belong to me because I happen to be a redhead, and that I lied to you about him not answering the door, is that it?" Her voice had become irritated and annoyed.

Oh boy. I felt sick again. "Of course not. Larry said they belonged to some other women he entertained. I just wanted to make sure I'd heard you correctly the first time, that's all. Green said he was planning on questioning you."

"Hmph. Well, thanks for letting me know. There are lots of redheads in the world, Heath. Some more natural than others."

"I know that, Liz. I'm sorry. Of course I don't really think you had anything to do with Larry's death."

"Are you sure?"

"I swear. I'm more sure of that than I am of myself."

"I wonder. Kind of funny you calling me up all of a sudden like to ask me about what happened after I already told you."

I felt tremendously guilty. "I'm sorry, Liz. I just wanted to make sure, that's all."

"Heath Barrington, how dare you? You're like a brother to me. You should know I would never lie to you."

"What about the time when you were sixteen and you told me you were going to Molly Stratmore's house to study, and I found you and Billy Sherman necking in Estabrook Park?"

"Oh, good grief! One time I lied to you, one time! But I haven't since."

"I know. I'm sorry. I'm all mixed up and very confused, and frankly scared sick. I just can't remember what happened that afternoon."

"Well, I have confidence in you. More than you do in me, it seems. I know you didn't kill Larry Crow."

"Thanks, Liz. And I do have confidence in you, I swear."

"Don't tell your mother you swear," she said, and then she laughed, and I knew she would forgive me eventually. Still, I had to wonder just who those red hairs really belonged to.

CHAPTER FOURTEEN

Tuesday Morning, August 12, 1947

I slept better that night than I had in a while. I actually woke up late, realizing I had forgotten to set my new alarm clock. I showered hurriedly and wolfed down one of Mrs. Murphy's doughnuts and a cup of black coffee for breakfast before rushing out the door. I signed in on the board downstairs at the precinct just after nine and took the steps two at a time up to my desk in the detectives' room. Alvin was out. I hoped he wasn't at Miss Caldwell's place, but even if he was, he'd most likely be gone by the time we got there.

In thinking about it, he was probably talking to Mr. Jarvis again over at the Grundy Market. I made a mental note to swing over there myself later. I spent the next several hours working on the petty larceny case, doing research, making phone calls, and clock watching. Finally, at ten after twelve, I signed myself out and pointed my car in the direction of Knapp and Franklin Place. I made it there in ten minutes and found a place to park in the shade of a gnarled old oak. I paced up and down the sidewalk a few minutes before finally deciding to walk to the bus stop on Juneau and Prospect to meet Alan. He was surprised to see me as he stepped off, a cloud of exhaust surrounding him as the old city bus ground its gears and pulled away.

"I thought I was going to meet you on the corner?" he said, waving the exhaust away.

"I got here early, so I decided to come your way. We can walk back together."

"I like the sound of that. How was your morning?"

"Uneventful. Though I finally got some actual work done on the larceny case."

"Good, that should make the chief happy."

"It's progress, anyway. But mainly I've been thinking about what I'm going to ask Mrs. Crow."

"And?"

I glanced over at Alan, so handsome in his police uniform and cap, and shook my head. "And I don't know, exactly. I'll wing it, I think."

We started out walking north on Prospect, Juneau Park just to the east of us on the other side of the avenue. It was a beautiful day, not too warm, not too cool, a nice breeze coming off the lake. There were only a couple of clouds in the brilliant blue sky, looking like lost little lambs in search of their flock.

"Did you have any lunch?"

"I packed a sandwich, and I bought a bottle of Coke from a street vendor. I ate on the bus. You?"

"No, but I'm too nervous to eat. I'll grab something later."

"Okay. What's the address again?" Alan said as we reached Franklin Place and turned onto Knapp Street.

"It's 829 East Knapp. Just past Marshall Street, kitty-corner from St. Paul's."

"St. Paul's is a great place. I've always loved the architecture."

"Me too. Let's pick up the pace, or our lunch hours will be long over before we even get there."

"Right." We walked quickly up Knapp Street until finally reaching 829, a three-story brown brick building on the south side of the street. The entrance was in between two wings and housed in a cream-colored vestibule. The directory inside the front door listed a Miss E. Caldwell in apartment 312. I buzzed and waited a brief moment before a woman's voice came over the tin speaker.

"Yes?"

"Milwaukee police, here to see Mrs. Crow," I said.

There was a long pause, so I repeated myself. Finally, a small, soft voice. "Oh, all right come on up." She buzzed us into the small lobby.

There was no elevator, just like at my place, so we climbed the two flights of stairs and found apartment 312 toward the back on the right. I knocked lightly on the door, answered promptly by a slight woman, probably in her mid to late twenties, wearing a simple, ill-fitting dress the color of dirt, for lack of a better word, that really didn't suit her. Her eyes were hazel dots set deep on either side of her tiny, upturned nose. She was pretty, with dark hair swept behind her ears, high cheekbones, and full lips the color of a soft pink rose. Her face was freshly made up, with just a touch too much rouge. She was trying to cover a bruise below her right eye.

"Miss Caldwell?"

"No, she's not home at the moment. I'm Mrs. Crow. Alice Crow."

"Oh, I see," I said. "You're the one we wanted to speak with. Mind if we come in?"

She looked doubtful but stepped aside just the same.

"Thanks." I removed my hat and Alan took off his uniform cap, which he set on a small table by the door, placed there for just that purpose, I was sure. The Caldwell apartment reminded me of the Crow place, but fixed up a little nicer, with more up-to-date furnishings. A rather delicious odor hung in the air and made my stomach rumble, remembering I hadn't eaten much yet that day.

"I thought we were through with the police. There was a Detective Green here before."

"I'm sorry to intrude, and I promise we won't keep you long. We just have a few questions to ask."

She heaved her shoulders up and down. "That's what the last fellas said. Might as well have a seat. I just finished baking some cookies."

We moved into the living room. "Thank you," I said, answering for me and Alan.

She seated herself daintily on the beige camelback sofa, smoothing out her dress nervously and crossing her legs at the ankles. After she was settled, we sat in comfortable large red and green chintz chairs on either side of a decorative fireplace, and I studied her carefully. She reminded me of a tiny little mouse, or perhaps a frightened bunny rabbit.

"So, you said you wanted to see me?" she said hesitantly, biting her lower lip before speaking.

"Yes, that's right. I'm sorry for the intrusion, and I promise we won't be but a moment. We just had a few follow-up questions to ask you about your husband's death."

"Okay. I guess that would be okay. Excuse my appearance. We weren't expecting company. Evelyn and me, I mean, Miss Caldwell. She's been so kind to take me in. She's at work now, at the library."

"I'm sorry we didn't call first." I decided she seemed more like a mouse than a rabbit. Definitely a little brown field mouse.

She looked at me, and then down at her ill-fitting, dirt-colored dress. "I wanted to pack a bag, to get some of my things, before I came here. But the police didn't want me touching anything. They wouldn't let me back inside my own apartment. So, I've had to borrow. This dress belongs to Miss Caldwell. Evelyn's a little bigger than I am. Not heavy, just athletic and strong. She doesn't have many dresses."

"You look fine, Mrs. Crow, truly," I said.

"That's very kind of you." She spoke so softly Alan and I both had to lean forward in our chairs to hear. "I've already talked to a detective, like I said. He didn't say anything about anyone else coming by."

I glanced at Alan and then back to her. "Just a follow-up visit, I hope you don't mind."

She shook her pretty little mouse head. "No, it's all right, I suppose. How can I help you?"

"First, please accept our condolences, Mrs. Crow. I'm sure this all must be a terrible shock."

She bit her lip again, the upper one this time. "Thank you. It has been a shock, something awful. And now I've got to make funeral arrangements, and I don't know what all to do. Larry wasn't a churchgoer, God knows, and he had no family I know of, except a brother somewhere out West. I don't know where exactly. I'm thinking of just a simple service. Probably not too many folks will come."

"Sudden death is always difficult to deal with, especially when it's a spouse," I said. "I'm Detective Barrington, and this is Officer Keyes of the Milwaukee Police Department. He'll be taking some notes while we talk. Is that all right?"

She looked doubtful but nodded.

"Good. Would you tell us, please, what happened last Saturday?"

She cocked her head to the side, and her dark hair fell away from her head on the right side. "What do you mean what happened? Larry was killed. You know that, I'm sure."

"Yes, I know that, but what exactly happened that day? I understand from what Detective Green told me that you'd been out and got home around two forty in the afternoon, is that right?"

"Yes." She straightened her head and moved her hair back behind her small right ear, with bare, delicate lobes that needed no ornamentation.

"Where had you gone?"

"Larry's been working nights again, to make more money, you know? We were behind on our rent. I offered to get a job, but he didn't want me working. So, he worked Friday night, the midnight to nine a.m. shift. He got home Saturday morning about ten. I fixed some breakfast for us. He doesn't like it if I eat before he gets home. He likes to have company when he eats. So anyway, I made us some pancakes, some coffee, and some juice, and we ate at the table in the kitchen."

"I see," I said gently.

"We finished about ten thirty, and he went in the bedroom to get some sleep."

"And what did you do?"

"I cleaned up the breakfast dishes, put things away, and tidied up, real quiet, of course. I decided to do some mending and some ironing. I was ironing one of his work shirts, thinking about doing some baking later, when he came back in the kitchen, wanting a sandwich."

"What time was that?"

"Oh, a little after noon, about a quarter past, I think." He was having trouble sleeping. I cut some bread and made him a sandwich, and he sat and ate it while I cleaned up again."

"Didn't you eat?" I said.

She shook her little mouse head. "No, sir. I wasn't real hungry. When I finished, he told me to get him a sleeping draught, like he usually does, and then he told me not to forget I had to leave soon. I didn't know what he was talking about, 'cause he'd never said nothing about leaving before that. He got angry with me, told me I forgot again, and when I told him I hadn't forgot, he just never told me, he..." Her hand went involuntarily to the bruise on her face.

"Did he strike you?"

She nodded imperceptibly. "Anyway, he told me I'd have to leave for a couple of hours, cause he had somebody comin' over at one o'clock and he didn't want me around. He told me not to come back until he called."

I shifted in my seat, knowing that someone was me. I could feel Alan looking at me, but I didn't return his gaze.

"Did he say who was coming? And did he mention anyone else he may have been expecting that day?"

She shook her little head once more, her dark hair falling here and there about her long, delicate neck. She moved the locks back behind her ears. "No, sir, he didn't. But Larry was like that, you know. Real private, hard to live with, and I wasn't about to ask him. I learned it's best not to ask questions. Agnes, she told me later, after it happened, that it was a man. She saw him."

"Agnes?" I said.

"Agnes Picking. She lives next door to me and Larry," Alice said.

"Were you surprised your husband had a man visiting?"

"Relieved, more like it. I thought it might have been a lady friend."

"Did he entertain lady friends at home often?"

Once more she shook her head. "Oh no, sir. Not very. Once in a while, maybe, I mean. We never talked about it, and I didn't really want to know. But he did have men friends come by sometimes to talk business."

"What kind of business would a janitor be talking about?"

"Larry was into all kinds of side businesses. And he liked to bet on the horses. He didn't like me knowing what he was up to, though, and like I said, I learned not to ask questions."

"How interesting. So, at a quarter past noon, he told you to get out for a while."

Her little head bobbed up and down this time. "That's right. He said I should leave by twelve thirty in case his appointment came early. I didn't have much time, and I still had to get dressed and do my makeup, and phone in a grocery order."

"Fifteen minutes is pretty short notice, I agree," I said.

"Well, he claimed he told me this the day before. I'd gotten used to it. It's how Larry was. I go to the library every Saturday afternoon, but normally I don't leave until one. I always like going there to see Evelyn. Sometimes we'll have lunch together in her office. I put on my blue dress and my yellow hat. I like blue a lot. It's my favorite color. It's so pretty, isn't it?"

Alan and I both agreed, as Alan scribbled furiously into his notebook. "I imagine blue suits you quite well, Mrs. Crow."

"Oh, well, thank you. I just have the one blue dress. I do like blue, though."

"So does Janey," I said.

"Who?"

"Sorry, nothing."

"Okay. Agnes, she's the neighbor lady I mentioned, was hanging up her laundry out on the back porch when I left. I do my laundry on Fridays, and she does hers every Saturday. That way we're not both using the line out back at the same time, you know?"

"Sounds like a good system," I said. "So, you did all your laundry Friday, and she was doing hers that day. Do you happen to recall what Mrs. Picking was wearing when you first saw her?"

"Wearing? Gee, I didn't pay much attention. Her green and white dress, I think."

"And was she still wearing it when you returned from the library, or had she changed her clothes?"

Alice scrunched up her little mouse face in thought. "I don't rightly remember, but I think she had on her navy dress when I got back. That's funny."

"Indeed," I said, shooting Alan a look. He made a notation in his notebook. "So, you went to the library."

"That's right, I go every week. Larry doesn't like it much, but he's glad to have me out of the house so he can sleep and do whatever else it is he does. Before I left, I remembered the last book I had taken out was overdue, so I ran down to the laundry to get it, and then back upstairs, hiding it in my handbag. Then I went out the kitchen door, leaving him alone."

"You have to hide your books in the laundry room?"

"Certain books, yes. The ones Evelyn recommends to me. Larry doesn't like me reading stuff like that. I felt awful my book was overdue, but Evelyn, Miss Caldwell, I mean, she didn't even charge me an overdue fee, on account of she's my friend."

"That was very kind of her."

"Evelyn is kind and gentle. She's the head librarian, you know."

"An impressive and important position," I said.

"Oh, yes. She even has a college degree, but she doesn't treat me like I'm stupid. She encourages me, and she's made me learn things and feel things I never have before. Or maybe I had, but I pushed them down, you know what I mean?"

"I think so."

"That's good. Most folks don't. But Evelyn understands. That's why I always like going there."

"I enjoy going to the library myself."

"You do?"

"Yes, I love to read."

"Larry says the stuff Miss Caldwell suggests is feminine propaganda or something like that. He doesn't care for her at all, even though he's never met her. But I like most of the books she gives me, even the stories, the made-up stuff, though most of what Evelyn likes isn't that."

"Stories and made-up stuff fuel the imagination, Mrs. Crow," I said. "I read the biographies, autobiographies, histories, and whatnot also, but I definitely enjoy a good fictional story, too."

She looked at me blankly. "Uh-huh. Me too, I think."

"By the way, you told the other detective your husband had telephoned you at the library. Why was that?"

"He did call me, yes."

"Why?"

"I was just sitting there at one of the library tables, reading my new book and perusing another one Evelyn had recommended, when he called. That means looking through it. Perusing."

"It's a good word," I said.

"Evelyn, Miss Caldwell, she taught me that. She's introduced me to all kinds of new books and authors, like I said. Folks like Gertrude Stein. Strong women. I admire them a lot."

"Understandable. Miss Stein was a talented, intelligent woman."

"Larry wouldn't have liked her at all—Miss Stein, I mean. He didn't like Evelyn, either. And Evelyn sure didn't like him."

"But you said they'd never met."

"No, sir, they hadn't. But I talked to Evelyn about him a lot, and she would get real angry at the things I told her. I finally quit talking about her to him because it just made him mad. Larry's a hard person to like and even harder to love, especially once you get to know him."

"I'm surprised you got married."

Alice looked embarrassed. "Well, when I was in high school, all the other girls had boyfriends, you know? But I never did. I didn't even want one. I thought something was wrong with me. I dated some after school, but it just didn't feel right. The men I worked with at the brewery were always asking me out, and I went a few times, but finally I made up a boyfriend who lived in California, just to get them to leave me alone. Then a few years later I met Larry, and he seemed nice enough. He told me I was pretty and made me feel special. All my old high school friends were getting married and having babies, and there I was, working at the brewery, living alone, with a pretend boyfriend. My folks liked Larry and pressured me to go out with him, so I did. We went out dancing and drinking, and then he brought me back to his place, and he did things to me. I remember the next day I felt violated, dirty, disgusted, even. I never wanted to see him again. But then, a few months later, I found out I was going to have a baby, so I got in touch with him. To my surprise, he offered to marry me, and I agreed. I didn't know what else to do."

"Understandable," Alan said.

She bobbed her head up and down. "Of course, I lost the baby shortly after the wedding, and Larry changed. I was afraid he'd leave me. Then after a time I hoped he would, but he never did."

"I'm sorry."

"Me too. I never talk about it much, except to Evelyn. We talk sometimes, in her office, and have tea, and lunch and stuff, and I tell her things, like I said. Things I couldn't ever tell nobody else, like what I just told you. Police are like priests, right?"

"I'm not sure I'd say that," I said.

"I mean, it's like going to confession. Police can't go around gossiping, can they?"

"Your secrets are safe with us, Mrs. Crow," Alan chimed in.

"That's good, I'm glad. I know they're safe with Evelyn, too. She's a real good listener. And she's helped me realize things about myself, and feel things I never did before or had pushed down, like I said earlier."

"She sounds like quite a woman. So, you were saying you were reading your new book…"

"That's right. I heard the phone ring at the circulation desk, but I didn't think much of it. Then Evelyn came over to me and said, real quietly of course, that Larry wanted to talk to me."

"And?" Alan said.

"Evelyn told me I could take it in her office and have some privacy, so I went back there and closed the door. He told me he was through with his appointment and it went real well, so I could come home. He said he would have called earlier but he fell asleep."

"I see," I said. Alan was still scribbling away in his notebook. "What time was it when he phoned you?"

She furrowed her brow in thought. "Gee, I don't know exactly. I got back home about twenty to three, so I guess he must have called around twenty minutes after two. After I hung up, I checked out my book, gathered up my things, and said goodbye to Evelyn. It was around two thirty when I left there."

"So his appointment left at one twenty, according to our sources," I said. "Since he had taken that sleeping draught, he must have fallen asleep shortly after, then woke up an hour or so later and telephoned you."

"I guess so," she said. "So, anyway, I hurried on home. As I was coming up the back steps, I saw Agnes was still on the porch. The kitchen door to our apartment was open a crack, which I thought was odd, but then I figured maybe I just didn't close it all the way. I slipped in as quiet as I could. I saw him right away. You can see the sofa from the back kitchen door. There was blood everywhere, and my kitchen knife on the floor, and I screamed."

"What then?"

"I just stood there screaming my head off. I tried to move, but I couldn't. Agnes came running in from the porch, and she saw what happened right away. She grabbed me and hurried me over to her apartment and locked both her doors. Then she called the police. She sat me down and tried to calm me. She got me some iced tea, but I was shaking so bad I spilled it down the front of my dress, the blue one. My only blue one. I just burst into tears then."

She seemed so small, so delicate. "Did your husband nap on the sofa often?" Alan said.

"In the summer he did. In the winter, he'd sleep in the bedroom after breakfast, but it gets hot in there in the afternoon in the summer, on accounta the window faces west." She brushed a strand of her thin hair away. "Of course, Larry had been drinking ever since he got home, and he took a sleeping drought, too, like I said. Pretty much what he always did."

"What was he drinking?"

"Bourbon. That's about all he drinks."

"But an empty beer bottle was found on the coffee table," I said.

"Was it? We keep beer on hand for Larry's guests. The fella that came to see him must have drunk it. Larry's not much of a one for beer, says it upsets his stomach."

"Unusual. You mentioned your neighbor earlier, a Mrs. Picking. Did she and your husband get along?" I said.

"Agnes? Oh, she's awful kind, but no, she don't like Larry one bit. Didn't like him, I guess I should say, huh? She's a war widow, you know. So sad. Guess I'm a widow now, too. I hadn't thought of that before. 'Course, she's real pretty and real sweet, so I don't think she'll be single long, even if eligible men are in short supply."

"Would you elaborate on her feelings for your husband?" I said.

"Would I what now?" She cocked her head once more, as would a dog, her little pink tongue even protruding from between her teeth and lips.

"Explain in more detail as to why she didn't like Larry."

"Oh, I see. Sure, well, Larry was always looking at her, you know? He didn't think I noticed, but boy I did. Once I even caught him touching her unmentionables on the laundry line. And he'd say things to her, too. She did her best to avoid him, and it's a real shame, 'cause I like Agnes, you know? She's my friend, and I don't have many of those anymore. Just her and Evelyn, actually. Larry drove the rest of them away."

"Mrs. Picking sounds like a nice lady," Alan said.

Mrs. Crow looked at Alan. "She is, but she's got a temper, let me tell you. A couple of times, I thought she was going to slug him. Larry, that is. Not that he wouldn't have deserved it. I'm glad she didn't, though. Larry would have hit her back, and he's pretty strong."

"Did your husband hit you often?"

Her eyes were red and filled with tears as her tiny hand went to the bruise below her right eye once more. "No, sir. Not much, anyway. Sometimes. If I made him mad, or if I woke him up when he was trying to sleep, or if I spent too much time at the neighbor's, or if he just drank too much. He gave me a black eye and a fat lip more than once. I had to wear my hat with a veil and heavy makeup every time I went out. But it was my fault for disturbing him or for doing something stupid, or for forgetting something. He told me what not to do, but sometimes it was just so hard."

"None of that was your fault, Mrs. Crow. No one deserves to be treated like that."

"That's what Evelyn says to me, too."

"Why didn't you just leave him?" I said as tenderly as I could.

She stared at me blankly, a few tears leaking out and falling down her cheeks, marring her rouge. "It's not that simple, Detective. Where would I go that he wouldn't have found me?"

"There must be someone, some place. What about here at Miss Caldwell's?"

She wiped away the tears, smudging her rouge. "Oh, she wanted me to. She was always after me to leave him and stay here with her, but I was afraid he'd find me. Larry threatened to kill me if ever I did leave. And I believe he would have, and maybe Evelyn, too."

"But you're here now."

"I am, and I'm so grateful. After Larry's death, the police asked where they should take me. Right here is the only place I could even think of, and Evelyn, she didn't even bat an eye, she just took me right in."

"Don't you have any family?" Alan said.

"No, sir, not anymore. My folks both died. So I had no place to go, you see? Still, I started saving money from the household account just in case."

"In case of what?" I said.

"In case I could leave somehow, figure out a place to go. If I could get away, leave town."

"So, you kept money out from the household account?" Alan said.

"That's right, a little bit over time. Larry would give me money to do the marketing and whatnot. I kept a few cents out every week, hoping he wouldn't notice. Pennies make nickels, you know? One time he gave me five dollars to buy groceries. I kept a nickel out of the change, but for some reason he got suspicious. He checked each item, adding up what they should be, asking me. I told him the can of tomatoes was twenty cents and he exploded. He went down to Grundy's and accused Mr. Jarvis of overcharging me, because they were really fifteen cents a can. Poor Mr. Jarvis ended up giving Larry the five cents. Larry and him didn't like each other much. Larry says Mr. Jarvis gave him a bad tip on a horse that cost Larry a lot of money, but Mr. Jarvis says it was the other way around. Anyway, next time I went in, I paid him back from my stash, I felt so bad. I knew I'd never be able to get away. I was terrified he'd find the money I'd hidden, terrified he would kill me if he did."

"How much had you accumulated?"

"Money? A hundred and two dollars and thirty-five cents, mostly in ones and change. I hid it in one of my hatboxes in the closet. After that happened, I thought all night about what to do. I barely slept. Of course, I don't sleep much anyway on account of his snoring. Since he started working nights again, I sleep better, not that I'd ever tell him that. Anyway, I thought I'd give the money away to someone needy, to the poor, you know? Get it out of the house before he found it."

"And?"

"I never got a chance to get rid of it."

"Last Saturday, did your husband seem any different? Did he act unusual in anyway?"

"Not really. He was tired and surly, as usual. I made him some food and got him a bourbon and rubbed his feet the way he likes. The way he liked. Then he went to bed. I have to be real quiet during the day when he's sleeping. I can't play the radio or have anybody over or nothing, so I do my sewing, or I do the baking, or I scrub the bathroom or dust, or anything I can do to pass the time that doesn't make noise. Sometimes, if I'm caught up in my chores, I'll steal a few moments and read. Larry doesn't like it much when I read, at least not the stuff Miss Caldwell gives me, like I said, so I keep my books in the laundry room downstairs in the basement. I read a few chapters when I'm doing the wash or when I'm caught up on my chores."

"What are you reading now?"

"I just started *The Company She Keeps*, by Mary McCarthy. It's about a young woman's search for identity."

"Seems fitting," I said.

"I suppose it does. Evelyn, Miss Caldwell, she recommended it to me. She suggested it when I was there the day Larry was murdered. Miss McCarthy is a good writer, kind of like that Gertrude Stein. I started reading it in the library before I came home, and then I checked it out, but I left it in the apartment, on the kitchen counter, I think."

"I'll have to read that one myself someday."

"It's real good. Miss Caldwell's been so nice to me since I got here, but there isn't much to do, really, especially when she's at work. I've been doing some baking and whatnot, but I miss reading and knitting. I had to leave all that in the apartment. I'm knitting Larry a scarf for Christmas." She stopped suddenly and then laughed nervously. "That's funny, isn't it? I was making him a scarf to keep his throat warm."

"Ironic anyway," I said, raising my eyebrows.

"Yeah." Her nose had started to run, and I handed her my handkerchief. "Of course, Evelyn has lots of books here, so I've been reading some of them, but most of them are real intellectual. I suppose my face is an awful mess," she said.

"We won't keep you much longer, Mrs. Crow," I replied. "Did your husband ever mention a notebook he kept? Or anything else he may have hidden around the apartment? And where he might be likely to hide something like a note he didn't want you to find?"

She looked at me blankly, her little mouse nose twitching. "A notebook? And a note? Gee, I don't know. I never thought about it. He has a cigar box in the hall closet he keeps things in, I know that," she said, blowing her nose into my handkerchief. "I'm not allowed to touch it. He keeps it locked, anyway."

The cigar box that the notebook was hidden in, I thought. "Yes. Did your husband smoke cigars, Mrs. Crow?"

"Larry? Oh, no. Camel cigarettes, that's all. He's had that cigar box for years. It had belonged to his dad. One of those old wooden ones, you know, from the Bodega Lunch Club in La Crosse, with a little padlock on it. That's where Larry grew up—La Crosse, on the Mississippi river."

"Pretty country. Any place else you can think of he may have hidden something?"

"Not that I can think of, why?"

"Just something we're following up on. Did your husband ever mention someone named Vinnie the Horse, by the way?"

She gazed at me thoughtfully. "Once last week I came into the living room from the bathroom, and Larry was on the phone. I heard him say something about, 'I'll get it to you, Vinnie, don't worry.' Then he hung up right away when he saw me. Do you think that could have been this Horse person?"

"Possibly. He may have paid a visit to your husband the day of Larry's death. He's a known cigar smoker, and your neighbor mentioned the man she saw was smoking cigars."

"You mean you think he was the one Larry had the appointment with?"

"It's a theory, Mrs. Crow. By the way, you don't own a cat, do you?"

"A cat? What a strange question. No, Larry doesn't like animals unless they're on a plate. I'd love to get a kitty, but I was always afraid of what he'd do to it."

"Maybe now you can," I said.

"Yes. That would be nice. Maybe two. Evelyn has a cat."

"Oh?" I said, glancing about.

"A calico named Toujours. She's a little timid around strangers, especially men, so she's probably hiding under the bed right now."

"I'm glad you have a friend like Miss Caldwell. If you think of anything else, anything at all, would you give me a call?" I handed her my card with my desk extension on it.

She took it rather timidly. "All right, I guess I could do that."

"Fine. Oh, and Mrs. Crow? Maybe don't mention that we were here to anyone, including the other detective, if it comes up."

"Why not?"

"Well, I'm not officially on the case. I'm just trying to help him out, and he doesn't like getting helped."

"I understand. I had a cousin like that. Too proud to accept help from anybody, so we all helped her in secret."

"Yes, that's how it is. We won't keep you any longer, but do call if you happen to think of anything else, okay?"

She got to her feet, smoothing out her odd, ill-fitting dress. "Sure I will. Here's your handkerchief, thank you so kindly." She held out my now damp handkerchief in her small hand.

I shook my head. "Why don't you keep it, Mrs. Crow? I'd like it if you would."

She closed her fingers around it tightly, and then she shoved it in the pocket of the dress.

"Thank you, Detective. You're very kind."

"Not at all, Mrs. Crow, my pleasure."

"Thank you for your hospitality," Alan said.

"I guess I wasn't very hospitable. I didn't offer you anything to eat or drink. Oh, but I made cookies this morning. Just a moment."

She disappeared back into the kitchen and I took advantage of the time to have a look around the apartment. The one and only bedroom opened directly off the living room, and it contained one full bed, neatly made, flanked by two nightstands, one of which held a book with the curious title of *Bachelor Women*. From the left side of the bed, a calico-colored tail protruded from beneath, swishing slowly back and forth. On the small dresser were trophies for women's tennis and golf, and on the wall, framed pictures of Babe Zaharias and Tallulah Bankhead, the latter autographed. A well-used tennis racket stood in the corner, next to a leather golf bag overflowing with clubs. The door to the bathroom was beside the closet. A pair of what appeared to be men's trousers and a necktie lay over the back of a small chair next to the window, along with a faded fedora. I stepped back into the living room just as Mrs. Crow returned with two freshly baked cookies on a plate. "Please have one, they're chocolate chip."

We willingly obliged, and they were delicious, though I was

careful not to get any crumbs on the floor. Holding the half-eaten cookies in our hands, we retrieved our hats at the door, and then bid her a good day.

Back out in the fresh afternoon air, we paused on the stoop to finish our cookies. "I can give you a lift back to Wisconsin and Wells," I said.

"Thanks, I'd appreciate that. I'd be late getting back otherwise."

"Right, let's go. I parked just up the street." We walked briskly along, each keeping pace with the other.

"What are your thoughts on Mrs. Crow?" Alan said as we crossed the street.

I pulled my hat low against the afternoon sun. "I feel sorry for her. She's so frightened, so alone."

"I'm glad she has Mrs. Picking. And Miss Caldwell," Alan said.

"Yeah, me too. I should like to know more about her, the librarian, I mean." I turned my car toward Wisconsin Avenue. "What are you doing after your shift?"

"Nothing special. Maybe spend some more time with my landlady's puppy. Why?"

"I was thinking I should pick up some groceries," I said.

"Okay, well, call me when you get home from there. I should be around."

"I was wondering if you'd like to come with."

He looked over at me as I shifted gears and turned the corner. "To the grocery store? I just went two days ago, and that's not exactly a romantic date."

"I wasn't thinking about a date. I was thinking about talking to Mr. Jarvis at the Grundy Market."

He dropped his head back against the seat back. "I should have known. What time?"

"You have to go back to the station to check out after your shift, yes?"

"That's right. I should be back by ten after five."

"Great. It's a quarter of two now. Meet me in the vestibule on the side after you sign out. We'll go from there. I phoned the market earlier. They're open until six tonight, and Mr. Jarvis is working."

"I'd say you're going to get us both in trouble poking around like this, but I don't think it would make a lick of difference."

I glanced over at him and smiled. "You know me so well, Alan. I'll drop you off at your corner, then I have to grab a sandwich and get back to my desk. Keep your thinking cap on!"

CHAPTER FIFTEEN

Late Tuesday Afternoon, August 12, 1947

I met Alan in the vestibule of the precinct right on schedule.

"How was the afternoon traffic duty?" I said.

"The drivers are crazy and getting crazier all the time. Anything new on the larceny case?"

"Yeah, in spite of my mind wandering all over the place, I made some real progress. I have to go to Racine on Thursday to interview someone involved. The Racine police are cooperating."

"The chief will be happy."

"Yeah, but he'll be happier when the Crow case is solved, and so will I. At least I think so."

"You think so?"

"I won't be very happy if it turns out I killed him."

Alan didn't say anything for a while as we left the vestibule and walked to my car. Finally, when both of us were sitting comfortably in the front seat, he turned to me and said, "I know you don't remember all that happened, and I know you have that bloodstained shirt crumpled up on the floor of your closet."

I started the engine, released the parking brake, and put the car in gear. "Ugh, don't remind me."

"No, I need to remind you, because you're torturing yourself, Heath. I know you didn't kill Larry Crow."

"How? How do you know? And don't tell me it's because you killed him, and don't tell me it's because I'm a nice guy."

Alan laughed as we pulled away from the curb and headed

toward State Street. "No, I didn't kill him and neither did you, and not because you're a nice guy, though you are. I know you didn't kill him because I know you, and you're not a murderer."

"Thanks, but you'll have to do better than that, Officer. No jury in the world will just take your word for it."

"Maybe not, but I've been giving it a lot of thought. You saw Larry at one and stayed there until about one twenty. When you left he was alive and well, correct?"

"Correct. Then I drove to that bar not far from his place and got drunk."

"Yes, you certainly did. From there you took a cab back to Larry's place. Knowing you, you probably wanted to confront him, keep him and Liz from going at it, tell him to go to hell, maybe even take a swing at him. But not kill him."

I stopped at a traffic light and looked over at him. "You can't know that. I had a motive. A very good motive. Our careers and our very lives were in danger."

"That's true, but it's just not in your nature. Maybe if he had you cornered, if there was no other way—"

"There *was* no other way, Alan."

"You couldn't have known that. You would have wanted to reason with him first, figure out a solution. It's how you operate. Killing would have been a last and final resort."

"So, if I didn't kill him what was I doing there?"

"Like I said, you went to reason with him and to protect Liz because she said she was heading to the Crow apartment. But when you got there, he was already dead."

"From the mysterious man hiding in the bedroom? Maybe Vinnie?"

"Maybe."

Or maybe from Liz, I thought, but then dismissed it. The light turned green once more, and I shifted gears and proceeded. "How did I get in if he was already dead?"

"The front door was most likely unlocked. Do you remember him locking it behind you when you left the first time?"

I shook my head, keeping my eyes on the road, as a yellow

Chrysler sedan pulled out suddenly from a driveway in front of me. Alan was right, the drivers were crazy lately. "Actually I left the door open when I left. I was angry. I just stormed out."

"So, you tried the door, it was unlocked, and you went in. You saw him on the sofa, you could see what had happened. You went to him, probably checked for a pulse, got blood on your hand, and wiped it on your shirt, hence the stain. You heard someone coming, maybe Mrs. Crow, and you fled, again out the front door."

"You have been giving this some thought," I said.

"I have. You told me you got back to the apartment the second time around two thirty, isn't that right?"

"Yes, as far as I can remember, which isn't much."

"And Mr. Crow telephoned his wife at two twenty, then presumably went back to sleep around the same time Liz supposedly was knocking on the door."

"Yes," I said. "But that doesn't exactly help my case. I could have come in at two thirty, killed him, and got out of there before Mrs. Crow came home again at two forty."

"I know, but you didn't. He was dead when you got there. You were drunk and in shock, so you left, probably roamed about the neighborhood in a daze, ending up in the park. Somewhere along the way, you got something to eat, then you had some more to drink. Eventually, you made your way home via a taxi, where you passed out."

"Well, it's logical and well thought out, but again, the jury is going to need more than that. They'll want facts and proof if I'm arrested."

"*If* you're arrested. You won't be."

"I wish I had your confidence. Here we are." I pulled my car into an angled parking spot just west of the front doors of the store and applied the parking brake as I switched off the engine.

"You'll find the real killer, Heath. I know it."

I put my hand on his knee and squeezed it gently. "*We'll* find the real killer, partner. And thanks."

We exited my car and walked down the sidewalk to the main entrance, which was on the corner of Twenty-seventh and State.

As soon as we entered the Grundy Market, we were hit right hard with the delicious smell of baked goods, temptingly displayed near the cash register by the front door, and I must admit it made my mouth water. There was also a faint, lingering smell of cigar smoke. The store was basically one large room, with an L-shaped counter on the left and shelves running around the perimeter, stacked to the ceiling with canned goods of every variety. In the center, dividing the store, were tables packed with bushel baskets of vegetables and fruits alongside sacks of flour, sugar, and containers of salt. There was a small refrigerated case in the back with some cheeses and dairy, but most everyone I knew got their milk and dairy products delivered. There was also a glass-enclosed meat case, but the best and freshest meats came from the butcher down the street.

Behind the cash register on the left stood a lean, tall man, almost completely bald except for a few long strands combed over from ear to ear. He had an eagle beak nose, which gave him a severe look, and large brown oval eyes like shiny pecans. Above his thin lips was a mushy mustache that tapered to a point and curled upward at each end. He wore a long white apron over a white shirt and white trousers, with a black necktie.

"Good afternoon, gentlemen!" he called out as we closed the door behind us, the bell over it jingling. The wood floor, running in wide planks perpendicular to the door, glistened. Out of the corner of my eye, I thought I saw the door to the back room close, but I couldn't be certain.

"Good afternoon. I'm Detective Heath Barrington, and this is Officer Alan Keyes. We're investigating the murder of Larry Crow."

"Oh, I see." The man's cheerful expression changed immediately. "There was another detective here this morning, fellow by the name of Green. He was here the other day, too. I have his card somewhere." He glanced about the register area before finally snatching it up from a spindle. "Yes, here it is. Detective Alvin Green. He said he was investigating Crow's death. I don't know what else you people want from me."

"I'm sorry to trouble you. We're working together, Green's a colleague. I promise not to take up much time. Are you Mr. Jarvis?"

I noticed the overhead light reflected off his bald head, and I wondered if he polished it every morning. "Yes, that's right. Ossip Jarvis, owner and proprietor, at your service. I took over from Mr. Grundy a few years ago when he decided to retire, but I kept the Grundy Market name."

"A pleasure to meet you, Mr. Jarvis. You have a nice store."

"Thanks. And you are?"

"Detective Barrington and Officer Keyes."

"I heard about the murder, of course, even before that Green fella got here."

I grimaced as I approached the counter. "News travels fast, especially bad news."

Mr. Jarvis picked up a bottle of Coke and took a sip before setting it back down on the counter. "I'm not sure Larry Crow being murdered is bad news."

"That's a matter of opinion, I suppose. I'm sorry to trouble you, but I would like to ask you a few more questions, if you don't mind."

"I guess not. As you can see, I'm not exactly bustling with customers at the moment, but like I said, I don't know what else I can tell you." He picked up his Coke again and made himself comfortable on a small gray metal stool behind the massive brass cash register.

"Thanks, just the same. I understand Mrs. Crow phoned in a grocery order on Saturday, the day of the murder. Is that correct?"

"Yes, that's right. I've known Mrs. Crow since she and her husband moved in to the neighborhood a few years back. She always comes here for her groceries or has them delivered, usually on Saturday afternoons. I offer free delivery to all my regular customers, you know."

"Very generous of you," Alan said.

"Just good business. When Mrs. Crow did come into the store in person, she always looked sad and troubled. Can't say I blame her, married to him. She's a pretty little thing, deserves better than what she got."

"You said she shops here regularly?" I said.

He brushed a few droplets of Coke off his mustache. "Every

week, sometimes twice a week. When she comes in she can usually only manage one box at a time. She has to walk four blocks home, then up a flight of stairs, you know. Her husband would certainly never lend a hand, so she has to buy frequently or have the items delivered. I do that for free."

"So you mentioned," Alan said.

"Right. He was a nasty man, her husband, I mean. He come in here once not long ago, all full of himself, trying to say I cheated his wife on the price of some canned tomatoes. Can you imagine?"

"That must have been upsetting," Alan said.

"You can say that again. He said I charged her twenty cents for a can of tomatoes instead of fifteen cents like I'd advertised in the paper. Called me a liar, he did. Waved the ad in my face, even."

"So, what happened?"

"I gave him the nickel out of the drawer just to get rid of him as he was causing a scene in front of other customers, but I didn't charge her twenty cents. My drawer was short a nickel that night."

"Did you have any other run-ins with him?" I said.

"A few. He didn't come in often. I think he thought grocery shopping was women's work, beneath him. But he'd stop by occasionally on his way to or from work for a doughnut or a pack of Camel cigarettes. He never had any money, always had me put it on his tab."

"Did he pay his tab?"

"Hmph," Mr. Jarvis snorted. "Not very often. He's a deadbeat. Or was a deadbeat. Now he's just dead!" With that he snickered a little bit and finished his Coke. He set the empty bottle in a wooden crate, which was half filled with others just like it.

"Someone told us you were angry with him because he gave you a bad tip on a horse that cost you a lot of money," I said.

"Who told you that?"

"Does it matter?"

"No, because it's not true. It was me that gave *him* the tip when he was in here one day, before the incident with the can of tomatoes. I thought it was a solid tip, but it turns out it wasn't and he got real sore, claims he lost a lot of money. 'Course, I don't gamble, and if I do, I do it legal like."

"Of course. You just pass on tips to your customers."

"Nothing illegal about that."

"There is if you get a kickback."

"I just do it out of the goodness of my heart."

"How generous of you. Do you remember what the time was when Mrs. Crow phoned in her order on Saturday?" I said.

"It was about a quarter past noon. I remember because I had just let Timmy go."

"Who's Timmy?" Alan said.

"Timmy Trotter. One of the Trotter boys, the youngest, I think. He does deliveries for me on his bicycle. But it was a slow day, so I gave him the afternoon off to play ball. I told him to check in around two thirty, after the game. So, yeah, Mrs. Crow called a little past noon. She was in a hurry, as she said her husband had someone coming over at one, and he wanted her out by twelve thirty. She said I should just come in the back way and leave the groceries on the counter. She gave me her order, and I jotted it down on my pad, like I always do." He pointed to an order pad next to the register.

"And you did the delivery yourself, I understand," I said.

"That's right, because Timmy was off playing ball. Since it was slow, I put a sign on the door and took the box over. When I'm out I usually get my sister to watch the store, but she wasn't available on short notice. Besides, Mrs. Picking is often outside on her porch on Saturdays, and she's a nice-looking dame."

"Mrs. Crow's neighbor," I said.

He smiled lecherously, a gold tooth shining. "That's right. She's one of my customers, too, though she always comes here to the store. She's a real tomato, ripe and fresh in all the right places, if you know what I mean."

"I'm familiar with her. She's an attractive woman."

"You can say that again, and I'm a single man, Detective. I was left at the altar over fifteen years ago, never did marry again. A dish like Picking, I notice. There's a few in the neighborhood, war widows, you know? Fern Garrwood, she's another one. Tiny little thing but curvy in all the right places."

"I'm sorry to hear that. About being left at the altar, I mean."

He shrugged. "Eh, it was for the best. She wasn't the lady I thought she was. She wasn't a lady at all, it turns out."

I raised my eyebrows and glanced over at Alan, who looked equally surprised.

"Really?" I said.

"No, sir. She was a tramp. She left the fella she left me for after only a year and took up with some traveling salesman from Chicago. I hear tell that only lasted six months. I lost track of her after that."

"Oh," I said. "I see. I misunderstood at first."

"So did I," Mr. Jarvis said. "I thought she was a lady, but I should have known better. My mother always told me a lady never scratches herself or spits, but Loretta did both, and often. Good riddance to bad rubbish. Ladies you marry, dames, well, you know."

"Not really," Alan said. "But as you said, Mr. Jarvis, it was for the best. Loretta just barely escaped."

"What do you mean by that?" He tugged on his mustache as he spoke.

"The two of you clearly weren't suited for each other," I said.

"Hmph, not hardly. What were we talking about before? I can't remember," he said.

"You were telling us that Mrs. Crow phoned in her order, and you made the delivery yourself."

"Oh yeah, that's right. I did."

"And what time was that?" Alan said.

"I left here about ten minutes of two, and I got to their place around two. I have a delivery van, but since they live close I decided to walk."

"If business was slow, why did you wait almost two hours to make the delivery?" I said.

"I had to eat my lunch, and I had a few customers come in. Besides, Mrs. Crow said her husband had an appointment at one, so I wanted to make sure I wasn't interrupting. I came up the back steps, off the alley. Mrs. Picking was on the porch, just outside her door, like I had hoped. She usually is on Saturdays, doing her laundry. She's got some nice gams on her, let me tell you."

I resisted the temptation to roll my eyes. "A tomato with legs, I guess you'd say."

"Yes, sir." He whistled. "She's a tough tomato, but I'll ripen her up one of these days."

"That tomato's ripe already, and she isn't for picking. Do you recall what was she wearing?"

"Wearing? A pair of quite shapely legs that went all the way up under her dress."

I sighed. "You, Mr. Jarvis, have a one-track mind. What color was that dress?"

"Damned if I know, but her legs looked smooth as silk. What does it matter what color her dress was?"

"Just trying to get the facts straight. Did you speak with Mrs. Picking?"

"Sure, we chatted briefly, but she's not so friendly. Then I knocked on the kitchen door of the Crow place, but there was no answer. So I just went in."

"Is that standard procedure?" I said.

"Most folks leave their back doors unlocked if they're going to be gone during a delivery. Especially if they have something perishable. Groceries don't do well in the summer heat."

"I suppose that's true. So you went into their kitchen," I said.

"That's right. I saw Mr. Crow right away, flat on his back, sleeping on the sofa, snoring like a buzz saw. I unpacked the groceries as quietly as I could, then took the box and left. I kept one eye on him the whole time, hoping he wouldn't wake up because I didn't feel like getting into any arguments right then. I guess he was done with his appointment."

"Do you always unpack for your customers?"

He shrugged. "Sometimes. Right now I'm short on boxes, so I figured I'd take it back and reuse it. Though I don't typically do the deliveries myself. Most of the time I have Timmy or some other boy, like I said."

"What time did you leave the Crow apartment?" Alan said.

"About ten after two."

"Did you happen to notice anyone else in or around the alley?"

"Nope. Nobody around anywhere. Too hot, I guess. I got back to my shop around two twenty, and Timmy was waiting for me. The ball game ended early."

"Do you recall exactly what Mrs. Crow ordered from you that day?"

"No, not exactly, but I can tell you." He picked up the order pad and flipped back a few pages, then scanned it briefly, moving his finger down the page. "Ah, here it is. A bunch of carrots, a can of peas, and a bag of sugar. I added it to their account, which is getting sizable."

"Credit can be a slippery slope."

"That's true, Detective. I gave her the sale price on sugar, even though it ended the day before. I remember how hard sugar was to come by during the war."

"I remember that, too, Mr. Jarvis. Everything was rationed, it seemed. Nice of you to give her the sale price," Alan said.

"I've got a sale on apples right now, the Macintoshes. Eighteen cents a pound, if you want some."

I picked one up from a display nearby, turned it over and then set it back down. "Uh, no thanks."

"Sale only goes two more days," he said, looking from me to Alan.

"Duly noted, but no thank you," I replied. "I could use a can of peas, though."

"Sure, they're on the back shelf, next to the stock room door."

"Right." I strolled back and found the peas on sale for fifteen cents a can, and picked one up, noticing the smell of cigars was slightly stronger back there. I returned with the can and set it on the counter.

"Anything else?"

"Not right now. By the way, would you mind if I used your bathroom?" I said.

He gave me an odd look as his eyes darted to the stockroom door and back. "It's out of order. I go upstairs to my apartment when

I need to. Sorry. There's a laundry up the street. You can probably use theirs."

"All right. We should get going then, I suppose. I thank you for your time. Here's fifteen cents for the peas."

"Thanks," he replied, ringing it into the register.

"All set, Alan?" I glanced over at him. He was bending over, examining the large glass jars of colorful and assorted penny candy beneath the register, right at a child's-eye view.

"I'll take a half pound of those gumdrops, Mr. Jarvis, if you don't mind," Alan said.

"Sure, those are nice and fresh, just got them in." He reached under the counter and put some of them into a white paper bag using a metal scoop, then placed the bag on the scale to the right of us, adding a few gumdrops once or twice, until it registered a half pound exactly. Then he tossed in a few more. "For good measure, on the house," he said.

"Thanks, much appreciated." He gave Mr. Jarvis a nickel and Mr. Jarvis gave him his change and the bag of candy, which Alan eagerly dug his hand into.

"By the way, I see you sell cigars. Willard Ponies," I said, pointing to a box of them on display next to the register.

"I try to carry a full line of cigars and cigarettes. Are you a cigar smoker, Mr. Barrington?"

"Once in a while I'll give one a try, but I don't smoke in general."

"A good cigar can be quite satisfying, and they're a profitable item for me."

"I bet. Sell many of the Willard Ponies?"

"Some. I have a few regulars that purchase them." His eyes flitted to the back of the store again for a brief moment.

"Do you happen to know a man by the name of Vinnie the Horse?" I said, picking up the can of peas I'd purchased.

"That's a funny name."

"He's a funny guy. Know him?"

"I don't think so. Maybe he comes in to buy cigars, but I can't say for sure."

"Uh-huh. Funny how you don't know him, yet you know he buys cigars."

"Just a lucky guess. You were talking about the cigars. Why are you asking about this guy?"

"I'm a curious sort. I hear tell he takes wagers on horses, among other things, and not the legal kind, either."

"Is that a fact?"

"That it is."

"Huh. I'll keep an eye out for him and let you know if I see him, then."

"You do that, Mr. Jarvis." We said our goodbyes and exited the store, the bell over the door jingling once more.

CHAPTER SIXTEEN

Tuesday Evening, August 12, 1947

I pulled my hat down over my eyes to shade them from the late afternoon sun hanging in the western sky, as Alan fished out candy from the bag in his hand.

"Looks like the laundry up the street is still open if you want to use the bathroom," Alan said.

I shook my head. "No, I'm fine."

"But you asked to use the bathroom just a minute ago."

"That I did," I replied.

"Well, then, want to go get some dinner?" he said, munching on more gumdrops. "Art's Diner isn't far."

"Looks like you're already eating dessert."

Alan grinned, and the sugar on his lips looked quite tempting.

"Life's short, eat dessert first, isn't that what they say?"

"Not according to my mother," I said, pulling out my pocket watch. "It's almost six. Dinner sounds good, but before that let's take a walk."

"A walk? You usually like to walk *after* we eat."

"I know, but it's a nice evening out, it's cooled down, still plenty of daylight left, and I feel like walking."

"Okay, sure. Where to?"

"To the Crows' apartment," I said. "It's close by, so we can leave my car here."

Alan groaned audibly. "I should have known you had an

ulterior motive. Do you think that's a good idea, Heath? Going back there again?"

"I wouldn't suggest it if I didn't think it was a good idea. You can stay here if you like. I won't be gone long."

"Nope, no chance. If you're walking, I'm walking. Let's go."

"Thanks," I said. "By the way, are you going to eat all those gumdrops yourself?"

Alan looked over at me and smiled once more as he licked the sugar off his lips. I would have liked to have done that. "Sorry, here, help yourself." He offered the little bag to me and I dug my hand in. The opening was a bit small, but I managed to get out several, popping them into my mouth one by one as we started walking. The red ones were my favorite.

"I'll just leave this can of peas in my car."

"Kind of a funny thing to buy."

"They were on display next to the stockroom door," I said.

"So?"

"Did you smell cigar smoke in there?"

"Not really, but I did smell that bakery."

"The cigar smell was faint, but stronger by the stockroom door. And when we first entered, I thought I saw someone go in there and close the door."

"And *that's* why you asked to use the bathroom. To see if he'd let you back there."

"Exactly. I wonder if the toilet is really out of order."

"Hmm, and he sells those Willard Ponies cigars," Alan said in between mouthfuls.

"Yes. I checked at the market near my place, and they only sell Bolivars and Cuabas. Ponies don't seem to be as popular."

"So you think Jarvis knows Vinnie the Horse?"

"It wouldn't surprise me. Jarvis strikes me as a bit of an unethical creep. Those Macintoshes he was pushing for eighteen cents a pound looked far from fresh, and the market by my place sells them every day for fifteen cents. And the peas I can usually get for ten cents a can."

"And that thing about the horse racing."

"I think Jarvis was lying about who gave who the bad tip. If I had to hazard a guess, I'd say Crow gave him a bad tip, Jarvis placed a large bet with Vinnie the Horse, the bet went south, and now Jarvis owes Vinnie a lot of money."

"Gee, that makes sense. And maybe Vinnie got Jarvis to kill Larry as payment."

"Maybe. But why? If Larry owed Vinnie money, too, killing him wouldn't help things. Unless Jarvis did it to get back at him for the bad tip and harassing him in front of his customers. Or maybe he thought that with Larry out of the way, he could finagle some cash out of Mrs. Crow."

"Ugh, so many things to think about. Makes my head hurt."

"I think it's all that sugar doing that. Here's my car. Let me put this can on the floor, and then we can go."

We walked on for several blocks at a moderate pace, arriving at the apartment building, 1812 West State Street, in just over ten minutes.

"Now what?" Alan said. "Surely the apartment is locked up tight with new locks."

"Without a doubt. But I'm not planning on going inside."

"Then what are we here for?"

I motioned him to follow me up the side street to the entrance from the alley that ran behind the building. "The Crows' apartment building is the third one from the corner," I said, as we walked along the narrow alleyway. When we reached the correct building, I stopped at the light pole and squatted down, examining the ground.

"What are you looking for?"

"This," I said, holding up a cigar butt. "There's two or three of them here on the ground. Curious. You finished with that bag of candy?"

"Ugh, yes. I ate the entire half pound."

"You're going to have a stomachache later to go with your aching head," I said.

He looked for all the world like a big, cuddly, blue-eyed puppy dog who had just gotten scolded for chewing up a sock. "I know, but I just can't help myself. I have a terrible sweet tooth."

I looked up at him and grinned. "It's okay, me, too. Give me the empty bag, will you?"

"Sure, what for?"

I scooped up two of the cigar butts with it, then put it in my pocket. "Possible evidence. Come on." I stood back up, and we climbed the wooden back staircase, which creaked accordingly under our weight. I hoped Mrs. Picking wouldn't notice or hear us.

When we had arrived at the back door of the apartment, I pulled out my pocket watch again. "Mr. Jarvis told us he left the store about ten minutes of two, and Mrs. Picking told us it was about two when she saw him on the staircase heading up to the Crow apartment, so the times match. Mrs. Picking also told us that it was about ten minutes after two when he left again. And Mrs. Crow spoke with Mr. Crow on the telephone at twenty after two."

"Okay," Alan said.

"By my calculations, Mr. Jarvis's story checks out. He left the Crow apartment at two ten, and that Timmy Trotter kid could verify he arrived back at the store ten minutes later. Mr. Crow phoned his wife at two twenty; therefore Larry Crow was alive and asleep on the sofa when Jarvis left at ten after two."

"So?" Alan said.

I shook my head, truly puzzled. "I don't know. If Mr. Jarvis didn't kill him, who did? Mrs. Picking or Vinnie the Horse, I'm guessing. Or maybe that mysterious man in the alley."

"What about Mrs. Crow?" Alan said.

"What about her?"

"She could have killed him."

"How? He was alive when Jarvis left him, and she didn't get back to the apartment until about a half hour later, at which time she screamed and Picking came running."

"Maybe she got home sooner and came in the front way, killed him, then left again and came up the back stairs."

"Possible. I suppose we should talk to that librarian and make sure she can vouch for what time Mrs. Crow left the library."

"Good idea. But even if she did leave when she said she did," maybe she came in the back door, grabbed the knife, slit his throat, dropped the knife, and then screamed."

"Not possible," I said. "She wouldn't have had enough time."

"Oh, I don't know, Heath. I think it could be done."

"Maybe. Let's get back to the car."

"Okay." We descended the stairs, then back down the alley and out onto State Street. As we walked, Alan suddenly stopped. "Time me."

I stopped, too. "What?"

"Just time me with your watch."

"I think the sugar's definitely getting to you, but all right." I took out my watch and said, "Go," wondering just what exactly he was going to do. It soon became apparent. He was pantomiming Mrs. Crow walking into the kitchen of their apartment, getting a knife and walking into the living room, much to the bewilderment of a couple waiting at the bus stop on the corner. Suddenly he slashed frantically at the air with the pretend knife, alarming the couple at the bus stop. When he had finished "murdering Mr. Crow," he dropped the pretend knife, mimed a scream, and then turned back to me and said, "Stop."

I walked up to him, tipping my hat to the couple, who hurriedly turned away. "Okay, point taken, forty-two seconds."

Alan beamed. "See?"

"Yeah, yeah," I replied as we started to walk again. "But you're forgetting something."

He cocked his head. "What?"

"Blood. When someone slashes someone's throat, the blood spurts everywhere, but no one mentioned Mrs. Crow having even a drop of blood on her, including Mrs. Picking, who was the first to see her."

"Hmm. Maybe she covered herself before killing him. A sheet or an apron or something."

"That would add to the time. She'd also have to dispose of it somewhere before she screamed. Want to pantomime that?"

"Funny," he said dryly.

"And where would she have disposed of a sheet or apron? Nothing was found in the apartment. Besides, even forty-two seconds is a long time. Mrs. Picking said she heard Mrs. Crow scream almost immediately after entering the kitchen door."

Alan looked somewhat disappointed. "Oh yeah, you're right. Then my money is on the Picking lady. She had motive and opportunity, and she seems as cool as a cucumber from what you've told me."

"Maybe so, Alan. And in a strange way, I hope you're right. At least, I hope it was someone else and not me. I hope you're right about that."

"I am right. Do you think Jarvis and Vinnie the Horse could have been in on it together?"

"That actually makes sense, if that was Vinnie hiding in the back room of the store tonight, but I can't figure out the angle. Why would Jarvis and Vinnie team up to kill Crow?"

"Yeah, I can't figure that out, either. Ugh, you were right about those gumdrops. I'll be eating a light dinner, if at all."

I laughed. "In that case, I'm buying."

"Thanks, big spender," Alan replied, looking slightly sick.

"Sorry, couldn't resist. Here's my car. Let's go eat. Maybe some broth or something will help you feel better. If not I've got some Coke syrup at home. Want to stay the night? That is, if your stomach is up for it."

He smiled, one hand on his stomach. "That is an invitation I can't refuse. My stomach and every other part of my body will definitely be up for it, one way or the other!"

We had dinner at Art's Diner, nothing fancy, but we had a booth to ourselves, and after some saltines and a bowl of vegetable soup, Alan felt and looked better. I picked up the check, and we went back to my apartment, arriving a few minutes before eight. Fortunately, no one was about in the lobby or halls, so I didn't have to worry about explaining Alan's presence that late at night. Hopefully we'd be as lucky in the morning.

CHAPTER SEVENTEEN

Wednesday Morning, August 13, 1947

With Alan's back to my chest, I slept better than I had in several nights. I felt safe, secure, and content. He woke before I did and got the coffee started in the kitchen. Eventually I got up, showered, shaved, and joined him for coffee.

"Good morning," I said, walking into the kitchen.

"Hey, sleepyhead. Coffee's ready."

"So I smell. Heavenly."

"I brought in your newspaper, too. Don't worry, no one saw me."

"Good, thanks. How'd you sleep?"

He grinned. "Heavenly."

I grinned back at him. "Me too. Stomachache better?"

"All gone, but I could use some breakfast. Want to eat in or out?"

"I'll fry us some eggs and make some toast while you shower and shave."

"Great, thanks. I'm glad you talked me into leaving a toothbrush and a razor here, along with some clothes."

"I was happy to empty out a drawer for you."

He put his arms around me and kissed me gently. "Give me a lift to the station after we eat?"

I laughed. "I think I'm heading in that direction, but I better let you off a block or so before the streetcar stop in case anyone sees."

Alan sighed. "Yeah, I understand. I won't be but a minute."

"I'll time you."

He gave me another light kiss and then headed for the bathroom, whistling a happy tune. After he left, I realized we might have been overheard through the kitchen vent, but there was nothing to be done about it now, and I wasn't going to let it spoil my morning.

The eggs and toast were ready quickly. I plated them and set them on the dining table along with a jar of my mom's apple preserves, some butter, salt, pepper, the last of Mrs. Murphy's doughnuts, two glasses of orange juice, and the coffee. Alan appeared shortly after that, dressed in his uniform, and looking clean and fresh.

"I'm starving," he said.

"You always say you're starving—unless you've just eaten half a pound of gumdrops, that is."

"Ugh, don't remind me." He glanced at the table. "Aww, you remembered I like my eggs over medium."

"I remember lots of things." Then my mood changed suddenly. "I just wish I could remember for certain what happened at the Crow apartment the second time I went back. It's all so hazy."

Alan put his hand on my shoulder. "Sit, eat, and forget about it. I told you what happened. We'll find whoever killed Larry Crow, don't worry."

I looked over at him as we sat down, putting our napkins on our laps. "Thanks. I don't think I could get through this without you."

"I'm glad to hear that. And speaking of, do you know tomorrow is the five-month anniversary of the day we met?"

I couldn't help but smile. "I remember that day well. March fourteenth. A dreary, rainy, miserable, wet, damp spring day that suddenly turned wonderful."

"We'll have to celebrate."

"Indeed. But first we have a case to solve, one way or the other." I glanced at the clock in the kitchen. "It's nearly eight. Let's eat, so I can get the kitchen cleaned up and we can be on our way."

"Yes, sir."

After the dishes were done and I'd strapped on my service revolver and put the bag of cigar butts in my pocket once more,

I sent Alan on ahead downstairs by himself, just in case any of the neighbors were about. It would look better if we weren't seen together. Almost as an afterthought, I dug out the bloodstained shirt from my closet and wrapped it in the morning paper, even though I hadn't read it yet. I tucked it under my arm, checked my reflection in the hall mirror above the telephone, then headed down, locking the door behind me. It was a warm, sunny morning, though the weatherman on the radio had said rain was expected later, and I thought that I probably should have brought my umbrella.

Alan was waiting for me by my car. Someone had taken my usual spot under the great-grandmother elm tree last night, so I had to park farther north, almost to Royall Place.

"All set?" I said, as I strode up to him and opened the driver's side door.

"If you're waiting for me, you're wasting your time," Alan replied.

"Anyone see you leaving?"

"Just the milkman on his rounds and an old black tomcat in the hall."

I laughed as he slid in next to me. "That's Oscar, Mrs. Ferguson's cat. I think our secret's safe with him."

"What's in the parcel?"

"The shirt," I said.

"Shirt? Oh, *the* shirt."

"Yeah. I figured I better get rid of it once and for all. Besides, that stain will never come out."

"What are you going to do with it?"

"I've been thinking about that. I think a trash can somewhere would be best. Untraceable to me, far from here." I tucked the package under the seat, put the car in gear, and made a left on Royall Place to Farwell, then another left, until we reached State Street, where I turned right, but instead of stopping at Eighth, I continued west.

"Where are you going?"

"The State Street branch of the library opens at nine this morning."

"Heath…"

"Just a slight detour, won't take long."

Alan sighed. "I should have known. I'll be late for my shift, you know."

"I can clear it with Evers. He owes me a favor, unless you want me to drop you at work first. I can handle the library on my own."

Out of the corner of my eye, I saw him shake his head. "No, the library it is. We're in this together."

I smiled as I accelerated west down State Street, glad the morning sun was to our backs. We found a parking spot close by, and side by side climbed the stone steps to the entrance doors, flanked by two carved sandstone lions. I pulled on one of the brass handles, which had been worn down to a soft, smooth brown, and we entered. As the door closed quietly behind us, I was immediately hit with that distinct library smell: musty, woody old leather and ancient pages. The odor of reams of paper also filled my nostrils. It was five after nine, and we were the first customers, apparently.

The State Street branch was small, the circulation desk sitting prominently in the center. Behind it, the stacks, where all those glorious books were shelved. To the left, the main reading room, complete with a fireplace and cozy nook. To the right, the children's reading room, also with a fireplace, but the librarian's office sat where the nook would be on that side of the building. A fierce-looking woman stamped books behind the circulation desk. She was solidly built, not fat, just tough and muscular. She looked up at us as we entered but neither commented nor smiled.

"Good morning," I said quietly.

"How can I help you?" she replied, still stamping, her voice soft but commanding. She wore her chocolate brown hair, streaked with wisps of silver, short and close to her head like a helmet, but it flattered her. She needed no makeup, as her complexion was clear and radiant. Her nails were short and unpainted but clean and neat. She had a pair of brilliant hazel eyes, set on either side of a small, thin nose. She was attractive in a fresh-scrubbed, natural way.

"I'm Detective Barrington of the Milwaukee police, this is

Officer Keyes. We'd like to speak to Miss Caldwell, please. Evelyn Caldwell."

She stopped in mid-stamp. A look of surprise crossed her face, then quickly went away. "I'm Miss Caldwell. What's this about?"

"We're investigating the murder of Lawrence Crow."

She set her stamp down and closed one of the books. "I already talked to Detective Green."

"Yes, I know. We're just following up. You're familiar with Mrs. Crow, correct?" I said.

"That's right. She told me you'd been to see her at my apartment. She's staying with me, as you obviously know."

"Yes. It was nice of you to take her in."

"Alice is a nice woman, and I consider her a friend. She doesn't have many friends. I told her a long time ago she could stay with me if she ever left her louse of a husband. I only have a one bedroom, but she knew she would be welcome. It's just me and my cat, Toujours. Alice likes cats, and Toujours likes her."

"Toujours, French for always, of course," I said.

"That's right. *Vous parlez Français?*"

"Uh, *un petit.*"

"*Vous devriez en apprendre plus, c'est une belle langue.*"

I could feel Alan looking at me, a slight smirk on his face. "I'm sorry, I don't know what that means. I studied it in school, but it's been a few years."

"It means 'You should learn more, it's a beautiful language.'"

"Oh, well, yes, *oui*, I should. You speak it well. How did you two meet? You and Alice, I mean."

"Here at the library. She's a regular. She comes in every Saturday afternoon and has been for the last couple of years."

She moved a pile of books to a cart. She was wearing a straight, dark brown skirt with a matching jacket over a white blouse, buttoned all the way up to the cameo at her throat. On her feet were flat brown leather loafers, very sensible. She didn't appear to be wearing hosiery.

"When did you last see her here?" I said.

"Last Saturday afternoon, the day her husband was murdered. She stayed a couple of hours, why?"

"I'm surprised you remember all that so easily," I said. "You must get a lot of patrons in here throughout the day."

"Of course we do. But Alice is a close friend, like I said, and a regular here. I always look forward to seeing her. When it's not busy we talk privately sometimes in my office."

"About what?" Alan said.

"Books, thoughts, politics, some private things. She's quite intelligent, you know. It doesn't come across at first because she's not well educated, but she's smart. There's a difference between educated and intelligent."

"I quite agree. Did you ever talk about anything else?"

"She talked about her husband sometimes, too. She was terribly afraid and unhappy in her marriage. She couldn't even bring certain books into their house. She had to hide them in the laundry room."

"Yes, she mentioned that. It's quite sad," I said.

"It's ridiculous, is what it is. Men." She gave each of us a disgusted look.

"Surely not all men," Alan said.

"Enough of them."

"You've never married?"

"No, and I don't intend to. Have you?"

"Me? Uh, no, at least, not yet," I said.

"I see." She looked from me to Alan and then back again. "I don't need a man. I can take care of myself, and I can take care of Alice better than she can. I told her many times she needed to act on her thoughts, to move. But as a wise person once said, 'The most difficult thing is the decision to act; the rest is merely tenacity.'"

"An excellent quote. Benjamin Franklin, I believe."

"You believe incorrectly, Detective. It was Amelia Earhart. If you want to check, you can see for yourself in the biography section."

I felt myself blush. "I stand corrected. I understand Mrs. Crow received a phone call while she was here that day, is that right?"

"That's right, she did. She was reading at that table over there, a new book we just got in I recommended for her. I answered the phone here at the desk. It was her husband, and he wanted to talk with her. We don't normally allow calls for patrons because it's too disruptive, but I make exceptions for Alice. I asked Miss Saunders to watch the front desk, and I took her back to my office so she could have some privacy."

"Did you stay with her?"

"No, I returned to the desk here." She looked disgusted again. "Alice never should have married him. Or anyone else. Men. I treat her better than he ever did. I know how to take care of her. He actually called to give her permission to return to their apartment because his appointment was over. Can you imagine someone giving you permission to return to your own home?"

"How do you know that's what he said to her?" I said.

Her eyelids flickered briefly. "Well, uh, she must have told me."

"Or you must have listened in on the extension here," I said.

Her pale face blushed crimson. "Alice is my friend, and she was afraid of her husband. If I listened in, it was only to make sure she was okay."

"I think I would do the same in your position, Miss Caldwell," I said.

"Thank you for that. I think you would have."

"Of course. So, what exactly did he say to her?"

"Well, he said, 'It's Larry, Alice. You can come home now. My appointment is gone.' Then she said something like, 'All right, I'll be home as soon as I can.' She sounded nervous and upset. Afraid of your husband, I think that's terrible."

"It is terrible. A terrible way to live."

"It's not my kind of living, Detective. She hung up and came back out here and asked me what time it was, and I told her it was twenty after two. She told me she needed to leave, so she gathered up her things, checked out the book she had been reading, and left."

"And that was about two thirty?"

"That's right. She seemed fretful and had a fresh bruise under her eye. It made my blood boil."

"Understandable. I can't imagine being married to Larry Crow," I said. "It must have been awful."

"You're lucky you're a man." She pursed her bare lips and looked even more agitated.

"I suppose I am." I glanced over at Alan and back to her. "Some people think so, anyway. Have you ever been to the Crow apartment?"

"No, never inside. I admit I went over once or twice, and hung around outside. I wanted to see what Larry Crow looked like and maybe try to talk to him if I got the chance, but I decided it would probably do more harm than good, so I never did."

"Probably a wise decision. Did Mrs. Crow ever mention a Mr. Jarvis? He's a grocer who made a delivery to their apartment last Saturday."

Miss Caldwell blinked several times and brought her right hand up to her cameo, which she fiddled with absentmindedly. "Jarvis? No, I don't think so. Why?"

"Just wondering. He was dropping off groceries there at two. Do you know him at all?"

"Me, no, why would I? I live in the opposite direction and do my marketing closer to home."

"Of course. Apparently, this Mr. Jarvis and Mr. Crow didn't care for each other much."

"Not many people *did* care for Mr. Crow," she said.

"Agreed."

"Just like library books, Detective, we all have due dates. Lawrence Crow's was a death overdue."

"That's not for us, or anyone, to decide."

"Perhaps, but he was taken out of circulation once and for all, and that's enough for me."

"On that, I can agree. Well, we won't take up any more of your time, Miss Caldwell. If we have any more questions, will you be here all day?"

"Actually no. I'm only working the morning. Alice is expecting Mrs. Picking this afternoon, and I'd like to be there. She's Alice's neighbor and she's coming to call."

"I see. Well, I appreciate your cooperation."

"You're welcome. Good day, gentlemen."

We turned and left, putting our hats on as we went down the steps toward the car. I pulled out my pocket watch. "Nine twenty. We should be at the precinct by nine thirty, not too late."

"Don't forget you have to drop me at the streetcar stop."

"Oh yeah, that's right. But don't worry, like I said, I can fix it with Evers."

"He owes you a favor, I know. That Miss Caldwell is interesting."

"I agree. She's one of the rare few who are educated and intelligent, I think. And she seems to care about Mrs. Crow a great deal."

"She doesn't seem to like men much."

"Do you blame her? It's a man's world, Alan, and it's a struggle for women to compete, to be considered equals. Men like Larry Crow and Ossip Jarvis are just two examples of what they're up against on a daily basis."

"Yeah, I guess so. I'm glad not all men are like those two. Maybe the world will change some day."

"Hopefully, for all of us. I noticed she seemed a bit unsettled when I mentioned Jarvis's name."

"Yeah, I noticed that, too. You think she was lying about knowing him?"

"I'm not sure. Maybe, but I can't figure out why."

I turned the car around and headed to the station. As arranged, I dropped Alan at the streetcar stop, then drove on by myself. He probably got there before me by the time I had parked. I signed in on the chalkboard downstairs, noting Sparrow was at the desk again.

"Good morning," I said, setting the chalk back down.

"Hey, Barrington. You're late this morning."

"Yeah, had something to do on my current case."

"You should have phoned in. I ran that Michael Hart for you, by the way. There's a few of them in town, but only one that was in the Navy. Lives over on Humboldt."

"That's probably the one. Anything?"

Sparrow shook his head. "Nope. Not even parking tickets. The guy's clean as a whistle. I think your cousin's safe."

"Good to know. Thanks for doing that."

"Sure, anytime. Get me some tickets to the ball game when you can."

"I'll do that."

"Thanks." He answered the ringing phone as he turned back to his typewriter. I went up to my desk in the detective's room, stopping first for a cup of coffee. I stole a glance in the direction of Alvin Green's desk. He was already at work, pounding away on his typewriter, hunting and pecking. Curious, I walked over to his desk.

"Good morning, Alvin," I said, as cheerily as I could under the circumstances.

He paused and looked up at me. "You're late. Again."

"You're right, sorry. I had to make a stop for work, and then I was talking to Sparrow downstairs. Anything new on the case?"

"You mean my case? The case that's none of your business?"

"Yeah, that's the one. I knew you'd know."

"Wise guy. Where were you last night? Say between six and eight?"

"Having dinner at Art's Diner on Wisconsin. I got home just a few minutes before eight, why?"

"Were you alone?"

I bristled. "No, Alan Keyes was with me."

"Alan Keyes. Figures. Anyone see you at the diner that can ID you?"

"Probably. They weren't very busy. Why the third degree about where I was?"

"Because Ossip Jarvis was found dead in his apartment above the store last night, two slugs in him."

"What?" I recoiled in shock and disbelief.

"He locked up his shop at six, and his sister found him dead a couple minutes after eight. He was in a robe and boxer shorts, reeked of booze. We found exactly fifty dollars in mostly small bills and change in one of the robe pockets and a half-empty pack of cigarettes, a cigar, and a book of matches in the other. The door was ajar."

"So, someone shot him?"

"That's usually what two slugs in him means, Detective."

"Did they find the gun?"

"Whoever did it must have taken it with."

I fidgeted with my tie. "You might as well know, Alvin, since you'll probably find out anyway, I did pay him a visit last night at his store, but I left him very much alive and was never in his apartment."

Green looked surprised. "What were you doing there?"

"Buying a can of peas."

"Funny guy. If I had to wager, I'd say you were nosing about, playing detective again in my case. Keep your nose out of it once and for all. If I can't pin these murders on you, I'll at least book you for obstruction of justice."

"My nose is clean. I was just trying to help."

"Yeah, right."

"So, you're trying to pin the murders on me?"

He sighed. "No, of course not. But if you *were* involved in any way, I won't hold back regardless what the chief says or feels."

"Fair enough."

"Maybe you went to his store last night to bump him off."

"Why would I kill Jarvis?"

"You tell me. The lab is analyzing the bullets they pulled out of Jarvis's chest cavity to see what type of gun they came from. Could be a .357 Magnum, just like your service revolver."

"If I *was* going to shoot someone, I wouldn't use my service revolver. I'm not that stupid."

"Maybe not, but you and Jarvis were both at the Crow apartment last Saturday. Maybe Jarvis saw you kill Crow and was blackmailing you. Maybe you went to his store to pay him off but decided to kill *him*, too."

"Jarvis wasn't blackmailing me and I didn't kill him, and I didn't kill Crow. But when I was in his store, I did notice a faint smell of cigars in the air, and I thought I saw a man going into the back room as I arrived."

Green glared. "Don't tell me. Vinnie the Horse again, right?"

I blinked several times, pondering how to reply. "Why not? Vinnie was a loan shark and a bookie, and word is Jarvis played the horses."

"And Vinnie killed Crow and Jarvis, I suppose. They picked up Vinnie late last night and booked him on suspicion of murder."

"Really? So, you think there's a chance—"

"We thought so, or we wouldn't have picked him up. But Vinnie has an alibi, albeit a crappy one, for last night when Jarvis was hit. Not much better than yours, actually, but it's an alibi. He claims he was at a poker game last night from about six to around eleven thirty. Schultz checked with a couple of the regulars, Watson and Jingles Johnson, and they backed him up. Of course, they all say they weren't playing for money."

"Naturally. Isn't Jingles locked up for counterfeiting?"

"Not anymore."

"Okay. So, you released Vinnie?"

"Not yet. Before we do, I've got a few more questions for him. Even if he didn't do the actual killing, he may still be involved. He may know something or someone."

I raised my eyebrows. "True. Where did they find him?"

"Again, my case. Not your business."

"Will you at least let me know what he says? If he confesses to anything?"

"Confesses to what? Killing Crow or Jarvis?"

"Either or both, I suppose."

"*If* he confesses it will be in tomorrow's paper. You can read it there."

"What about the prints on the beer bottle? And the ashes in the ashtray? Any results?"

Green continued to pound the typewriter keys harder than necessary, until at last he pulled the paper and its carbon out of the machine and laid them on his desktop. Only then did he look up at me, a scowl on his face. "Has anyone ever told you you're annoying? The beer bottle *did* have Vinnie the Horse's prints on it. And the ashes in the ashtray were a mix of cigarette and cigar, brands undetermined. It's one of the reasons we picked him up, if you must know."

My eyes lit up. "That proves Vinnie was in the Crow apartment, just like I said. Hiding in the bedroom."

"It proves he was there at some point, not necessarily while you were there. You're still a suspect. I plan on heading over to the cab company this afternoon. They wouldn't tell me anything over the phone, nothing without a warrant, so I had to wait on Judge Kohler."

"Alvin—" His mood and attitude toward me had turned much colder since the last time I'd seen him, and I couldn't put my finger on why.

"What time did you leave the grocery store?" he said.

"About five minutes to six or so. He was getting ready to close, I think."

"Uh-huh. And you went directly to this Art's Diner after you left Jarvis's store?"

"More or less."

"I don't like more or less, Barrington."

"We took a walk around the neighborhood first, it was a nice night."

"Kind of a queer thing to do, but you're a queer fella. I'll check with the folks at this Art's Diner and see if they can ID you and Keyes. What time did you leave there?"

"About fifteen minutes to eight. Not enough time to drive back to the Grundy Market."

"Probably not, *if* you left at fifteen to. Remains to be seen. By the way, where was your cousin, Miss Valentine, last night?"

"I don't know, but I do know she wasn't at the Grundy Market or Jarvis's apartment."

"Sure, Barrington, sure. Jarvis's sister said she saw a man and a woman leaving his apartment right before she found him dead, and they were in a big hurry. Maybe the two of you are in on this together."

"We're not. I don't know where she was last night, but she wasn't there, and she's not involved. Ask her yourself."

He stood up and stared at me eye to eye. "I will this afternoon, after I get back from the cab company."

Suddenly I remembered the cigar butts in my pocket, and I pulled out the paper bag. "Oh, I almost forgot. I found these around that light pole in the alley behind the Crow place. They're cigar butts."

"The light pole in the alley. Where the mystery man was reported by Mrs. Picking."

"That's right, the mystery man who was smoking cigars. It proves he was there."

"It doesn't prove anything, Barrington, not hardly. They could have been dropped by anyone at any time. Lots of people come and go through that alley, I imagine—delivery men, service guys, vagrants, you name it. How did you come by these?" he said, peering into the bag I had produced and set on his desk.

"I found them. I just happened to be in the alley, and I noticed them. I scooped them up in the bag, so they haven't been touched. I thought maybe you'd want to have them analyzed, see if they're Willard Ponies."

"You just happened to be in the alley? And I'm the Easter Bunny. I told you before, don't tell me how to do my job. That Picking woman said the mystery man in the alley wasn't the same guy in the hall. She said he was shorter and stockier."

"True, but it wouldn't hurt to be sure. If they aren't Willard Ponies, the identity of the mystery man is still a mystery, but he could be the killer."

"I'm still not convinced there even *was* a man in the alley. Didn't I hear you have some kind of appointment in Racine for your larceny case?"

I stepped back. "Yeah, tomorrow morning at nine."

"Safe travels." He sat back down, put a fresh piece of paper and carbon in the typewriter, and began assaulting the keys once more. It looked like he chewed his nails.

"Right, thanks. I'll just leave the bag there in case you decide you want to do something with them." He grunted, and I realized I would get no further with him, so I went back to my own desk and tried to focus on my report to date and to come up with a line of questioning for my Racine witness, Mr. McElroy. I typed a page, threw it away, started over, then threw it away, too, and over, and over. Finally, Spelling wandered by on his way to the water cooler.

"Have stock in a paper company, Barrington?"

"Funny, Spelling. I'm just having trouble concentrating."

"You can say that again. From the looks of your trash can, you've gone through about a ream of paper."

I glanced at the now overflowing basket beside my desk. "Yeah, I guess so."

"What time is your appointment in Racine?"

I glanced up at him. "Nine tomorrow. And I've got a lot of research to do before that."

"That stinks, but better you than me."

"Yeah, so you've said." I was restless, frustrated, and couldn't concentrate. I really wanted to talk to Alan and tell him about Jarvis's murder, but I knew that would have to wait until he was off duty. With a large sigh, I pushed away from my desk and walked down the hall to the lavatory to relieve myself. Then I walked over to the window in the hall and looked down at the street absentmindedly. Hoping to clear my head, I took the stairs down and went out the side door onto the sidewalk. I hadn't signed out, but it was just a break. I'm not much of a believer in providence, but just then I saw Alan rounding the corner, heading back to the station. At the sight of me, he quickened his pace.

"Heath! Where are you off to?"

"I was going to ask you the same thing. Aren't you on traffic duty again today?"

"I am, but I forgot my whistle, so I was just going to get it."

"It's almost noon."

"I know. I was making do without it but decided to grab it on my lunch break. Chet's covering for me until I get back. What's up?"

"Green just told me Jarvis was shot dead last night in his apartment above the store."

A look of surprise and shock crossed his face. "The grocery guy? You're kidding."

"I wish I was."

"But we were just there last night."

"I know. There goes one of the suspects."

"But who shot him? And why?"

"I'm not sure. Apparently it happened sometime between six, when he closed up the store, and a little after eight, when his sister came over and found him."

"Jeepers. So maybe it was Vinnie. I could see him doing it, and you thought he was in the back room while we were there."

"Yeah."

"Why, though? Why would Vinnie kill Jarvis?"

"Maybe because Jarvis owed Vinnie money from that bad race tip. After Jarvis closed, they went up to his apartment to settle up."

"And Vinnie shot him. I don't get why he would, though. If Jarvis paid him the money he owed, why kill him? And if Jarvis didn't have the money to pay him, what would killing him accomplish?"

"Good questions. But I just had another thought. Green said he thought maybe Jarvis saw me kill Crow and was blackmailing me, so I killed Jarvis. What if Jarvis saw Vinnie at the Crow apartment, figured Vinnie murdered Crow, and was blackmailing him? And Vinnie shot him."

"That makes sense."

"Yeah, though something's still not right. Jarvis was found in boxer shorts and a bathrobe, with exactly fifty dollars in the robe pocket. Why would he be dressed like that if Vinnie had gone up to the apartment with him? He would have had to have changed out of his clothes while Vinnie was there."

"You don't suppose—"

"That Jarvis and Vinnie are homosexuals? I suppose it's

possible, but if that's the case, Jarvis certainly put on a good act last night."

"But that's what we do, right? Put on acts? I mean, we all do," Alan said.

"To some extent, yes, we have to in order to survive. But maybe instead Jarvis was actually expecting a lady friend, maybe someone like Mrs. Picking."

"Mrs. Picking? But she hated Jarvis."

"Like you said, Alan, don't we all put on acts? Green said Jarvis's sister saw a man and a woman leaving the apartment right before she found him. Maybe it was Picking and Vinnie working together."

"Gee, that could be! She set him up and Vinnie shot him. That would explain why Jarvis was dressed like that."

"It would, but I've got some more thinking to do. You'd better get your whistle and grab something to eat."

"Okay. Have time to join me?"

"Not just now. I may walk up to the drugstore and get a bite."

"Sounds good. Keep me posted on any new developments."

"I always do. I'll call you after your duty shift."

Chapter Eighteen

Early Wednesday Afternoon, August 13, 1947

I watched him enter the station, then I started walking east slowly, meandering, really, looking in shop windows, shading my eyes with my hand as I had left my hat on the hook behind my desk. An older woman in a burgundy dress and matching hat walked by, fanning herself with a magazine she must have just purchased at the corner drugstore. I paused at the drugstore's picture window and admired the display of Ivory soap stacked in the shape of a giant white swan, surrounded by little toy swans. As I stood there, a smart-looking woman and what appeared to be her young daughter emerged from within the store. The girl stood beside me, her face and nose pressed against the window glass. In her right hand, she held an ice cream cone that had already begun to drip down in the summer heat, and under her arm she clutched a picture book.

"Lydia, eat your ice cream before it melts," the woman said. "And don't get any on your book. We have to return that to the library."

"Did you see the swan, Mommy? It's made out of soap!" the girl replied, her cone still dripping.

"Yes, Lydia, I see. And we're going to need a lot of that soap to clean you up once we get home. Don't get any on your dress because we don't have time to go back and change."

"There's toy swans there, too. Are they boy swans or girl swans?"

"I don't know, dear. Swans all look alike to me. I can't tell the boys from the girls."

"Well, I want one. Can I buy that with my piggy bank money? I've been saving my pennies, and you always say pennies make nickels."

"Not today, Lydia. Let's go, we still have to stop at the haberdasher's and the library." She held out her hand and the little girl took it, finally licking at her cone as they stepped away and moved off down the sidewalk.

I took out my handkerchief and wiped the back of my neck before putting it back in my pocket. With one last look at the swan, I turned and pulled open the door of the store, listening to the bell as it jingled overhead. The soda jerk, dressed all in white, smiled at me as the door closed.

"Good day, sir."

I nodded in his direction. "Good day. Hot out there."

"Yes, sir. Though it may rain later, according to what the radio says."

"They're frequently wrong. There's not a cloud in the sky, but we could use some rain."

"We could. Anyway, we have conditioned air in here. Can I get you something?"

I felt my stomach rumble and realized I was hungrier than I thought, so I took a seat on one of the swivel stools and glanced quickly at the lunch specials. "The fried egg sandwich, please, and a large Coke."

"Coming right up." True to his word, it was set before me in mere minutes. I devoured it in even less time and gave him my money, telling him to keep the change.

"Thanks. Anything else?"

"No, thanks, I'll just have a look around the store."

"Sure thing. Ivory soap is on special, just so you know."

"Yes, I saw the display in the window. Very eye-catching."

"Mrs. Lundt does all those herself. Real artsy."

"She's the proprietor?"

"The proprietor's wife. Nice folks. Though Mr. Lundt won't

give me an allowance for my laundry, and it's hard to keep these whites white working here. One drip of chocolate syrup and I'm done for."

I smiled. He couldn't have been more than seventeen or eighteen years old. "I suppose so." Just like the little girl and her ice cream cone.

"I keep a spare apron and shirt in the back, just in case. Mr. Lundt's a stickler for cleanliness."

"Keeping a spare is a good idea, then. I guess it's always a good idea. Is there a pay phone nearby?"

"Sure, mister. Back by the pharmacy counter."

"Thanks." I went down the narrow aisles, past hair tonics, talcums, toothpastes, compounds, and creams to a telephone booth at the very back. I stepped inside and closed the door, which turned on a small overhead light. I flipped through the phone book hanging down on a small black metal chain. Locating the number for the Grundy Market on State Street at last, I dropped in my nickel and dialed the exchange. A woman answered on the second ring.

"Grundy Market, how can I help you?"

"Oh, hello. This is Detective Barrington with the Milwaukee Police. I'm looking for Mr. Jarvis's sister."

A long pause. "This is his sister, Violet. What do you want?"

"I understand you found your brother last night."

"Just a moment." There was a slight pause, and I heard her finishing up with a customer before she returned. "I did. He didn't answer when I phoned last night, which I found odd as he had asked me earlier if I could loan him a hundred dollars. I told him I could manage forty, and he said to bring it by last night but to call first. So I stopped over to check on him when he didn't answer the telephone, and found him dead on the floor in the living room. It was quite a shock. The police say it was probably a robbery."

"That's possible. I'm sorry."

"So am I. He wasn't the greatest brother in the world, but he was family, my family. I wasn't going to open the store this morning, but I have nothing else to do, and I needed to take my mind off everything."

"That's understandable. In the event it wasn't a robbery, can you think of anyone who would want to harm your brother?"

"I already went over this with a Detective Green. Why are you asking me the same questions? What did you say your name was?"

"Barrington. Detective Heath Barrington. I'm just helping out on the case."

"I see. Well, like I said, he wasn't the greatest brother, and he wasn't the greatest human being. He didn't have many friends, but I can't think of anyone at the moment who'd want him dead. If I do think of someone I'll let you or that Green fella know."

"That would be most helpful."

"I did tell the other detective I saw two people scurrying away from the building and into a car as I was coming up the sidewalk last evening, though, if that means anything. They pulled away real fast."

"What kind of car? Did you see the license?"

"Some kind of sedan, dark color—blue, I think. Didn't see the license, though it was a Wisconsin plate. It was a man and a woman. They jumped in the car and took off in a hurry. Seemed suspicious."

"Excellent. Good. Thank you, Miss Jarvis."

"Pigg."

"Pardon me?"

"It's Mrs. Pigg. I'm married."

"Ah, yes, sorry, Mrs. Pigg. Goodbye."

"Goodbye."

We disconnected, I heard my nickel drop down into the repository, and I exited the phone booth. Interesting, very interesting.

The soda jerk was busy making a root beer float as I left the store, but he still managed to call out a "Thanks for coming in," as I went out the door.

CHAPTER NINETEEN

Later Wednesday Afternoon, August 13, 1947

The heat and the bright sun hit me all at once, even worse because I was now walking west back to the station. I shaded my eyes with my right hand and hurried as quickly as I could, wishing I'd brought my hat.

When I reached the police station, I saw a tall, slender fellow just exiting the building. He was well dressed in a slightly rumpled light gray three-button pinstripe suit, pink and black striped tie, a black pocket square, and a wilted pink carnation in his lapel. On his well-shaped head he wore a white fedora with a black band of satin ribbon. I sidled up to him as he paused to light up a cigar, and he gave me an eye. He looked haggard, tired, and in need of a shave, but still attractive. I knew instantly who he was, though I was surprised to see him on the street and not behind bars. I decided on a subtle, somewhat deceitful approach.

"Vinnie the Horse, right?" I said. "What are you doing here?"

He dropped the match on the sidewalk, took a puff on the cigar, and blew out the smoke through his nose as he looked me up and down. "Cops had me in for tea and a slumber party. Do I know you?"

I shook my head, glad we were standing in the shade of the building. "Not directly. But I know people who know you, and I've seen you around. I think we played poker once a while back. I lost."

His eyebrows went up a touch. "I don't recall playing cards with you."

"I'm not as good a player as you, and I don't play much. I lost more than I wanted to. We only played once. Watson and Jingles Johnson were there, too."

"Huh. Jingles is a lousy player and a sore loser, but he loves to play. I guess you do look kinda familiar."

"It was pretty dark around the table that night."

"Yeah, I don't do so well in bright sunlight."

"Same here, and I lost my hat on a wager this morning."

He stared into my eyes. "I didn't catch your name, friend."

"They call me Duck," I said, using a nickname Alan had given me when we were in Chicago.

"Huh, never heard of you. How do you know Watson and Jingles?"

"Jingles helped me, shall we say, on a printing issue, if you catch my drift."

"Yeah, he's a top-notch counterfeiter. Gotta watch him when he pays his poker bets."

I laughed. "I bet. I'm fairly new here in Milwaukee, Vinnie. I was doing business in New York, but Knuckles Falcone ran me out on the rails," I said, referencing a known criminal in the Big Apple I'd heard about.

"Knuckles Falcone is not a guy you want to mess with. Not if you want to live."

"I was lucky he just drove me out of town. I spent some time in Chicago after that, then came up here," I said. "I got tired of being a small duck in a big pond, so to speak. Nice suit."

"Thanks, imported. I got it in Chicago, speaking of. Little place called Blount's. Ever hear of it?"

"Sure. In the Edmonton hotel," I said. "Run by Victor Blount."

"Yeah, so you know it, huh. Closed now, though."

"Yeah. Somebody bumped him off."

"Word gets around. If you knew Blount and Falcone, and you're in with Watson and Jingles Johnson, I guess you're all right."

"Thanks. I knew Larry Crow, too."

"Oh yeah? The guy was a bum. Got what he deserved," Vinnie said, taking an even bigger puff on his cigar.

"I agree. Though he had something of mine I wanted back."

Vinnie laughed, but it came out as more of a snort. "You and me both. A grand he owed me. Was supposed to be paying me back over time."

"You saw him last Saturday at his apartment?"

"Yeah, I saw Crow Saturday. I left some prints on a beer bottle, and the cops even found cigar ashes in the ashtray that they were able to pin on me. Go figure."

"Careless. Not like you, Vinnie, from what I hear."

He puffed out his chest a little. "Glad to hear my reputation precedes me. But it wasn't carelessness. I had no idea someone was going to bump him off, so I had no need to wipe off prints and worry about my cigar. I just dropped in on him to encourage him to pay up, if you know what I mean. A friendly visit."

"Yeah, sure," I replied, trying to sound equally tough. "Cordial."

"But while I was there he got company, some appointment he had made. Crow said it was a cop, a dick. Go figure. Larry entertaining cops. I had to hide in the bedroom. After the cop left, Larry told me he had something on this particular cop and was trying to get money out of him so Larry could pay me what he owed."

"I wonder if he got any money out of the dick."

"Not that day he didn't." He looked me up and down. "What are you doing here at the police station, by the way, Duck?"

"Visiting the cops. They want to know about my relationship with Crow."

"And what relationship was that, buddy?"

"Business. He had something I never did get back, like I said earlier. Now that he's dead, I probably never will."

"Probably not."

"You hear about Jarvis?"

"The grocer? Yeah, I heard somebody shot him last night. Cops asked me about that, too. Thankfully, I have an alibi."

"They're probably going to ask me about him, also. We bet on a few fillies together once in a while, spent some time together."

"Nice of you to show up voluntarily for questioning."

"I try to cooperate. I find it gets me places."

"Uh-huh. I don't recall Crow or Jarvis ever mentioning you. Or Watson and Jingles, for that matter."

"Why would they? They didn't talk about you to me, either."

Vinnie seemed to ponder that for a moment. "Guess you're right."

"I'd like to know who bumped them both off," I said. "Cops called me this morning and told me to come down for questioning."

He furrowed his brow and squinted at me. "Kind of funny sounding. I wasn't aware they telephoned suspects and gave them verbal invitations."

"I'm already pretty well known by the police here, unfortunately. They know I usually cooperate, and I don't think they think I'm a suspect. I think they just want information from me more than anything else."

"Huh. I don't like stool pigeons, Duck—or stool ducks."

I feigned an offended look. "Me? I don't squawk. I talk in circles, make them think they're getting information out of me, just to stay in their good graces. Coppers are generally pretty stupid and detectives are even dumber."

He relaxed his brow and laughed. "You can say that again. But somebody squealed on me, and I wouldn't be surprised if it was my no-good brother. They picked me up at his place around midnight. I had to spend the night here, and I don't sleep too good in jail. I have a delicate back."

"But they let you go."

He took the wilted carnation out of his lapel and tossed it in the gutter. "Yeah. They made me promise to behave and give them my new address. No solid evidence to hold me, and they know I got good lawyers. I've been down this road a time or two before, you know. The cops gave me the old song and dance about not leaving town. Personally, I think they just want to watch me and see if I slip up and give them more concrete evidence. They think I know something."

"When did you last see Jarvis?"

"Last night, no secret. He owed me five hundred on a horse. I went to his store to collect, and I bought some cigars while I was there. Of course the cops showed up and I had to hide in the back room. All this hiding ain't good for my reputation. I don't like it."

"What did they want with Jarvis?"

"They asked him about Crow. Real nosy. I didn't see them close up, but it was a plainclothes dick and a uniform. By the time they left, I had to hightail it to my poker game."

"At least you got your five hundred."

Vinnie chuckled and snorted. "Not hardly. Jarvis had two seventy-five on him, which he handed over. Said he'd get me the rest in twenty-four hours."

"I heard he had fifty bucks in cash on him when they found him."

"Do tell. He swore he gave me everything he had. Maybe he rounded up another fifty from someplace else after I saw him. Or somebody else. Or maybe he was holding out on me, though I figure he was smarter than that."

"Word on the street is he was bumped off last night sometime between six and eight."

"Could be. Like I told the cops, he was very much alive when I left him. I went downtown to my poker game. Got there a few minutes past six, and got back to my brother's place a few minutes before midnight. The cops were waiting for me. I don't know why they would think I'd kill Jarvis or Crow, seeing as how they both owed me money. Somebody's been knocking off all my cash cows, and I don't like it."

"I know the feeling, buddy. Well, nice chatting with you, Vinnie. I guess I better get inside. I don't want to keep the coppers waiting." I pulled out my pocket watch. It was just after one thirty.

"Yeah, right. They're funny about stuff like that. Nice talking to you, Duck. Look me up if you ever want to do business or know someone who's a little short on cash, if you know what I mean. I'm in the market for some new clients now that Crow and Jarvis are gone. The boys in the fifth ward generally know where to find me. Ask at Pop's Pool Hall."

"Thanks."

"And if you ever feel like another game of poker, I'll go easy on you the first couple of hands. But right now I aim to have a hot shower and a shave, and a word or two with my brother before I chat, so to speak, with a certain lady." He took another puff on his cigar, tipped his hat, and then meandered down the sidewalk.

When he had gone, I entered the building, taking the stairs two at a time up to the detectives' room. Green was still at his desk, or most likely, back at his desk after questioning Vinnie, looking defeated. I nodded to Perkins, Gray, and Schroeder and walked over to Green, who didn't acknowledge me, if he noticed at all.

I made myself comfortable in his guest chair without being invited. I figured he wouldn't mind. Finally, I drummed my fingers on his desktop rapidly, which at last caused him to look over at me, an annoyed expression on his face. The bag with the cigar butts was gone.

"What do you want this time?" he said irritably.

"How did it go with Vinnie the Horse?"

"You know I can't talk about that with you. I've already said too much today." He leaned back in his chair and crossed his arms over his stomach, his unbuttoned suit coat falling to the sides as he glared at me.

"You talk about it with the other detectives. Perkins, Gray, Schroeder, even Spelling. We all talk about our cases with each other."

"You trying to be funny?"

"No, I don't think so."

"The other guys aren't suspects in the case," Green said flatly, as if I were stupid.

"Am I still a suspect? So, Vinnie didn't confess."

"Yes and no."

"Yes and no?"

"Yes, you're still a suspect, and no, Vinnie didn't confess, even though his prints were on the bottle and he admitted the ashes in the ashtray were his. He claims Crow was alive when he left, and we've got nothing concrete to hold him on at this point. Happy now?"

"Ecstatic. Who else you got?"

"Besides Vinnie, there's you, Mrs. Picking, and your famous mystery man in the alley. By the way, I trotted my butt down to the lab with your bag of butts. As a favor to you, Fletcher dropped what he was doing and did a comparison analysis with a Willard Ponies. They didn't match."

"Oh, well, thanks for doing that. So, the mystery man wasn't Vinnie. I kind of figured he wasn't. That actually makes sense, believe it or not, with my new theory."

"Of course it does. And one of *my* new theories is maybe it was your cousin, Elizabeth Valentine."

"She had nothing to do with it."

"Of course you'd say that. Then who did? Unless you're here to confess, I'll admit I'm stumped. Vinnie could have done it, but Crow was worth more to him alive than dead. Picking? I just don't know. She doesn't seem the type."

"But there is no type when it comes to murder," I said. "You know that."

"Yeah, yeah. First chapter in the detective's handbook. But still, my strongest suspects are you, Picking, and your cousin. I spent yesterday talking to Jarvis at his store and Mrs. Crow at her friend's apartment. I admit I had started to consider Jarvis, but then somebody shot him."

"Huh. Well, maybe Picking did it in cahoots with Vinnie."

"Is that your new theory? Well, ain't that something? I'll put out warrants for them both right now."

I shrugged. "Have any better ideas?"

"As a matter of fact, I do. I need to pay a visit to the Boynton Yellow Cab Company, the company you took from that bar on the day of the murder. Judge Kohler's clerk just delivered the warrant to me so I can go through their records from Saturday. And then I want to talk to your cousin, officially. I know you don't drive a dark blue sedan, but maybe she does."

I felt a bead of sweat break out on the back of my neck. "She doesn't. She doesn't even own a car."

"Minor detail. Cars can be obtained."

"That's true, of course. But I have another theory, if you're open to it. Stronger than Picking and Vinnie together, and certainly stronger than me and my cousin."

He brought himself forward now and propped his right elbow on his desk, resting his chin in the palm of his hand as he stared at me. "All right, I'll bite. What?"

"I've been thinking is all, and shopping, and talking to a very interesting, well-dressed fellow and a soda jerk. It's a beautiful afternoon. Care to take a drive with me before you go to the cab company?"

"To where?"

"To see a man about a horse, and to see Mrs. Crow, her neighbor, and her roommate. If what I'm thinking turns out totally wrong, I'll drive you to Boynton's myself."

Alvin blinked slowly, still staring at me, and sighed. Finally he sat up, covered his typewriter, and put away the file he had open on his desk. "Sounds like I've got nothing to lose."

"And I have everything to lose."

"All right, let's go, then. She's staying at a friend's place." He consulted a page in his pocket notebook. "A Miss Evelyn Caldwell, 829 Knapp Street. I'll drive."

I smiled. "Sure, just let me grab my hat."

CHAPTER TWENTY

Later Wednesday Afternoon, August 13, 1947

It was a short drive, and we found a parking spot right out front of Miss Caldwell's apartment building. My lucky day. At least I hoped it was. As we climbed the front steps of the stoop, Alvin looked over at me. "So, why are we here?"

"Following up on some thoughts. You know, Alvin, it's a good day for ice cream."

He wiped a bead of sweat from his brow and glanced up briefly at the sweltering sun. "I'll grant you that. According to Janey, any day is a good day for ice cream, even in the winter. But what does that have to do with the price of eggs?"

"Just don't drip chocolate sauce on your shirt," I said as I pushed the button for the Caldwell apartment. "Unless you have a spare."

"Damn it, Barrington, you drive me crazy sometimes."

I grinned. "Thanks. And you know what goes great with chocolate syrup and ice cream? A good book from the library. And if you save up your pennies, they make nickels, and you can buy more ice cream."

"I take it back. You don't drive me crazy, I think you *are* crazy," he said, shaking his head.

"By the way, did you know male and female swans look almost identical?"

"Have you been drinking again?"

A gruff woman's voice crackled over the speaker before I could answer him. "Yes, hello?"

"Detectives Green and Barrington to see Mrs. Crow," Alvin said.

"Oh." Nothing but silence followed.

Alvin buzzed again. Finally, the door clicked and we entered. As we climbed the stairs to the third floor, I said, "Since you'll soon find out, I suppose I should tell you I've been here before."

Alvin stopped, his left foot on one carpeted step, his right on the other, and looked at me hard. "What do you mean, you've been here before?"

"I admit I did a little investigating on my own, that's all," I said sheepishly.

He scowled. "That kind of shit can get you kicked off the force, Barrington."

"Why? I didn't do anything illegal. I just paid her a visit."

"In an official capacity? Questioning suspects without authority? Like you did poking around Jarvis's store last night, talking to him?"

I pushed my fedora back on my head and faced him head-on, as best I could, balancing on the steps. "Look, Alvin. I have a personal interest in this case. Two personal interests in this case, actually. Me and my cousin, Liz. We're both suspects, and I have to prove neither of us did it."

"That's my job. Or at least it's supposed to be."

"I know, I'm sorry. But wouldn't you do the same if you were me?"

"I'm not you in any way, shape or form. And as I said before, the situation would not be reversed. I would never put myself in the situation you're in."

"And as I believe I said, never say never, Alvin. Look, I'm not saying you're not a good detective, because you are. But sometimes two heads are better than one. I've barely been sleeping nights, trying to make sense of all this, trying to figure out who really killed Larry Crow and Jarvis, and trying my damnedest to convince myself it wasn't me."

"Wouldn't you know if you killed them or not?"

I let out a deep breath. "I didn't kill Jarvis. And normally, yeah, I would know if I'd killed Crow. But as you know, I had quite a bit to drink that afternoon. And events after that were, and still are, hazy. But I think I've finally got this all figured out, so just let me help you help me, okay? Please?"

He didn't say anything at first. He just stood there, staring at me, breathing in and breathing out. Finally, he brought his left foot down to the same step as his right. At last, he took a breath and spoke, his voice gruff but soft. "All right, but you'd better know what you're doing. And if this doesn't pan out, we're going straight to the cab company with the warrant."

"Right, thanks, Alvin. I owe you one."

"You owe me two."

"Glad you're keeping track," I said.

We got to the third floor, and I knocked on the door of the Caldwell apartment. Miss Caldwell answered, dressed in a pair of men's trousers and a white shirt with the sleeves rolled up. On her feet were the same brown leather loafers she'd been wearing before.

"Gentlemen. You came together this time," she said.

Green shot me a look before answering. "Yes. Sorry to disturb you once more. May we come in?"

She stepped aside. "Of course. Let me take your hats."

Everything was pretty much the same as it had been the other day, except there was no delicious odor of cookies baking this time and the air was stifling in the afternoon heat. The windows were open, but there was little breeze, except from a small electric fan on the table.

Miss Caldwell placed our hats on that same side table and ushered us into the living room, where Mrs. Crow was sitting in one of the chairs flanking the fireplace and Agnes Picking was on the sofa, balancing a cup of coffee and a saucer on her knee.

"You know Mrs. Crow, of course," Miss Caldwell said, "And this is Mrs. Picking, Alice's neighbor."

"We actually also both know Mrs. Picking," I said.

"Oh, I see. May I bring either of you some coffee or some lemonade?"

I directed my attentions to Miss Caldwell. "No, thank you. I see you didn't have any trouble taking the afternoon off."

"I'm the head librarian. I can take time off when necessary. Alice told me yesterday Mrs. Picking was going to be stopping by, so I decided to be sociable and come home early. Miss Saunders has the day off, but I left Mrs. Schmidt in charge. She's quite capable."

"And you changed your clothes."

"My work attire is not very comfortable, Detective. A man's home is his castle. Do you know who first said that?"

"Uh, no."

"King Henry VIII upon his return to the throne after he had his wife Anne Boleyn decapitated. Men."

"Horrible."

"Disgusting. But the quote is accurate, and I dress as I like when I'm in my castle. Anything wrong with that?"

"No, not at all. I feel the same way. You heard Ossip Jarvis died last night?"

"The grocer? How awful!" Mrs. Picking said. "What is happening in that neighborhood?"

"Terrible news. But I imagine he had enemies. He wasn't a very nice man," Miss Caldwell said.

"What makes you think it wasn't an accident or a health related issue?" I said.

Her face went white, then red. "It was on the radio this morning. WBSM. They had it on the news."

"That can be checked, but I suppose it makes sense. It wasn't in the *Sentinel*."

"Go ahead and check, but why would I lie about it?"

"Good question," I said. "The library is so quiet, I'm surprised you'd have the radio on."

"I have a radio in my office. Sometimes when I'm on a break, I close the door and turn it on low, mainly to hear the news."

"Okay," I said, turning to Mrs. Picking. "Nice of you to pay a social call."

"Yes, well, I hadn't heard from Alice since the murder, and I thought I would see how she's getting along. I brought her some flowers," she said, gesturing to some yellow roses in a vase, which sat on the mantel next to a bowling trophy, a cigar, and a pile of books.

"Neighborly of you. I'm glad you're here, actually. I want to go over a few things, and your memory may prove invaluable. We would like to talk with each of you."

Alvin and I made ourselves as comfortable as we could next to Mrs. Picking on the sofa, which appeared to be quite overstuffed, and Miss Caldwell took a seat next to Mrs. Crow, crossing her legs with her ankle on her knee.

"Talk to us about what?" Miss Caldwell said.

"The murders of Larry Crow and Ossip Jarvis."

"Not much to talk about, I don't think," Miss Caldwell said. "Larry was murdered by some unsavory character he probably owed money to. Mr. Jarvis might have been the same thing."

"So, an open-and-shut case. Perhaps the same unsavory character killed them both. The same man Mrs. Picking saw lurking about the alley that day," I said.

"Perhaps," Miss Caldwell agreed.

"I knew it! I just knew it! I should have called the police the second I saw him," Mrs. Picking said. "Shifty, hanging about like that, hat pulled down low."

"It makes sense," Miss Caldwell said, ignoring Picking.

"It does, but things aren't always what they appear to be, are they, Miss Caldwell?"

"What do you mean by that?"

"'Things are not always as they seem; the first appearance deceives many.' Phaedrus. One of the inner circle of Socrates. You can look it up if you like. Should be in the Greek history section of your library."

"I'm familiar with the quote, Mr. Barrington, and I know who Phaedrus was, but what does he or his quote have to do with anything?"

"Just that the man Mrs. Picking saw lurking about the alley the last few days may not have been all he seemed. He may not have been there at all."

"Not there?" Mrs. Picking said, setting her cup and saucer down. "But I saw him. What do you mean?"

"It means he thinks he's being clever," Miss Caldwell said, scowling. "But Mrs. Picking says she saw a man, and whoever he was must have slashed Larry's throat and then shot Jarvis to death."

"It does make sense. How did you know Jarvis was shot? Surely that wasn't on the radio."

"Well, uh, actually I think they did say he was shot."

"Yes, I think so," Mrs. Crow said, who today was in a dark green frock that didn't fit much better than the dirt colored one.

"Again, that can be checked. Mrs. Crow, you told me the other day when you got home from the Grundy Market, you entered the kitchen door of your apartment and immediately saw your husband dead on the sofa. Is that right?"

"Yes, why?"

"And then you screamed."

She nodded her little head, her mouse nose twitching. "Yes, sir. It was such a shock, you see. It was awful. There was blood everywhere."

"I can imagine. So, you came in the kitchen door and saw him. Is that correct?"

"Yes, sir, but I don't understand why you're asking me that."

"You didn't set anything down first?"

"What would I set down? As soon as I walked in, I saw him." She shuddered a little.

"I see. And if I could verify something Mr. Jarvis told me about the order you phoned in to his store the day of the murder," I said.

Mrs. Crow looked nervously at Evelyn. "Oh?"

"Yes. I recall him telling me you ordered a bunch of carrots, a can of peas, and a pound of sugar that day. Is that correct?"

She wiped her palms on the fabric of the green dress. "Yes, I believe that's right."

"Was there anything else?"

"No, just those three things," she said.

"Why are you asking all this, Detective?" Miss Caldwell said. "Mrs. Crow is just a nice woman who has been through a terrible ordeal. She had nothing to do with either of these deaths."

"I'm just curious, that's all," I said, and then I looked back to Alice. "Funny you ordering a bag of sugar when your canister was full already."

"Oh. I, uh, planned on doing some baking."

"Without eggs? I didn't see any in your kitchen."

"I forgot the eggs, I guess. Silly of me."

"Wasn't it? How big was the box those items came in?"

"Standard size, probably. Though I don't really know. He took the box with him, why?"

"Who did?"

"Mr. Jarvis took it after he delivered the groceries," Alice said.

"How did you know he made the delivery and not his usual boy, Timmy?"

She shook her head, trembling lightly. "I don't know, maybe Agnes told me when I got home. I don't remember."

"Is that correct, Mrs. Picking?"

"I really don't remember, either. Everything happened so fast, and it was a terrible shock."

"Of course. By the way, what were you wearing that day, Mrs. Picking?"

"What was I wearing? What difference does that make?"

"Just curious. Do you remember?"

"Well, yes. I had on my green and white dress at first, but it's gotten a little snug and it was warm. I took off my stockings and changed into my blue linen dress in the afternoon."

"That makes sense, I suppose. Mrs. Crow, you do remember the groceries were unpacked on the counter."

"I saw the items on the counter, yes."

"The box he used is probably still in the back room of his store," I said.

"Maybe. That would make sense if he planned to reuse it, but again I don't understand these questions," Mrs. Crow said.

"Miss Caldwell, would you happen to have a bunch of carrots, a can of peas, and a pound of sugar? Oh, and a grocery box?"

She looked puzzled. "Why, yes, of course, in the kitchen."

"Would you be so kind as to put those three items in the box and bring the box out here?"

"Whatever for?"

"If you wouldn't mind, please."

She looked at me with an odd expression, but finally agreed, uncrossing her legs and getting to her feet. "Well, all right, just a moment." She went into the kitchen, reappearing a few minutes later carrying the box.

"Thank you so much," I said, standing and taking the box from her, which I set on the coffee table. "You may be seated."

"I think I'll stand for a while."

"Suit yourself."

"Is this box about the same size as the one Mr. Jarvis delivered to Mrs. Crow's apartment on Saturday, Mrs. Picking?"

She gave it a brief once-over and then nodded. "Yes, exactly the same, I'd say."

"Interesting. The carrots, sugar and can of peas barely take up any room in the box at all. In fact, you have to peer over the edge to even see them. If you were standing talking to someone, they wouldn't see anything inside."

"What's your point?" Miss Caldwell said.

"My point is that Jarvis stopped to chat with you, Mrs. Picking, on Saturday on his way to the Crow apartment, and you remarked to him that the box appeared to be close to overflowing with groceries."

"She exaggerated, clearly," Miss Caldwell said, folding her arms under her bosom as she leaned against the mantel.

"Maybe, but certainly she saw a box much fuller than this one," I said.

"So what?" Miss Caldwell replied, scowling again.

"It was definitely full to the brim and more. I could see the bunch of carrots sticking up, even from my seated position," Mrs. Picking said.

"Yes, I recall you mentioning that," I said. "And, Mrs. Crow, you just told us you didn't set anything down. You came in, saw your husband on the sofa, and screamed. And almost immediately after that, Mrs. Picking came in and hurried you off to her apartment. Yet when Detective Green and I were in your kitchen, I couldn't help but notice your library book on the counter, the one you yourself told me you had just checked out. Mrs. Picking said she saw you bringing it home with you, isn't that right?"

"Alice had it under her arm," Mrs. Picking said.

"She just forgot she had set it down in the shock of the moment," Miss Caldwell said.

Alice quickly agreed. "That's right, I just forgot. I must have absentmindedly set it on the counter as soon as I walked in the door, right before I saw him."

I looked over at Alvin. "Think that's a possibility?"

"Maybe, but it seems unlikely. As I recall, the book was sitting next to the bread box, which is pretty far into the kitchen. I'd be surprised if you couldn't see your husband from there, Mrs. Crow. In fact, you yourself said you didn't even get the door closed."

"I took a few steps toward him. I couldn't believe my eyes."

"I see. So, you did see him right away, then took a few steps in, set your book down, and screamed," I said.

"Sure, that's right." Her left eye started to twitch.

"All right, so that's how it happened. So what?" Miss Caldwell said. "She got confused."

"I find it interesting, Mrs. Crow, that you brought the book into the apartment at all, especially that one, *The Company She Keeps*. You yourself told me your husband didn't like you reading books like that. You had to hide them in the basement. Yet on Saturday, you marched right in with the book in hand."

"I guess I forgot I had it with me."

"Did you forget? Or did you already know he was dead, so it wouldn't matter? Did you come in the back door, check to make sure your husband was indeed dead on the sofa, set your book down, and then scream?"

"What do you mean, 'check to make sure her husband was indeed dead'?" Mrs. Picking said, looking from her to us.

"Why don't you tell us, Mrs. Crow?" I said.

Her lips trembled, her eye twitched fiercely, and her face went white. I thought at first she might faint.

"I don't know what you mean," she said at last, quietly, her voice cracking.

"Let me see if I can help. Mrs. Picking, you stated Mr. Jarvis made his delivery at two and left at approximately ten minutes after. By his own testimony, Mr. Crow was asleep and snoring on the sofa when he left. Jarvis went directly back to his store."

"Yes, that's correct, though I'm not sure if he went directly back to his store or not. He didn't say where he was headed next," Mrs. Picking said.

"His delivery boy, Timmy, met him at the store at two twenty, so apparently he did," I said.

"Yes, yes, that sounds right," Mrs. Crow said. "And Larry telephoned me at the library at twenty past two. He was definitely alive after Mr. Jarvis left."

"Was he?" I said. "Clever of Jarvis to think about asking you the time as he left, Mrs. Picking. That way you were sure to recall. And, Mrs. Crow, I'm sure you made a point at the library of making sure Miss Caldwell knew that it was twenty past two when you supposedly received the phone call from your husband."

"What do you mean, 'supposedly'? I answered the phone," Miss Caldwell said.

"How do you know it was really him?" I said.

"Because he said so. He said, 'This is Mr. Crow. I'd like to speak with my wife, Alice.'"

"And seeing as how you'd never met him, you had no reason to doubt that it was indeed him. Very believable. Then Mrs. Crow supposedly spoke with him in the office."

"Again with the 'supposedly.' What are you getting at?" Miss Caldwell said, bristling.

I looked at Alice. "What is your telephone number, Mrs. Crow?"

"My phone number? KLesmer Lake 4285, why?"

"That's what I thought. I checked with the phone company.

There were no completed phone calls from that number to that branch of the library that day."

She brought her hand up to her eye as if to try and stop the twitching. Her lips trembled.

"Who really called you that day, Mrs. Crow?"

"Don't answer him," Miss Caldwell said, taking her seat once more next to Alice, her hand on Alice's knee.

"Cat got your tongue? My guess is the call came from the Grundy Market. It was Mr. Jarvis, pretending to be your husband in order to give himself an alibi."

"Why would he need an alibi?" Mrs. Picking said.

"Because he murdered Larry Crow," I said.

"And case closed," Miss Caldwell said. "Jarvis murdered Crow."

"Yes, he did," I said.

"Mr. Jarvis murdered Mr. Crow?! You mean he did it while I was sitting on the porch? And then he calmly came out and chatted with me?"

"I believe so, yes, Mrs. Picking."

"But what about the man in the alley?" Mrs. Picking said. "The shady-looking character?"

"That was someone else entirely."

"But I'm afraid I don't understand. Why would Mr. Jarvis do that?" Mrs. Picking said. "And didn't you just say Larry was still alive when Mr. Jarvis left? Jarvis himself told me Mr. Crow was snoring on the sofa."

"That's what Jarvis wanted people to think, yes."

"But Mr. Crow's throat was slashed. I saw blood all over the place when I rushed in," Mrs. Picking said. "If Jarvis killed him, how come there wasn't any blood on him when he left? Jarvis was dressed all in white and not a drop of blood anywhere. I would have noticed."

"I've no doubt when he left the Crow apartment he was spotless, Mrs. Picking. Being in the grocery business requires a certain level of fastidiousness."

"So, how could he have killed him?"

"He unpacked Mrs. Crow's groceries from the box that was filled to nearly overflowing, but there was something else in there underneath the groceries—a pair of gloves, a fresh apron, a new shirt, maybe even a clean pair of pants. He put on the gloves and the apron, grabbed the knife, and slit Larry Crow's throat. Then, as you mentioned, Mrs. Picking, blood spurted everywhere. He dropped the knife, put the bloody apron and gloves in the box, and maybe even changed his shirt and pants. He went to the bathroom and washed off his face, using the washcloth and towels that had been hanging on the towel bar. Seeing they had traces of blood on them, he took them with, leaving the towel bar empty. Then he left, carrying the now supposedly empty box, being sure to check the time with you, Mrs. Picking."

"You use that word 'supposedly' an awful lot, Detective," Miss Caldwell said.

"Sorry, it's just a good word that happens to fit. With a search warrant, we can go over the back room of his store, his other aprons and clothes, and any delivery boxes he may have. I imagine we'll find traces of Lawrence Crow's blood somewhere."

Alice, I noticed, had started to cry.

"Would you like to tell us your side of the story, Mrs. Crow? Tell us what really happened?"

She looked over at Miss Caldwell, who shook her head vehemently.

"Don't tell them anything, Alice. They're just guessing."

"I think you'd like to tell us, wouldn't you, Mrs. Crow?" I said as softly as I could. "Explain, please. In fact, why don't you start at the beginning?"

She looked at me, tears streaming down her cheeks, as we all stared at her. "The beginning, sir?"

"Of that day. Last Saturday. As I recall, your husband got home from work that morning, the two of you had breakfast together, then he went to lie down in the bedroom. You did some ironing and mending, then he got up, you made him a sandwich and got him a sleeping draught, and then he told you to leave the apartment and not come back until he called you because he had someone coming at one. He claimed he had told you this the day before and when you disagreed, he struck you. Is that correct?"

"Yes, sir," Alice replied, her voice so soft.

"But just before you left, you phoned in a grocery order to Mr. Jarvis, is that right?"

"That's right."

"But it wasn't just a grocery order, of course. You'd arranged it all in advance. And I think you hadn't even thought about what to order before you called, probably because you were nervous and hadn't expected Larry to ask you to leave earlier than you usually do. That's why you ordered a pound of sugar, even though your canister was full. You rattled a few items off the top of your head."

"I don't know why I thought of sugar, peas, and carrots. Funny how the mind works sometimes."

"Yes it is. You had planned to go to the library as you do every Saturday, and you knew Larry would take the sleeping draught as he usually does, and Mr. Jarvis would come in at two, when hopefully Larry would be sound asleep. He'd stay no later than ten after, and then he would call you at the library when he got back to the store, letting you know through code that Larry was dead and you should go home, arriving at twenty minutes to three. By phoning in the order, you were letting him know all systems were go."

"That's ridiculous," Miss Caldwell said. "Why would they go ahead with a scheme like that if her husband had an appointment that day at one? Why would Jarvis risk coming into the apartment? The appointment may have still been there."

"That's true, but there really was no risk. If Larry had been awake, or if his appointment was still there, Jarvis would just unpack the groceries, take the box, and leave."

"To try again another day," Green said, finally contributing to the questioning.

"Yes, but it had to be on a Saturday, because Alice told Jarvis Mrs. Picking did her laundry on Saturdays and would most likely be on the back porch to help with his alibi. And the weather had to be good, no rain, isn't that right?" I looked at Alice, who was still crying, her nose running. I held out my handkerchief to her. "Mrs. Crow?"

She nodded almost imperceptibly as she took the handkerchief I offered, like she had the last time I was here. Good thing I had a large supply of them. "Yes, that's right. Mr. Jarvis told me the fact that Larry had an appointment that day was actually a good thing. He thought the police might finger whoever it was Larry had the appointment with."

I shuddered involuntarily at the thought, and I felt Green looking at me. "Smart thinking, but a terrible thing to do to the innocent man Larry was meeting."

"I said that too, afterward," Alice said, "but Mr. Jarvis said they wouldn't be able to prove anything against whoever it was."

"Men have been hanged for less, Mrs. Crow," I said.

"You don't have to tell these men anything more, Alice," Miss Caldwell said. Then she looked at us. "It sounds like Mrs. Crow will be needing a lawyer. So, I think we're finished for the time being."

Mrs. Crow glanced over at her then, and held up her tiny little hand. "No, Evelyn, it's all right. They know…things. I want to talk about it."

"I'd advise against that, Alice, please."

"Thank you. I know you're looking out for me. You were just trying to help. To be kind. But I have to do this. For me. You wouldn't understand." She turned back to me and Alvin.

"Go on, Mrs. Crow," Alvin said.

"It seemed like it would be so easy."

"When did you and Mr. Jarvis first plan all this?"

"It started out almost as a joke, you see? Mr. Jarvis made a delivery to the apartment, and Larry happened to be out. We'd just had a nasty fight and he'd stormed off after breaking a bowl my mother had given me. By the time Mr. Jarvis arrived with the groceries, I had calmed down some, but Larry was still gone. I asked Mr. Jarvis if he thought he could repair the bowl, but he said it was in too many pieces. Then he asked me if I had anything else that needed doing for a little extra money. Painting, repairs, errands, that kind of thing. I jokingly said I couldn't think of anything unless he wanted to kill my husband, because I was angry and I had a hundred dollars stashed away. I knew Mr. Jarvis didn't like Larry, and he clearly needed money."

"The hundred dollars was the money you had saved to escape. Pennies make nickels, I believe you said."

"That's right. Mr. Jarvis laughed when I suggested it, but the next time I saw him, he said he had come up with a plan. He explained it all, and then told me what I'd have to do. He told me I could pay him fifty dollars up front, and fifty when it was over. I was scared, terrified, really. Terrified about what would happen if he killed him, terrified of what would happen if he didn't. To be honest, I actually thought about killing Larry myself lots of times before, but I always chickened out. And I could never figure out how to do it. I thought about poison, but that seemed like they'd figure out it was me."

"Okay," I said. "I think I understand. Go on."

"Sometimes I thought maybe I'd just leave, disappear. Never go home again."

"That's something you could have done, Mrs. Crow," I said.

"I know. I thought about it many times. But it wouldn't really solve anything, would it? Even if we got divorced, he'd just marry someone else eventually and do the same things to her. And I was afraid he would track me down and kill me, no matter where I went. He had to be stopped."

"I'd say he did," Alvin said.

"But I also told myself we'd do it only if someone showed me a kindness. I thought that would be a sign I didn't deserve to be treated the way Larry treats me."

"No one deserves to be treated the way you were, Mrs. Crow," Alvin said.

"I agree," Miss Caldwell said.

"So do I," I added.

Alice dabbed at her eyes. "You know, Larry could be real nice sometimes, like when he first found out I was going to have a baby, and he married me. I never thought he'd do that. Of course, he changed once I lost the baby. He got real mean. But then again, sometimes he was sweet as sugar. Once he brought me flowers for no reason. Store-bought ones, not ones he picked from somebody's garden or stole from the cemetery. I never knew how he was going to be."

"Typical behavior of men like that. They keep you guessing, throw you off guard," Alvin said, looking angry.

"He did that real well, Mr. Green. I was feeling poorly, sorry for myself, crying, that day. I was a mess by the time I got to the library. But then I saw Miss Caldwell, here. Evelyn." She reached over and took Miss Caldwell's hand in hers. "She could see I'd been crying, and she saw the fresh bruise on my face. She put her arms around me and gave me a good, long hug and kissed my cheek and stroked my hair. And she let me return my book and didn't charge me the overdue fee. And then she recommended *The Company She Keeps*, by Mary McCarthy."

"And her waiving the fee and suggesting the book, especially that particular book, was your sign?" I said.

"That's right. It had to be, didn't it? An act of kindness."

Mrs. Crow smiled then, just a small smile, but it spoke volumes. "Evelyn has been just wonderful through all this."

"So, you sat down and waited for the signal, the phone call from Jarvis pretending to be your husband."

"Uh-huh, that was Mr. Jarvis's idea, too. Of course, I was a nervous wreck, and I think Evelyn could tell."

"And after the call you went back home."

"Yes, I was just sick the whole way. When I reached the back door I commented to Agnes that it was ajar, but she didn't seem to think much of it. Nonetheless, that's what Mr. Jarvis told me to say. He said that was part of the plan."

"How so?" I said.

"I don't see how any of this is relevant or your business, Detective," Miss Caldwell said.

"Nonetheless, please continue, Mrs. Crow."

She glanced over at Evelyn once more, but Miss Caldwell only scowled in our direction. Then Alice turned her attentions back to me and Alvin. "Well, the overall plan was that we would make it seem like a burglar or one of Larry's business associates killed him, by leaving the knife out and the back door ajar. He had to use a knife rather than a gun so there wouldn't be any noise. Larry knew a lot of strange men, and a lot of them didn't care for him. And like I said before, Mr. Jarvis figured the fact that Larry had an appointment at one that day made it even more likely."

"I see," I said, rather irritated. I wondered what the two of them would say if they knew the man Larry had the appointment with was me.

"Then I went on in the kitchen from the porch. I saw him right away, on the sofa, flat on his back, his throat cut open like a pig's. I'd read about that in a book. It's amazing what you can find in the library. I knew there would be a lot of blood, but it still surprised me to see how much there actually was, and it was *everywhere*." She laughed suddenly, which I found a bit disturbing. "I'm sorry, it's not funny. But my first thought when I saw the blood was that Larry was going to be mad if I couldn't get it cleaned up, but then I realized he wasn't ever going to be mad or hit me again. He looked frightful, and his eyes were partially open, staring at me blankly. I thought for a second he was alive, but then suddenly I knew he wasn't. I set my book down on the counter, and then I screamed."

"So, what happened after you screamed?"

"Agnes heard me."

"I certainly did," Mrs. Picking said. "It sent a shiver right through me."

"She came running in the back door and saw Larry and the blood right away, just like Mr. Jarvis said she would. She grabbed my arm, and we went to her apartment and she locked her doors. Then she telephoned the police."

"You and Mr. Jarvis had it planned well. Premeditated murder," I said.

"You mean you knew he was dead? It was all faked, your screaming and everything?" Mrs. Picking said. "I can't believe it." She shifted her body just slightly, moving away from Mrs. Crow, her face pale.

"I'm sorry, Agnes, truly. I was just following Mr. Jarvis's directions," Alice said. "But the scream, I think, was real. I'd planned on faking it, but when I saw him dead, I couldn't control myself."

"Please don't say anything else, Alice," Miss Caldwell said, softer this time. "Not without a lawyer."

"I would definitely advise getting one, Mrs. Crow," I said. "When did you first tell Miss Caldwell about all this?"

"Oh, Evelyn had nothing to do with it, and that's the truth. When I showed up at her door last Saturday with the police, she could tell I needed a friend. I was so scared. We talked a long time, well into the night. I told her Larry had been murdered, but I didn't confess who had done it. I wanted to, but I just couldn't. I also told her I owed Mr. Jarvis fifty dollars, and that I was supposed to bring it to his apartment Tuesday night at seven. That would have been last night."

"The other half of his payment," I said.

"That's right."

"Why wait until Tuesday?" Alvin said.

"Just to make sure the police were all done hanging around and stuff, and I figured it would be easier for me to get there. I'd have to take the number five bus from here."

"Okay." I looked at Miss Caldwell. "Weren't you wondering why Mrs. Crow owed Jarvis such a large sum of money?"

"I was curious, but it wasn't my business. I thought maybe she was just paying off her grocery bill."

"On a Tuesday night at seven o'clock, after the store closed," I said, and then I looked back at Mrs. Crow. "So, what did Miss Caldwell say when you told her what had happened?"

"Well, she offered to drive me to Mr. Jarvis's apartment, which was a lot easier on me than taking the bus."

"Did she know you were going to kill him?"

Mrs. Crow's eyes grew wide. "Oh, no, not at all. Evelyn didn't know nothing about that. I didn't even know at that point I was going to kill him."

"Alice!"

"It's true. But she did say she was worried about my meeting with Mr. Jarvis."

"Why is that?"

"Because she was going to a man's apartment by herself at night to give him fifty dollars in cash. I offered to accompany her, but she said she had to go alone, though she agreed to let me drive her," Miss Caldwell said.

Mrs. Crow squeezed Miss Caldwell's hand. "Evelyn worries about me. She keeps a gun in the drawer of her nightstand, and she told me to put it in my purse for protection, just in case, along with the fifty dollars. I don't like guns, but I agreed to make her happy. I think it was a few minutes to seven by the time we got to Mr. Jarvis's apartment. Evelyn waited in the car."

"So you went up to Mr. Jarvis's apartment above his store alone."

"That's right. He answered the door wearing just his underwear, no shirt, and a bathrobe, which was hanging open. I went in, and he closed the door behind me. He offered me a drink, which I declined. He'd been drinking quite a bit. I gave him the other fifty dollars, and he counted it and stuffed it in his bathrobe pocket. Then he told me one hundred dollars in total wasn't enough. He said he wanted at least a thousand dollars because the cops were snooping around and he'd taken a big risk."

"A thousand dollars is a big jump from a hundred."

"I know. I was panic stricken. I told him I didn't have that kind of money, but he said I should be collecting on Larry's life insurance and pension soon. I said I needed that money to live on. He said if I didn't pay him, he would go to the police and tell them I killed Larry. I wasn't thinking straight. He kept leering at me and touching himself in places he shouldn't. I tried not to look, but he kept talking and moving closer to me."

"Disturbing," I said.

"Yes. He told me I was pretty, and that made me sick. His behavior reminded me of Larry. I wanted to leave, but he was blocking the door. He said maybe we could work something out.

He said I owed him for killing Larry. He came at me all of a sudden then, grabbing my hair and pawing, touching me, trying to kiss me. I pushed him as hard as I could and he fell, then I took the gun out of my purse and shot him. I didn't mean to, honest. It just went off. Twice. Then I stepped over his body and left."

"Alice, for God's sake, shut up. You shot him in self-defense when he tried to rape you," Evelyn said.

Mrs. Crow wiped away her tears and lifted her chin. "That's right, I did. And I'm not sorry. And I'm not sorry Larry's dead, either. Evelyn's been nicer and kinder to me than either of them ever were. She's more than a friend to me, and I'm not ashamed to say it."

"And, Miss Caldwell, when you heard the shots, you left the car and went running up to the apartment, correct?"

"Yes, I did. My heart was racing. Alice was just coming out of the apartment, still holding the gun. I took it from her, put it in my pocket, and hustled her down the stairs into my car."

"A dark blue sedan. And you were dressed similarly to the way you are now, maybe even a man's hat on?"

"That's right. Why?"

"From a distance in the twilight, you could be mistaken for a man."

"That's a terrible thing to say, but I suppose it's true."

"Just like Mrs. Picking mistook you for a man in the alley when you hung around waiting to see Larry Crow, all the while smoking your cigars."

"I'm not denying it. I suppose there's no use now."

"What brand of cigar do you smoke, Miss Caldwell?"

"White Owl, why?"

"Just curious. I found out they weren't Willard Ponies."

"I don't understand," Mrs. Picking said. "The man in the alley was you, Miss Caldwell?"

"That's right. I wanted to see what the weasel looked like and maybe set him straight, threaten him if he didn't ease up on Alice, but I eventually thought better of it."

"Well, mother of pearl, and you smoke cigars? I never!"

"Well, now you have, Mrs. Picking," I said.

"So that's what you meant, Detective, when you said he wasn't a man." Mrs. Picking looked like she might faint.

"Exactly," I said. "Miss Caldwell is a swan. An intelligent, fierce swan." I turned back to Alice. "I'm afraid we'll have to take you downtown, Mrs. Crow. You're under arrest for the murder of Ossip Jarvis and your husband. Miss Caldwell, we'll need a formal statement from you, but I don't believe you'll be charged. Mrs. Picking, you're free to go, but don't leave town."

"I'll phone for a black-and-white," Alvin said as he got up and walked toward the telephone niche by the door.

"Alice isn't a criminal, Detective," Miss Caldwell said. "She's a victim. You have no idea what she's been through, how terrified she was for her life. That first night, that Saturday, I held her in my arms in bed, and she trembled almost until dawn. If necessary, I'll confess to the murders."

"That's very noble of you, Miss Caldwell, and I believe you would, but hopefully that won't be necessary. Just give your statement, testify at the trial as to what Mrs. Crow has been through and to her character, and chances are things will turn out okay."

Miss Caldwell stood and looked at me straight in the eyes. "You're not a bad sort, Barrington, for a man."

CHAPTER TWENTY-ONE

Early Evening, Wednesday, August 13, 1947

When the officers had taken Mrs. Crow away, Green and I escorted Mrs. Picking to the door while Miss Caldwell changed her clothes to go downtown and give a formal statement. Mrs. Picking looked stunned.

"I can't believe Alice or Mr. Jarvis would do such a thing," she said quietly, her voice quavering.

"Desperate people do desperate things sometimes, Mrs. Picking," I said, as I retrieved our hats from the table and handed Alvin his.

"But still, Alice is so sweet, so innocent."

"I know that. She'll need your friendship now more than ever. Please be there for her. Don't abandon her."

Mrs. Picking looked up at me, a hint of tears in her eyes. "Her husband was a foul man. He got what he deserved, and it sounds like Mr. Jarvis did, too. I will be there for Alice now and always, Detective, as will Miss Caldwell, apparently."

I smiled at her as we stepped into the hall. "Alice said you were a good friend, and I would say she's right. And as for Miss Caldwell, well, more than friends is even better."

Alvin and I turned then and walked back down the hall. We took the stairs slowly, neither of us saying anything. When we reached the ground floor, we walked out into the afternoon sunshine, pulling our hats low to shade our eyes. The weatherman had definitely been wrong about the rain, but it was hot and humid. We went down the front steps to the sidewalk, where Alvin stopped abruptly. He had thrust his hands in his front pants pockets, and he looked troubled.

"What's wrong?" I said, stopping beside him.

He tilted his head back a bit and looked at me. "Besides you?"

"What's that supposed to mean?"

He didn't answer right away. Then he looked away from me. "I didn't want it to be her."

That got to me. I wasn't the only one who felt for Mrs. Crow, obviously. "I think I know what you mean, Alvin."

He turned back to me then, but it wasn't a hard look. Instead it was rather soft. "There's no concrete evidence against Mrs. Crow, you know, as far as her husband. Nothing a jury would stand behind, anyway. Miss Caldwell is right about self-defense against Jarvis. And you know as well as I do the phone company doesn't keep records about what calls were made and completed and from which exchange," Green said.

I shrugged. "I know they don't, but I figured Mrs. Crow didn't know that."

Alvin sighed. "Yeah, good bluff. Second chapter in the Detective's Handbook."

"I took a chance. Sometimes they pay off."

"Sometimes they do. I've seen cases like this before, you know. The woman goes to trial, a jury finds her guilty, and she gets life in a women's prison."

"She may not," I said. "Jarvis was the brains behind it, and he did the actual killing of Larry Crow, Alvin. Premeditated, in cold blood. And like you said, Alice can claim self-defense against Jarvis."

"You sound like an attorney," Green said.

"And you're not sounding much like a police detective right now. I like Alice Crow, too, but the fact remains she was involved."

"She was following Jarvis's orders. As you just said, he's the one that did the murdering. She wasn't even there. She was just an accomplice."

"Actually she was only an accessory to murder," I said. "Accomplices are present at the scene of the crime, accessories are not. It's a lesser charge. I checked with a friend of mine in the DA's office."

"Aw, what do you care? You'll be cleared regardless."

"Why do you care so much?"

He pulled his hands out of his pockets and paced up and down the sidewalk a while before stopping in front of me, his brow furrowed in sweat. "Because. Because this same thing happened to my big sister, that's why. She was fifteen years older than me. I was just a kid, but I saw what he did to her. She killed him, finally, when he came at her one night after he'd been drinking. But I watched her get arrested, go to trial."

"I'm so sorry. What happened?"

"Because of the self-defense she didn't get life, thank God. But it was awful for her, for all of us, and she's never been the same. Guys like that, guys like Larry Crow and Jarvis, they deserve what they get, just as Miss Caldwell said."

"I agree with you, but we can't be judge and jury, Alvin. We can only do our jobs."

He sat down then, right in the street, his butt resting on the dirty cement curb, and put his head in his hands. "She had no choice, Barrington. Nowhere to go, nowhere to run, nowhere to hide to escape him. Crow would have killed her."

"You don't know that for certain."

"And you don't know for certain he wouldn't have. It's happened too many times before. And like she said, even if she escaped, there'd be someone else, another wife, another girlfriend, another victim of his abuse."

"The law is the law, Alvin. We can work to find a way to protect women like Alice Crow, but we can't ignore the law. It's our job."

He didn't say anything for several minutes. Slowly then, he raised his head and looked at me. "Yeah, I suppose I know that. I suppose I knew that even as I was saying it. You're right, Heath. Why are you always right?"

I sat down beside him on the dirty curb, to hell with my pants. I'd never seen this side of Alvin Green before. "I'm not always right. I wish I was, but I'm not."

He looked over at me, a queer expression on his weary face. "Yeah, you're probably right about that, too."

I laughed at the ridiculousness of it all, and suddenly he laughed, also.

"Look, Alvin, I know we don't always see eye to eye, but I respect you. You had to make the arrest. You had no choice."

"I know it. But it goes against my beliefs. What if, God forbid, my daughter Janey ever ends up married to a louse like that?"

I shook my head. "She won't. And for what it's worth, I think Alice will be okay. I like her, too. She's a kind woman who was in a bad spot and couldn't see any other way out."

He looked over at me, his face sad. "Thanks. I appreciate that."

"I'm just a cop, a detective doing my job, the same as you."

His expression changed again. "Only you're not the same as me." He reached in his suit coat pocket and took out his wallet. "I have something you may be interested in, by the way."

"Oh?"

He extracted a well-worn piece of paper that looked familiar from the bill compartment. "I found it in the Crow apartment the day you and I were there together, while you were poking about in the bedroom and using the bathroom."

"Where did you find it?"

"You're not the only good detective on the force, you know. I figured you were looking for something, and I wanted to know what, which is one of the reasons I decided to let you back in there. I thought to myself, where would I hide something in that tiny place? Then I remembered I hid a bracelet from my wife once that I'd gotten her for Christmas. She's a notorious snoop when it comes to gifts, so I've gotten pretty good at hiding things. I taped it to the wall, just above the door frame, inside the closet. She never found it and was genuinely surprised Christmas morning."

"I wouldn't have thought to look there."

"It was just a hunch. Sometimes I get lucky, too," Alvin said.

He handed the piece of paper to me. It was the note Crow had found in the garbage and hidden in his apartment to blackmail me with. I glanced at it, then folded it back up and put it in my pocket.

"And you kept it in your wallet? Not exactly protocol for handling evidence, Alvin."

He looked over at me. "Eh, I didn't really ever think you were the killer. But I hung on to it just in case."

"Thanks for that, truly. It means a lot to me. I even had doubts about myself. You didn't have to give that note to me."

"I know. Now you owe me three."

I smiled. "Thanks."

"I read it, you know," he said, staring down at the sewer grate between his legs and spitting expertly into it.

"The note?"

"Yeah. I had to see what it was all about."

"Oh. I see."

Suddenly it all made sense why he had become so distant and cold to me ever since we left the Crow place together.

"What now?" I said, my stomach sick again. "I had hoped that note would never see the light of day."

He looked over at me. "I can imagine, but don't worry, I'm not going to tell anyone. It's your business, not mine, and you have the note back to do with as you please. But you may want to see a doctor about, well, you know."

"Sure," I replied, uncertain of what else to say.

He stared at me. "It's an illness, Barrington. A mental illness. I did some research on it after I found the note. A good psychologist can help you. Your friend, too. No one has to know. Use an assumed name, go out of state, maybe Illinois."

"Yeah. Thanks for the advice."

"I hope you take it. You really are a good detective. By the way, no hard feelings, but I'm rescinding that dinner invitation. I don't want you around my daughter."

I bristled. "It's not like that, Alvin. You don't understand."

"I guess I don't, nor do I want to. Just the thought of it makes me sick, to be honest."

"I'm sorry to hear that."

"I'm leaving the force. Dottie's mother in St. Paul isn't doing too well, and Dottie wants to be closer. St. Paul has an opening in their detective division, and the pay is better."

I stood up, brushing off the seat of my pants, and Alvin did the same. "I see," I said. "Sorry to hear about your wife's mother, but congratulations on your new job."

"Yeah, thanks. You'll probably be glad not to have me around."

I shook my head. "I thought we worked well together, Alvin."

"I will say you're a good detective, for what it's worth. How did you know? About Mrs. Crow, I mean, and everything else?"

"I didn't know for certain. Some of it was bluff, like the phone call records. But it was actually something Alan Keyes said that got me to thinking."

"Keyes, of course. It's not normal, Barrington, or right or moral. But I guess you two make a good team. As for me, I prefer to work solo. Let's get back to the station. I have a report to finish."

CHAPTER TWENTY-TWO

Thursday Morning, August 14, 1947

After my Racine appointment regarding the larceny case, I stopped back at the precinct and filled in the chief with what I had so far. Overall he was pleased, and I was making good progress on the case. He was also happy at the conclusion of the Crow/Jarvis case. I had let Alvin take the credit for solving it, so now I figured I only owed him two. The Chief told me my friend Grant Riker, the policeman I had worked with on a previous case, would be promoted to detective in Green's place. I made a mental note to congratulate him and then returned to my desk to call Liz, hoping she'd be home.

"What's buzzin', cousin?" I said.

"Me! Buzz, buzz. How are you?"

"Better, much better. Knowing I'm not a murderer is a big relief."

"I should think so. And what about me?"

"I never really thought you killed Larry, Liz, you know that. I just had to follow through on every possibility."

"I'll forgive you, perhaps, if you buy me a chocolate soda."

"Deal. I'm almost finished for the day. I promised Alan we'd go to a movie tonight, because it's our five-month anniversary, but perhaps the three of us could get a soda together, and you could join us for the movie if you like."

"I would like that very much, but I don't want to be a third wheel."

"You won't be. He wants to meet you."

"Then it's a deal. And I look forward to meeting this Alan."

"Good. We'll pick you up about six, okay?"

"I'll be waiting."

I hung up the phone, covered my typewriter, put my files away, and grabbed my hat. Once I had signed out downstairs, I got in my car and picked Alan up at the streetcar stop.

He was all smiles as he climbed in beside me. "Hey, Heath."

"You seem to be in a good mood," I said.

"Another workday done, a movie to look forward to, and spending time with you on our five-month anniversary. What's not to be happy about?" he said.

"I agree," I said, putting my car in gear and heading in the general direction of the east side of town. "Liz wants to meet you. I thought perhaps we could all go for a soda at Lemke's pharmacy, and then the movie. What do you want to see, anyway?"

"I'd like to meet Liz, too. I feel like I already know her. As far as a movie, gosh, there's so many good ones. *The Ghost and Mrs. Muir*, *Dark Passage*, *A Double Life*..."

"How about *Dark Passage*? I like a good Bogart and Bacall film."

"Deal," Alan said. "I guess I won't have time to go home and change out of my uniform."

"You have a change of clothes at my place, remember?"

Alan grinned. "Oh, yeah!"

We arrived back on Prospect Avenue within fifteen minutes, and I was happy to see my favorite parking spot was open under the great-grandmother elm tree. I put the parking brake on, turned off the engine, and then reached under my seat, extracting the bloodstained shirt wrapped in newspaper.

"I thought you were going to dispose of that," Alan said, looking at it.

"I was, but I guess I forgot about it until just now. I probably still should, as that stain will never come out."

"Not unless you use scissors."

"Wise guy."

We exited the car and Alan followed me up to my apartment.

When he and I had both changed our clothes and the bloodstained shirt had been deposited down the trash chute, Alan emerged from the bathroom and walked over to my dresser, where my autographed picture of the actor William "Billy" Haines was tucked up in the corner. "What are these?" he said, picking up the figurines Liz had brought back for me from Paris. "I noticed them the other day but forgot to ask you about them."

"Those are Health and Happiness. Liz got them in Paris for me. They're voodoo dolls."

He picked one up and looked at me, a queer expression on his face. "I didn't think you put much stock in voodoo and spirits and all that."

I shrugged. "I don't. Or I didn't. I don't know. But so far I'm in good health, and with you and Liz in my life, and Larry Crow's and Ossip Jarvis's murders solved, I couldn't be happier, so who am I to argue?"

Alan grinned as he set the figurine back down next to its mate. "Works for me. All set?"

"Just about." I locked my service revolver away in the nightstand, and we grabbed our hats as we headed down the stairs and out the door. We climbed back into my car and drove the short distance to Liz's place. She was waiting on the corner, looking radiant in a dark blue dress and a yellow beret, with low yellow heels to match, a white clutch, and white gloves. I parked the car next to a mailbox, and we got out so I could introduce them.

"Elizabeth Valentine, I'd like you to meet Alan Keyes. Alan, this is my cousin, Liz," I said.

"So, you're Alan Keyes. You're even more handsome than Heath said," Liz said, beaming at him and taking his hands in hers, her clutch tucked beneath her left arm.

Alan blushed. "Gosh, and you're awfully pretty, Miss Valentine."

"Call me, Liz, please. I insist. I feel like I already know you so well, even though we've just met."

"Gee, thanks. And please call me Alan. I'd like it if you would."

"Then I will."

"That's a fetching chapeau, Liz," I said. "Something else you brought back from Paris?"

She laughed gaily. "Of course!"

"No wonder your bags were so heavy. You must have bought a whole new wardrobe. I haven't been abroad since before the war..."

"Time for a return trip, my darling. Maybe we can all go together."

"That might be fun," I said.

"It *would* be fun!" she said. "So, what movie are we seeing?"

"*Dark Passage*, starring Bogart and Lauren Bacall. Okay with you?"

"Okey dokey," she replied. "I adore Lauren Bacall. *Dark Passage* is playing at the Oriental. Let's have a soda at Maxwell's on Farwell. We can walk there from here and then on to the Oriental. I expect you to buy me popcorn, too."

"Fair enough, my lady. Shall we?"

The three of us strode down the sidewalk, Liz in the middle.

"So, cousin, I hear you solved the case of Larry the louse's murder," she said, looking up at me. "And that Mr. Jarvis's death, too, though you kindly gave Alvin Green the credit."

"Well, it was a group effort. Alan here is the one who originally thought it may have been Mrs. Crow."

"That poor woman," she said. "I really feel for her. I know what Larry was like, and I think he only got worse over time."

"Yes," I replied. "Ossip Jarvis planned and did the actual killing, but Alan is the one that suspected Alice Crow was involved. I never really did until much later."

"I guessed," Alan said.

"What made you think so, Heath?" Liz said.

"Lots of little things that finally added up. I heard a little girl say pennies make nickels, which is what Mrs. Crow had said about saving up the one hundred dollars, and I wondered what became of that money. Alice said she never had a chance to get rid of it, and she had it hidden in one of her hat boxes, but Green made no mention of it when he went over the inventory with me of the Crow apartment. He even said specifically that they had looked in the hatboxes. Then

Green told me they found Jarvis with fifty dollars in small bills and change in his bathrobe pocket, the other half of a down payment on a murder, I figured. And then there was Mrs. Picking stating the grocery box was overflowing. That didn't jive with what Jarvis said he had delivered. There was also the library book on the counter and the clean white clothes."

"Clean white clothes?" Liz said.

"Jarvis was dressed all in white when he made the delivery. When a soda jerk mentioned how hard it is to keep his uniform clean, I thought about that grocery box again, and what could have been in it besides groceries to make it seem so full."

"A change of clothes, of course. Good thinking, Heath. I wonder what made Jarvis do it?" Alan said.

"A chance to earn a hundred bucks and knock off someone he hated. Plus, I think he figured he'd be able to get her into bed. According to Alice, he tried to right before she shot him."

"Gee, that's something," Alan said.

"Yes. The final piece was a comment I overheard about male and female swans looking alike. It got me to thinking perhaps the mystery man in the alley was actually a mystery woman, namely, Miss Caldwell."

"Why would you think that?" Alan said.

"I saw men's clothes in her apartment, and she struck me as rather manly when we saw her in the library. Hey, I just thought of something," I said.

Both Alan and Liz looked at me. "What?" they both asked at the same time.

"This is the first case we've worked on together where you didn't think all of the suspects did it collaboratively, Alan."

"Funny," Alan said. "But that actually did cross my mind. I dismissed it quickly, though."

"Why is that?"

"Because you were one of the suspects, and to a degree, so was I. And Liz."

I laughed and clapped him on the back. "Yeah. Thanks again for believing in me, even when I doubted myself. Both of you."

"Of course. I never doubted your innocence. Unlike you doubting mine." She glanced up, her eyes narrow.

"You're not going to let that go, are you?"

She smiled then, a twinkle in her eye. "Not until I get my chocolate soda, anyway. And maybe a double. And my popcorn, with extra butter."

"Fair enough, cousin, fair enough."

I looked at Alan over the top of Liz's head. "I'm still mad at myself for not destroying that note I wrote you instead of throwing it absentmindedly into the trash."

"You couldn't have known Crow would find it, Heath. But yeah, I guess we have to be ever vigilant. Remember that picture that nice lady took of the two of us in Chicago with my camera when we were down there for the weekend?"

"Yeah, sure, at the museum," I said.

"I had it framed and put it on my nightstand."

"Aww, that's sweet," Liz said, interrupting. "I'd love to see it."

"It's a nice picture. But my landlady came in to check for pests. The guy across the hall had mice. Anyway, she saw the photo and asked me about it."

"What did you say?" I said.

"I said it was a friend, that's all. I hate not being able to be open about us."

"Me too, but hopefully someday, slowly, that will change."

"Kind of like Mrs. Crow," Alan said.

"What do you mean?" Liz said, interrupting once more and looking up at each of us in turn.

"She was afraid, living in a loveless marriage. No one to talk to, no one to tell. Maybe someday that will change, too."

"I know exactly how she felt," Liz said.

"All we can do is work to make those changes happen," I said.

"And what will happen to her now?" Liz said.

"She is under arrest, accessory to a murder in the case of her husband. And murder one for Ossip Jarvis. It will go to trial. I'll testify, and so will several others. I'm sure you'll be called, Liz, to give testimony as to the type of abusive person Larry Crow was.

Violent, dangerous, and criminal. They may even call Vinnie the Horse to testify."

"That would be something," Alan said.

"It will say a lot to the jury that Crow and Jarvis were associated with someone like Vinnie," I said. "Miss Caldwell gave her statement, and she'll be called to testify, too. Alice claims Evelyn knew absolutely nothing about what happened, and she never told her anything."

"You believe that?" Alan said.

"No, not entirely. But I don't think Caldwell knew anything in advance, including that Alice was going to kill Jarvis."

"So, you think she'll get off?" Alan said. "Mrs. Crow, I mean."

I shook my head. "I don't know for certain, but I think it's possible her charge for Jarvis's death and Larry's may be reduced to manslaughter, or she may get off entirely."

"How?" Liz said.

"A lot depends on how her attorneys decide to present it. I think they'll go for temporary insanity for Larry's death and self-defense for Jarvis. They'll say Alice was not responsible for her actions because of the psychological trauma her husband inflicted on her over the years, and that she was unable to understand the implications of her actions and therefore can't be held criminally liable. And they'll probably say Jarvis was the instigator."

"I think there's something to that," Alan said.

"I *know* there's something to that," Liz added.

"So do I. And perhaps she'll move in with Miss Caldwell permanently and live happily ever after. Word is Miss Caldwell is already working on raising funds for Alice Crow's bail."

"Who's this Miss Caldwell, exactly?" Liz said.

"A friend of Mrs. Crow's, a librarian who seems pretty keen on her, and I'd say the feeling is mutual."

"Oh, that's really nice. I'm glad she has someone for when she gets out."

"Me too. But the outcome of the case will also depend on the prosecuting attorney. He will try to spin it a different way, of course. Regardless, I think Alice Crow will be okay. In my opinion, all she's really guilty of is half-jokingly suggesting a murder to Jarvis, and later defending herself from him. Anyway, she's free from her husband and Jarvis at last."

"Yeah. We're all free from Larry Crow at last. Like I said the other day, it was the only way," Liz said.

We waited on the corner as a bus rumbled by, and then we crossed west on Kenilworth Place toward Farwell.

"I wonder," I replied.

"I wonder if you'll spring for extra whipped cream on my double chocolate soda, cousin. I'm in the mood to celebrate."

"You're always in the mood to spend my money," I said with a laugh. "By the way, how's that unemployed friend of yours? The one you met on the ship."

She glanced up at me, shading her eyes with a gloved hand. "Mike? He called. I knew he would. We have a date for Saturday night."

"Of course you do," I said. "I ran a check on him at the station, by the way. He's okay."

"Of course you did," she said, laughing. She looped her arm through Alan's and leaned in toward him. "Now then. Tell me how the two of you met. I want to know every detail!"

MYSTERY HISTORY

The Bee's Knees, the cocktail Heath introduced to Liz, is a favorite of the author's along with the St. Germaine and Champagne drink that Liz mentioned and, of course, a good martini—though with a blue cheese–stuffed olive rather than a pickle. The Bee's Knees, which dates back to Prohibition, is made with gin, lemon, and honey. The lemon and honey were used to improve the taste of poor quality bathtub gin, and the name refers to 1920s slang meaning top-notch.

The Pfister Hotel mentioned in the book still exists in Milwaukee. It is a grand and beautiful upscale hotel, and one can have high tea there, as the author and his husband, along with their friend Mary, have done, just like Heath and his aunt Verbina.

The incident Liz mentions about her father driving a bus and deciding on the spur of the moment to drive the city bus to Kentucky is based on a real incident that happened in 1947. A man named William Cimillo took his bus from New York to Florida without permission and, fortunately, without passengers. The bus company filed charges, but the public rallied to support him, and the charges were dropped.

The Cudahy Tower building, where Aunt Verbina lives, still exists on Prospect Avenue and has been converted to exclusive condominiums, many of which overlook Lake Michigan.

Art's Diner is fictitious, though it is based on numerous diners of the time, many of which are serving food and slinging hash even to this day.

Party lines were common in the 1940s, especially during the war years when copper for the wires was in short supply. A party line was shared by multiple subscribers, and anyone on the party line could pick up their telephone and listen in to someone else's conversation.

The *Girls Aplenty* magazine Heath sees in the Crow apartment is a nod to book three, *Death Checks In*, which is where this fictitious pin-up magazine is first mentioned.

The *Kon-Tiki* raft expedition actually did crash into a reef in August of 1947.

Willard Ponies cigars really did exist in the 1940s, as did White Owl cigars.

The State Street branch of the Milwaukee Public Library system was created for the purposes of this story. The closest library to where the Crows' apartment would have been is the Central Library, which is a much larger, grander building on Wisconsin Avenue. Most branch libraries in 1947 Milwaukee were located in modest storefronts until the 1960s, when the library system began a program to replace the storefront libraries and build new buildings throughout the city.

There's a subtle nod to the TV show *Friends* in this book. The restaurant Heath and Alan have lunch at is called Schwimmer's, and their waiter's name is David, who states he's the owners son, making him David Schwimmer, who played Ross on *Friends*. The waiter also mentions he works so much he doesn't have time to spend with his friends at the coffee shop.

William "Billy" Haines was a sex symbol and huge movie star with MGM in the early thirties, fired for refusing to pretend he wasn't gay.

About the Author

David S. Pederson was born in Leadville, Colorado, where his father was a miner. Soon after, the family relocated to Wisconsin, where David grew up, attending high school and university, majoring in business and creative writing. Landing a job in retail, he found himself relocating to New York, Massachusetts, and eventually back to Wisconsin, where he currently lives with his husband.

His third book, *Death Checks In*, was a finalist for the 2019 Lambda Literary Awards. His fourth book, *Death Takes A Bow*, is a finalist for the 2020 Lambda Literary Awards.

He has written many short stories and poetry and is passionate about mysteries, old movies, and crime novels. When not reading, writing, or working in the furniture business, David also enjoys working out and studying classic ocean liners, floor plans, and historic homes.

David can be contacted at davidspederson@gmail.com or via his website, www.davidspederson.com.

Books Available From Bold Strokes Books

Death Overdue by David S. Pederson. Did Heath turn to murder in an alcohol-induced haze to solve the problem of his blackmailer, or was it someone else who brought about a death overdue? (978-1-63555-711-4)

Every Summer Day by Lee Patton. Meant to celebrate every summer day, Luke's journal instead chronicles a love affair as fast-moving and possibly as fatal as his brother's brain tumor. (978-1-63555-706-0)

Everyday People by Louis Barr. When film star Diana Danning hires private eye Clint Steele to find her son, Clint turns to his former West Point barracks mate, and ex-buddy with benefits, Mars Hauser to lend his cyber espionage and digital black ops skills to the case. (978-1-63555-698-8)

Cirque des Freaks and Other Tales of Horror by Julian Lopez. Explore the pleasure of horror in this compilation that delivers like the horror classics...good ole tales of terror. (978-1-63555-689-6)

Royal Street Reveillon by Greg Herren. In this Scotty Bradley mystery, someone is killing the stars of a reality show, and it's up to Scotty Bradley and the boys to find out who. (978-1-63555-545-5)

Death Takes a Bow by David S. Pederson. Alan Keys takes part in a local stage production, but when the leading man is murdered, his partner Detective Heath Barrington is thrust into the limelight to find the killer. (978-1-63555-472-4)

Accidental Prophet by Bud Gundy. Days after his grandmother dies, Drew Morten learns his true identity and finds himself racing against time to save civilization from the apocalypse. (978-1-63555-452-6)

In Case You Forgot by Fredrick Smith and Chaz Lamar. Zaire and Kenny, two newly single, Black, queer, and socially aware men, start again—in love, career, and life—in the West Hollywood neighborhood of LA. (978-1-63555-493-9)

Counting for Thunder by Phillip Irwin Cooper. A struggling actor returns to the Deep South to manage a family crisis but finds love and ultimately his own voice as his mother is regaining hers for possibly the last time. (978-1-63555-450-2)

Survivor's Guilt and Other Stories by Greg Herren. Award-winning author Greg Herren's short stories are finally pulled together into a single collection, including the Macavity Award–nominated title story and the first-ever Chanse MacLeod short story. (978-1-63555-413-7)

Saints + Sinners Anthology 2019, edited by Tracy Cunningham and Paul Willis. An anthology of short fiction featuring the finalist selections from the 2019 Saints + Sinners Literary Festival. (978-1-63555-447-2)

The Shape of the Earth by Gary Garth McCann. After appearing in *Best Gay Love Stories*, *HarringtonGMFQ*, *Q Review*, and *Off the Rocks*, Lenny and his partner Dave return in a hotbed of manhood and jealousy. (978-1-63555-391-8)

Exit Plans for Teenage Freaks by 'Nathan Burgoine. Cole always has a plan—especially for escaping his small-town reputation as "that kid who was kidnapped when he was four"—but when he teleports to a museum, it's time to face facts: it's possible he's a total freak after all. (978-1-163555-098-6)

Death Checks In by David S. Pederson. Despite Heath's promises to Alan to not get involved, Heath can't resist investigating a shopkeeper's murder in Chicago, which dashes their plans for a romantic weekend getaway. (978-1-163555-329-1)

Of Echoes Born by 'Nathan Burgoine. A collection of queer fantasy short stories set in Canada from Lambda Literary Award finalist 'Nathan Burgoine. (978-1-63555-096-2)

The Lurid Sea by Tom Cardamone. Cursed to spend eternity on his knees, Nerites is having the time of his life. (978-1-62639-911-2)

Sinister Justice by Steve Pickens. When a vigilante targets citizens of Jake Finnigan's hometown, Jake and his partner Sam fall under suspicion themselves as they investigate the murders. (978-1-63555-094-8)

Club Arcana: Operation Janus by Jon Wilson. Wizards, demons, Elder Gods: Who knew the universe was so crowded, and that they'd all be out to get Angus McAslan? (978-1-62639-969-3)

Triad Soul by 'Nathan Burgoine. Luc, Anders, and Curtis—vampire, demon, and wizard—must use their powers of blood, soul, and magic to defeat a murderer determined to turn their city into a battlefield. (978-1-62639-863-4)